Book 2 of the *Mahabharata* series

SHAKUNI & THE DICE OF DOOM

MALLAR CHATTERJEE

Readomania

Readomania Publishing
A division of Kurious Kind Media Private Limited
908, Vishwadeep Building, District Centre, Janakpuri,
New Delhi – 110058
books.readomania.com
email: contact@readomania.com
Facebook: facebook.com/iamreadomania
Twitter: twitter.com/iamreadomania
Instagram: iamreadomania

First Published in 2019 by Readomania

This book is a work of fiction. Any resemblance to real persons, living or dead, or actual events or locations, is purely coincidental.

ISBN: 978-93-858547-9-8

Typeset in Palatino Linotype by Shine Graphics
Printed in Delhi

Readomania

India has traditionally been the land of storytellers and a lot of us have an inherent skill of creating good plots, good stories and good narrations. With a little encouragement and support, many more authors will be widely read and attain a place in the sun. This is the essence of *Readomania*—an initiative that nurtures emerging stars of the literary world.

It would not be an exaggeration to say that *Readomania* is the talent hunt in fiction. It goes a step beyond by not just identifying the talent but also nurturing it and showcasing it to the world. In the process, we have created a powerhouse of content.

Readomania has four principal interest areas—traditional print publishing, online library of short stories and poetry, literary events and products.

The print publishing works towards delivering good quality content to the readers. We publish good authors in meaningful anthologies, novels and works of narrative non-fiction. Our books stand out for their perspectives, the plots, the language and most importantly their ability to enrich lives.

Take a break, read something nice, write something beautiful. Read our books or visit us at www.readomania.com and enjoy a whole new world of literature.

To my

Baba (Dr Alok Chattopadhyay)

&

Ma (Smt Sahana Chattopadhyay)

—the mighty pillars that hold me aloft with unwavering support.

Author's Note

'I see with sympathy
The swollen veins on his brow, showing
How exhausting it is to be evil.'

Bertolt Brecht

Shakuni is the villain-in-chief of the *Mahabharata* whose unscrupulous machinations spelled disaster for the great Kauravas. But what made him so desperately vengeful against the Kuru family? *Maharshi* Vyasa never mentioned it clearly in his story, nor did he throw much light on the other aspects of Shakuni's personality than his deviousness. His provocative silence subsequently invited interesting speculations in some regional versions of the epic.

I have used a small reference from the Indonesian (Javanese) version of the *Mahabharata* to assume the reason behind Shakuni's rancour and knitted a fictional story around it, taking some creative liberty. This story leans against a philosophy that human evil is probably begotten more by exogenous inducements than innate defects. Perhaps human turpitude is all about wrong, inappropriate reactions or responses.

While writing the book, I had to consult a variety of study materials including the works of Dr Dipak Chandra, Dr Nrisingha Prasad Bhaduri, Indrajit Bandyopadhyay and Maggi-Lidchi Grassi. I am deeply indebted to all of them.

I am fortunate enough to have received blessings, good wishes, inspiration and even inputs from many people—my teachers, cousins, friends, colleagues and senior officers—

who have contributed, in their very own and different ways, to the making of this book. My parents, my wife and my son have been like a formidable bastion wherefrom I can fancy waging my own war. I think it will be ostentatious to reveal my true feelings for them.

When I was writing my first book, I was completely sure that no one was going to publish it and I wrote it for a personal satisfaction. But on a beautiful October morning in Delhi (2016), I would get a strange call from a certain Dipankar Mukherjee. It will not be an overreaction should I flag the moment as life changing. As a matter of fact, I can never thank Dipankar, the editor Indrani Ganguly and Team Readomania enough. I sincerely feel that Indrani and her editorial team comprising Rima Kar Ghosh and Piyusha Vir have given my manuscript the best possible shape. I want to thank Sourish Mitra as well for the beautifully designed cover. And last but not the least, a very special thanks to eminent author Ms Sutapa Basu for her astute advice.

This book is a work of fiction based on the story of the *Mahabharata*. No comments, interpretations or explanations given in this novel are in any way meant for hurting or disrespecting any religious/social/popular sentiments and existing spiritual concepts.

MALLAR CHATTERJEE
Kolkata
July, 2019

'They think my dice are infallible.
Little do they know
that I myself have been a die
rolled to unleash
this mayhem...'

Background

Gandhara

The Gandhara kingdom was a mountainous state located to the north-west of Bharatavarsha. The Gandharas were an intelligent people. However, though Gandhara was a part of the extended Aryavarta, many orthodox Aryan kingdoms would find the Gandharas unchaste as their customs, rituals and lifestyle often differed from the mainstream Aryan system.

Subal was the king of Gandhara. He had a number of sons and one daughter called Gandhari. Shakuni was Subal's eldest son and was famous for his outstanding intelligence. There was a myth that Shakuni could impeccably identify a person just by seeing his shadow once! He was the pride of Gandhara. Although he was not particularly great as a warrior, Shakuni was an astute military strategist. His skill in dice games, however, was proverbial. He regularly resorted to deceptions for winning dice games and no one could detect his tricks. But he played such games only for fun and to hone his extraordinary mental abilities.

King Ugrasen of Mathura invited King Subal to attend his beloved niece Devaki's *swayamvara* ceremony. There was a political will behind this invitation which was to mend the difficult relations between the Gandharas and the Vrishnis. Subal accepted the invitation and detailed Shakuni to visit Mathura on his behalf. As instructed by his father, Shakuni visited Mathura to be present during the function.

In Mathura, a life-changing incident befell Shakuni. He became a different person with completely different priorities.

Hastinapur

The powerful Hastinapur kingdom was ruled by the Kauravas—the descendants of Kuru the Great. The Kuru king Pratip had three sons—Devapi, Bahlik and Shantanu. Devapi became an ascetic in his early youth and left the kingdom. The second son, Bahlik, was made the king of Vahik *Desh* (a kingdom located west of Hastinapur) while the youngest, Shantanu, became the king of Hastinapur. Shantanu's first wife was Ganga who bore him Devavrata—an extraordinary personality and an unparalleled warrior. But in spite of his merit and popularity, he could not succeed his father to the throne.

Shantanu had fallen in love with a much younger Satyavati—the adopted daughter of a fisherman. The fisherman put a condition that Shantanu must secure the throne of Hastinapur for Satyavati's son. In order to facilitate his father's marriage to Satyavati, Devavrata surrendered all his rights to the throne and also remained a bachelor throughout his life to avert any potential feud between his children and those of Satyavati in the future. In recognition of his outstanding sacrifice, the gods gave him the name 'Bheeshma'.

Shantanu and Satyavati had two sons—Chitrangad and Vichitraveerya. Chitrangad was killed in his youth by a Gandharva of the same name. Vichitraveerya became the king but he was grossly incompetent. It was Devavrata who was actually ruling over the kingdom, as a regent though. However, Vichitraveerya died childless due to sudden illness. In order to get a suitable heir to the throne, Vichitraveerya's young wives—Ambika and Ambalika were asked to bear sons through *Niyoga*. They reluctantly agreed to bear *Rishi* Vyasadeva's (Satyavati's son from her pre-marital union with *Rishi* Parashar) sons. But their sons were flawed, unfortunately. While the older Dhritarashtra was born blind, the younger Pandu was an albino. Vyasa's union with a maid of Ambika begot Vidur who would grow into an extremely wise and righteous man. As the eldest Dhritarashtra was blind, Pandu was anointed as the crown prince with Devavrata as the regent and Vidur as the adviser.

When Dhritarashtra and Pandu reached marriageable age, Devavrata started looking for suitable brides for them.

Mathura

The Yadavas had many clans like the Vrishnis, the Andhakas, the Kukuras, the Haihayas, the Chedis, the Bhojas and so on. The Vrishni Yadavas were the most prominent among them. They ruled over the kingdom of Saurasena, named after Shurasen, their king. Mathura was its capital city. The Vrishnis did not prefer hereditary monarchy as the mode of governance. Instead, they governed their land through some unanimously selected chieftains who were as good as kings.

After Shurasen's death, his good friend Ugrasen was chosen by the fellow chieftains as the head of the state and like Shurasen, he was a just ruler. Ugrasen had an adopted son, Kansa and a niece, Devaki who was more than a daughter to him. Kansa was a devious man who had ambitions of becoming the king of Mathura. Shurasen had one son, Vasudeva, and four daughters. Shurasen gave away his eldest daughter, Pritha, to his childless friend Kuntibhoja, a Bhoja warlord. Kuntibhoja renamed Pritha as Kunti after adoption.

Devaki and Vasudeva (the parents of Lord *Shri* Krishna Vasudeva) loved each other secretly. Though Ugrasen liked Vasudeva very much, he never saw him as Devaki's husband. As Devaki reached the marriageable age, Ugrasen arranged a *swayamvara* ceremony for Devaki to choose her husband from many suitors. But an untoward incident happened during the ceremony.

Prologue

The young man was waiting with bated breath. He was standing behind a dense bush that was beautifully cropped in the shape of a lotus petal. He was getting impatient.

A light footstep was heard. He became all ears and tried to peep through the bush.

She was coming!

The man blinked a couple of times quickly so that he would not have to bat an eyelid for quite some time, for he did not want to miss even a single glimpse of that girl.

She was now fully visible. She gracefully walked towards a couch-shaped rock and quietly sat on it with her back to the man.

The man knew what she would do now. She would sing a song in a low voice looking at the setting sun. The voice of the girl was like the sound of a flute and the tune was too dulcet to forget.

The man had come prepared today. He wanted to tell the girl something very important and also had brought a precious gift for her. He clenched his fist around a black leather satchel hanging from his shoulder. The gift was inside the bag.

He had been staying in this city for the last seven days as an honourable guest. On behalf of the host, the girl—a royal herself—had been looking after all the esteemed invitees including this man. He was smitten by her looks and charming personality at the very first sight. Within a few days, his infatuation had turned into a deep, consuming love. The girl perhaps realised that. Her behaviour towards him seemed to have been extra kind—at least the man felt so. He had made up his mind that he would formally propose to her today. He was very much confident that she would not refuse.

The girl, meanwhile, started humming a tune and the man was listening, spellbound.

Suddenly, the man felt something squirm near his feet. With a start, he looked down. It was a snake—easily the biggest he had ever seen! The dreadful serpent crept rapidly through the neatly mowed grass of the garden. It was slithering towards the rock that the girl was sitting on.

His girl was in danger! Without a second thought, the man dashed forward as fast as he could.

The girl was completely lost in her singing. The snake, by then, had reached the rock and was climbing over the boulder's jagged surface. The man, panting, reached the place almost at the same time. Without thinking anything, he grabbed the girl from behind and pushed her on the other side of the rock and in the act tumbled over her. The snake changed its direction quickly at the commotion and disappeared into a cranny.

The girl, crimson with astonishment and rage, could not just believe what had happened. She got up quickly, trembling. The man also got up with some difficulty. The girl's doe eyes were now smouldering with fury. The man realised that he had been misunderstood.

'H...how dare you! You...you...,' the girl was stammering.

'Please...please, understand. There was a...,' the man faltered and pointed his finger towards the snake that was no more there. The only proof of his innocence was lost.

'Shut up, you scoundrel!' the girl's voice, though not raised much, was spine-chilling. Her beautiful face contorted with a searing anger.

She called me a scoundrel! How could she!

Though there was still some light in the sky, it was already all dark for the man. He tried to make a desperate last attempt to save the day, 'Believe me, *Devi*, please. I just tried to save you... I just....'

'I don't need to be saved! You tried to molest me actually. You thought I was alone and helpless. I always knew, you had it in your mind. I saw it in your eyes the very first day I met you. You have been stalking me here for the last two days. I noticed everything but didn't care simply because you happen to be a guest. But I could not even imagine you'd stoop so low and dare this much!'

The girl's affronts were flogging the crestfallen man. Meanwhile, some armed guards showed up.

Surprisingly, she calmed down a notch and took a step towards the man who stood like a lifeless effigy. She said in a rather low voice, 'I could have you beheaded right now, but our noble culture grants immunity to an officially invited foreigner, regardless of his crime. Just get lost and never dare show me your face ever again.'

One of the guards placed his hand very roughly on the man's shoulder. The man was not used to such a brusque touch—from a socially inferior person at that! He turned around sharply and rammed his knuckles straight into the guard's chin. The guard fell down on the ground like a severed tree trunk.

The other sentinels pounced on the young man like hungry wolves showering punches and kicks in torrents. He put up a brave fight but they were too many for him. The man was brutally thrashed. Then, one of them held him by the scruff of his neck and made him stand up. The others lifted their blades to hack him into pieces.

The battered, bloodied man knew his time was come. He had no strength left to stage a fightback. But before he died, he had to see the girl's face for one last time. He looked at the girl who was standing like a marble statue. Her peculiar countenance seemed like a mystery to the man. Was she feeling sad for him? The man's heart thumped. Did she have a place for him in her mind, however small? The man felt light for one fleeting moment, completely oblivious of his present situation.

He did not know that the girl herself had been in trouble for quite some time. She did not want to get involved in any untoward incident further.

'Don't kill him! He has been punished enough already,' the girl's tired voice floated in the air.

'*Deviji*, this man should not live. He dared touch you!' One guard said with folded hands, asking for the permission to slaughter him.

'No! This petty rascal happens to be a foreigner and a guest. Have you all forgotten that tomorrow is my best friend's wedding? Do not spoil the happy mood of the city with any violence.'

Petty rascal! Me? She dared call me a rascal?

The young man felt as if his mouth had been filled with ashes. Was that what he had craved for? He felt he would have better been left dying a painful death than to survive on her clemency. He hated himself.

The swords came down immediately. The guards took their hands off the man. One showed him the exit without saying anything. Another grabbed him by the collar and gave a savage push. He wobbled a little before regaining his balance and walked away at a snail's pace, with his head sunk into his chest.

By the time he reached the exit gate, he had a completely different taste in his mouth. A bitter malice had welled up to his lips now.

He turned back once. The guards were still watching him. The girl was not there anymore. She had left.

While he deserved to be feted for saving the girl's life, these bloody people presented him with an insult worse than death!

Today was their day alright; but he would have his, too. And on his day, he would give them back much more than what he got today. He swore to take a devastating revenge on the girl and these proud people. He spat out a blob of spittle that landed on a beautiful red rose.

You will have to pay for this. You are very proud of your 'noble culture', no? My foot! I shall destroy the entire clan you are so proud of and make you watch the ruin!

The girl's pretty face surfaced in his mind for a moment. Tears brimmed in his eyes. He was being burnt and drenched at the same time. The man left the place in a huff. He wished he could leave this damned city at once but that was not possible. He must attend tomorrow's function by any means to avoid a scene. Otherwise, he would have a lot of explaining to do, even to his own people.

The special gift he had brought for the girl could not be delivered.

Part i

I

Devaki was looking a little restless now. She had so far been an epitome of poise and grace. Dressed in the most expensive silk and bedecked with dazzling jewellery, she was looking like a goddess. She was the beloved niece of Ugrasen, the Vrishni king of Mathura.

Her feathery fingers were clutching at the heavy garland with unnecessary tightness. She was looking at the doorway through the corner of her eyes. Was she expecting someone to come?

Devaki's *swayamvara* ceremony was just about to begin. The inaugural dance and music performances by the best artists of Mathura had just concluded. The guests were gearing up for the main attraction. Devaki—one of the most desired girls of *Aryavarta*—was to choose her husband from a number of admirers now. She would soon start roaming around with the garland in her hand. She would choose her life partner by garlanding him. This was the most awaited and exciting moment of the ritual. Every lovestruck young man was nervously watching the girl, expecting the garland to fall on his shoulders.

But Devaki was not moving. She was taking time. The guests were getting impatient. Even Ugrasen himself could not understand why his niece was not making a move.

'*Kanya* Devaki, start walking. Everybody is waiting, can't you see?' Ugrasen whispered.

Suddenly a strapping, robust man stormed into the hall. Though middle-aged, he moved with an unbearable swagger.

He was well-known to Ugrasen who stood up from his seat and shouted a surprised greeting at him, 'Good heavens! How come you are here, Shini? What a pleasant surprise! Come, come bless my daughter, she is choosing her husband today.'

Saying this, Ugrasen introduced the stranger to the assemblage: 'O my esteemed guests, please allow me the liberty and pleasure of introducing to you this extraordinary gentleman who is a jewel among the Vrishni Yadavas. He is *Shri* Shini. He is a cousin of the late King Shurasen.'

Shini—an outstanding warrior—did not really need an introduction. Most of the guests either knew him or had at least heard of him. He bowed to Ugrasen reverentially and said in a rumbling voice, 'O *Maharaj* Ugrasen, please accept my apology in advance. I am going to do something which may not please you very much. I shall take Devaki with me now. I shall get her married to my dear nephew Vasudeva. They are deeply in love and are meant for each other.'

Ugrasen stood nonplussed. It was not that he did not like Vasudeva. On the contrary, the young boy had impressed him very much by his intelligence and pleasant manners. But Ugrasen actually never thought of him as Devaki's husband.

Shini took a step towards the guests and issued them a brave warrior's challenge.

'Here, I take the girl away with me. If anyone has any objections, come forward and fight me.' Saying this, Shini unsheathed his enormous sword.

'Anyone?' Shini shouted haughtily.

No one responded. Shini's reputation as a warrior deterred the guests from taking meaningless risks.

'Very wise of you,' grinned Shini.

Turning around, he addressed Devaki spreading his hand towards her. 'Come *Kanya,* I shall get you the man of your life.'

With a delighted smile, Devaki held his arm. They started to walk towards the exit. Ugrasen was scratching his head as he could not understand whether to stop or allow them.

'Stop!' An irate shout was heard from the crowd.

Shini turned back flashing a crooked smile, 'Ah…at least there is someone here with some guts. Good! But who is it?'

It was Somadatta, the crown prince of Vahik *Desh*. The young, courageous prince came forward with a crescent-shaped cavalry sword in his hand. His face was red with anger.

'You simply cannot take her away like this,' screamed the young prince.

'Oh, really? Can't I?' Shini asked sarcastically.

'At least you have to defeat me before doing that.'

'So be it. Let's then have a quick fencing game.' Saying this, Shini slashed the air with a wild swing of his sword.

Somadatta rushed in with the upraised sword and pounced on Shini, who quickly side-stepped with nimble footwork. Although slightly off-balance, Somadatta still managed to bring the sword down on Shini's head dangerously. Shini parried the blow by holding his sword horizontally overhead. Somadatta quickly freed his sword from the lock and tried to jab Shini in the throat. But again Shini moved his head aside with an amazing body feint and held Somadatta's wrist with the left hand. A right-handed Shini easily twisted his arm even with the weaker left hand and headbutted him in the face.

Somadatta's head reeled. With a bleeding nose, he was down on his knees. But he was not to give up so easily. He got up immediately on his feet and desperately lunged at Shini's jugular like a leaping snake. Shini did not expect such a spirited fightback from Somadatta. Although he managed to step aside, he could not save himself completely. Somadatta's sword grazed his shoulder leaving a deep cut.

Shini looked at the wound on his shoulder. It was smarting and bleeding. The sight of his own blood infuriated him. He came back to his elements. With a jerk of his shoulder, he got rid of the *uttariya* that covered his torso. Shini now stood bare bodied. He looked severe.

Drawing blood on his formidable opponent, Somadatta got a little carried away and came too close to Shini for another assault. But an enraged Shini did not give away any more chance to his rival. He struck on Somadatta's sword so powerfully that the blade broke off from the handle and flew away quite a distance before falling on the floor with a clink. A stunned Somadatta blankly looked on at the bladeless hilt held in his hand. Shini kicked Somadatta in the stomach. Somadatta fell down on the floor clutching his belly with both his hands. The fight was over.

Somadatta was wallowing on the floor helplessly. But Shini's anger had not yet died down. He mercilessly kicked Somadatta in his face again. He rolled over on the ground with his face smeared with blood and the dust from Shini's boot.

The humiliation was unbearable. The Kshatriya princes and aristocrats present there were appalled at Shini's ungracious behaviour. However, fearing a similar treatment, nobody dared voice any protest.

'Feel obliged that I have spared your life. Go home and take some medicines!' Shini mocked at his fallen rival.

He held Devaki's hand tightly and stormed out of the hall. Devaki turned back for a moment and looked at Ugrasen's face with an unspoken apology. Ugrasen looked totally vacant. He was sensitive enough to read Devaki's mind. He realised that she herself desired Vasudeva and her present sense of guilt would soon be lost into the blissful marital romance that her future promised.

Somadatta was still lying prone, battered and humiliated. One man slowly came out of the throng of dumbfounded guests. He walked up to Somadatta with measured steps and bent down to hold his hands.

'Get up, *Kumar* Somadatta. I am Shakuni from Gandhara.' He said with a low, dry voice.

'Shakuni!' Somadatta wiped the dripping blood from his nose and mouth and said in a choked voice, 'If you are a friend, please do me one favour. Dig your knife into my chest and carry my corpse to my father. I simply can't go home carrying this humiliation on my back!'

Shakuni almost whispered, 'I am neither your friend nor your enemy—at least not yet. I just wanted to tell you that you need to live to get avenged, *Kumar* Somadatta. Go home. The battle has just started!'

There was something in his voice that gave Somadatta the strength to get up on his feet.

2

King Bahlik stormed into his son's luxurious bed chamber.

His son was seated on a gem-encrusted chair, his face buried into his palms. On a massive marble table before him were kept a big glass jar and a golden chalice. There was a reddish liquid almost at the bottom of the jar. Bahlik could easily identify the liquid from the distinct smell wafting in the air. It was *madhvika*! His dear son had taken to the intoxicating liquor right from the morning itself.

Bahlik stood with his arms akimbo and glowered at Prince Somadatta, who poured the remaining liquor into the chalice and downed it in a single draught, completely ignoring his father.

'What the hell is this, Soma? Why are you so upset? You've lost only a minor duel. We are Kshatriyas; we win some fights, we lose some—what's the big deal? Have you forgotten how many battles you have won already? You must not take this defeat so seriously, *Putra*,' the king said softly.

'Minor defeat, huh? *Pitashri*, do you know what that bloody Yadava did to me? After knocking me down with a shot, he kicked me again on my face—here, just see!' Somadatta excitedly pointed at the bluish lump just under his left eye.

Bahlik's jaws stiffened. Kicking a floored opponent was truly unpardonable. How dared Shini do that to his son? He should have better killed Somadatta, instead of inflicting such mortal humiliation. Bahlik clenched his fist around the scabbard hanging from the waistband. He took some time to digest this. But he knew that he must not show his own anger lest the already upset son get excited further. He asked carefully, 'What do you want to do?'

'I want to slaughter those Vrishnis, *Pitashri*. I want to raze their city to the ground, at any cost!' Somadatta stood up and screamed at the wall. He was breathing like a mad bison with his handsome face twitched in fury.

Bahlik, for once, felt pity for this immature youth. *These youngsters want to solve everything with brawn.* He decided to teach his son a little bit of politics now.

'Do you know anything about these Vrishni Yadavas, Soma? Before scurrying for revenge, you must know their strength. Sorry to inform you that our army would not survive even a full day before them. Moreover, despite the fact that the Yadavas have so many factions and internal feuds, in case of emergency you shall invariably find them united and invincible,' Bahlik said with a grim face.

Somadatta impatiently shouted, '*Oho*, why should we go to war alone? We shall field our Devavrata and his Hastinapur army along with us. Who can beat our Devavrata? I am sure he will support us. After all, we too are from the same family!'

'I am much more aware than you that we too are Kauravas. You don't need to remind me that. I know my nephew very well. I am sure that Devavrata won't help us in this particular case.'

'Why? He is so fond of me…,' Somadatta asked like a child.

'Because he is far more intelligent than you. Hastinapur cannot afford to court enmity with the Yadavas—especially the Vrishnis—right now. Hastinapur has old disputes with Panchala and is wary of the rising Magadha as well. Mathura is kind of a buffer state for Hastinapur to remain secure both from Panchala and Magadha. Devavrata has to be on good terms with the Vrishnis.'

'Then? Can't we seek help from Jarasandha of Magadha? Or the Panchalas?'

'Absolutely not. Jarasandha is a friend of Kansa. He has got his two daughters married to Kansa, who is the last word in Mathura, despite his father Ugrasen's presence. You can say, Mathura and Magadha are fast allies now. And we should not try to befriend the Panchalas simply because that would offend our Devavrata. Moreover, though I know Prishat likes me personally, I am less confident about his son Drupad who is going to be anointed as the next Panchala king very soon. Things are not very encouraging on that side, my dear!'

'Then what should I do, *Pitashri*, have a bellyful of good food and jump safely into my mother's lap to be caressed and cuddled, completely digesting the insult?' Somadatta barked at his father.

Bahlik did not react. He was pacing up and down, with his hands clasped at the back. He was seriously worried. His son's humiliation had revealed a serious flaw in his foreign policy. He had never made serious efforts to build up a separate clout of his Vahik kingdom. He had always preferred to stay under the shadow of Hastinapur, relying too much on his Kaurava lineage. Somadatta's defeat was a good lesson for him.

'If you want revenge, you have to have patience, only patience. This wait could be inordinately long—may extend even beyond one generation.'

'What do you mean? Tell me quickly,' Somadatta appeared interested.

Bahlik sat on an upholstered couch and reclined comfortably. His eyes were glaring.

'We must look west, instead of the east. We have to slowly build up a strong confederacy around us.'

'How? With whom?'

'We too have many friends, Soma. Madra kingdom is our natural ally. Shalya has developed into a fearsome warrior and leads a very strong Madra army. He will be on our side, for sure. Chandravarma and his son Sudakshina of Kamboja are good friends of mine. The Tusharas and the Yavanas are also indebted to me. Briddhakshatra of Sindhu can also be approached. He is an amiable man and we have good trade terms. The only point of concern is Gandhara.'

Somadatta had been listening with interest. With the mention of Gandhara, his face darkened again. He said, 'Right, *Pitashri*. That Subal is very cunning. Although his son Shakuni behaved very nicely with me in Mathura, I think we should not trust him. He is actually a fox!'

'That's very close to what I myself believe. But we must have Subal and Shakuni on our side, by any means.'

'But we should never trust those mountain scorpions!'

'We have to. And that is because of Shakuni only. I shall tell you why later.'

Somadatta sprang up. 'Fine, then. We should start sending emissaries to these kingdoms at once.'

Bahlik burst out laughing, 'What for, Soma? We are not going to any war tomorrow. I told you we'd have to wait pretty long for the revenge. No need to rush now.'

Somadatta sat down frustrated. Bahlik understood that he had not been able to instil much hope in his son's mind. He thought a little biting his lip and decided to divulge a secret he had kept only to himself thus far.

Bahlik cleared his throat and sat on the couch. He began in a low voice, 'What I am going to tell you now, must never go beyond this room, mind you.'

Bahlik now had Somadatta's complete attention. He continued, 'I shall tell you a story. I had an elder brother named Devapi. He was a peculiar man—never interested in anything royal. He had ascetic tendencies right from the childhood. Quite early in his youth, he contracted leprosy which disqualified him for the throne. He left the kingdom and started residing in a dense jungle near Hastinapur. There he met many *rishis* and ascetics and apparently acquired certain psychic powers.

In his absence, my father offered me the throne of Hastinapur as I was the second son. Before my coronation, I went to meet Devapi in the jungle to seek his blessings. I was very close to him. He, meanwhile, had become a famous soothsayer. He forbade me to accept Hastinapur's throne and advised me to settle on this land, Vahik *Desh*, to set up a new kingdom. This land had been won by my father, with the help of Jarasandha and his father Brihadratha. I obeyed Devapi, for I had great respect for him and his psychic abilities. I refused the throne of Hastinapur and told father that I wanted to sit on the throne of Vahik, instead. Father agreed and my younger brother Shantanu—Devavrata's father—was made the king of Hastinapur, while I shifted here.'

'But, why did he advise you against Hastinapur's throne? After all, Hastinapur is a more powerful, prosperous and influential kingdom than ours,' Somadatta asked with genuine curiosity.

Bahlik took a good swig of water and resumed the story, 'Devapi told me that Hastinapur was doomed. Eventually, serious tension will crop up within the family. Relationships will strain and tragedies abound. Unbridled corruption will become an accepted norm of the royal culture. Jealousy, malice and hatred will pollute the air inside the royal palace. Then a foreign agent would arrive at Hastinapur with a specific mission. He would cause a rift within the house. Finally, two equally powerful factions will emerge inside the Kuru family and they will fight a bloody civil war between them. The breakaway group will attack Hastinapur with supports from Panchala and the Vrishnis—the most formidable clan of the Yadavas. Mind you, your enemy Shini happens to be a Vrishni! Obviously, we will have to fight against them to defend Hastinapur, supporting the other camp. In order to avenge your humiliation, I am now waiting for that war to take place. I will gradually start building up a fast alliance with the north-western kingdoms of Bharatavarsha and the Uttarapatha to ensure their support in future. In that battle, you or your descendants will get a chance to settle scores with Shini or his descendants. You need to wait till that moment as it is not possible for us to embark on any adventure against the Vrishnis right now.'

Somadatta was listening with rapt attention. His mood had changed completely. He asked, 'But *Pitashri*, how can you be so sure about Devapi's prophecy? Has any of his predictions already come true?'

'Good question. Devapi had said that all troubles in Hastinapur would originate from an amazing act of sacrifice committed by a great scion of our Kuru dynasty. He did not name the person, nor did he describe the act of sacrifice. When I learnt that Devavrata had renounced all his legitimate rights to the throne of Hastinapur and pledged celibacy, trust me Soma, I had goosebumps all over my body! Devavrata is not only great—he can be easily considered as the greatest Kaurava ever born. You don't know him. I do. I know what he is capable of. I know what material he is. And just see what followed next. Both his step-brothers died young. The wives of one of those step-brothers had to be impregnated through *Niyoga*. And what was the result? Dhritarashtra was born blind, and Pandu, albino. Nothing in that family is going right.

One of Devapi's predictions has already proved correct and I firmly believe—so will the others.'

Somadatta now asked the most obvious question, 'Didn't you ask him about the outcome of the war?'

'I did. But his reply was quite cryptic. He said with a wry smile that the side with the most intelligent man will win the war, regardless of the comparative military strength.'

'The most intelligent man?'

'Yes. Can you understand now why I desperately want Shakuni on our side? His brainpower is unmatched. The Gandhara kingdom has been blessed to have him. We already have the illustrious Devavrata. With both Devavrata and Shakuni on our side, our victory should be ensured as per Devapi's prediction. And with that your dream of punishing the Vrishnis will be fulfilled.'

'Hmm,' Somadatta started walking up and down slowly. His drunkenness was totally gone. 'So, where do we go now?'

'See, your personal aspiration for revenge is a rather small matter. But your defeat at that Vrishni's hand has been an eye opener for me. It's a blessing in disguise, perhaps. If Hastinapur is in trouble, we cannot stay aloof. We must start our own preparations with an eye to the future. First, I need a very special grandson!'

'Sorry?' Somadatta was taken aback at this unexpected suggestion.

'You heard me. If you don't get a chance to defeat Shini, at least your son can defeat Shini's son or grandson and avenge your humiliation. You have to worship Lord Shiva and get a mighty son with his boon. Side by side, I have to secure Shakuni's support. That is most important.'

'How would you go about it?'

'I have a plan. Devavrata is looking for a bride for Dhritarashtra. But as Dhritarashtra is blind, no one is willing to get his daughter married to him. I will advise Devavrata to set up an alliance with Shakuni's sister Gandhari. And if that is done, Shakuni will be ours, forever!'

Somadatta was getting more and more confused. He was feeling like a clueless child lost in a convoluted labyrinth. He asked with eyes bulged, 'But why should Subal agree to give his daughter to a blind Dhritarashtra?'

'For that, we need to conduct a fake war with support from Devavrata's army. I will rake up the old border issue with Gandhara over that unadministered hilly land that had once been ruled by the Sakas. They gifted that land to me before leaving the place for good. The Gandharas claim that land to be theirs. We will now occupy that land with an army led by Devavrata. The Gandharas will come under pressure. Then we will put forward the condition—either give Gandhari to Dhritarashtra, or perish. And we shall give away that useless land to Gandhara as a "return gift"—a token of courtesy. How's the idea, Soma?' Bahlik grinned impishly.

Somadatta's head was reeling. He could not say anything. Perhaps this was the right way to survive in this vicious world! He never knew his father had this much cunning. And he thought *Shakuni* was a fox!

'I will have to send an urgent message to Hastinapur now, apprising Devavrata of my plan. He will surely like the idea of a Gandhari-Dhritarashtra alliance. He will have to come here soon and set up the drama of an invasion. We have to hurry otherwise the beautiful Gandhari will be married off to someone else. I must take your leave now,' Bahlik got up and walked hurriedly towards the door.

He stopped mid-way, as if he just remembered something important. He turned back and asked Somadatta hesitantly, 'Er...tell me one thing. Why did you try to fight Shini alone, while the others did not say anything? Did you have a thing for Devaki?'

Somadatta coughed suddenly. He moved his palm quickly over his face—probably to hide his immediate spontaneous reaction—and curtly said, 'That is not an issue, *Pitashri*. Why should Shini enter a *swayamvara* ceremony uninvited and abduct the girl forcibly? That too not for himself, but for his nephew! Let alone the meek Ugrasen, even the mighty Kansa did not protest! It was nothing but a sinister Vrishni conspiracy to conduct a fake *swayamvara* ritual while everything was fixed beforehand. It was utterly humiliating for all the kings and the princes present there. But no one dared protest. I did, for I could not tolerate such an insult. Tell me, did I do anything wrong?'

Bahlik nodded and left the room. He had to send an important message now to Hastinapur requesting Devavrata to come at the earliest.

King Bahlik had completely ignored the two guards standing just outside the room with lofty spears in their hands.

He did not know that one of those guards was of Gandhara origin and he had been all ears overhearing their discussion.

The guard was eagerly waiting for his duty hours to be over so that he could pass on to his master in Gandhara a very important piece of information he had just been privy to.

3

'Pitashri wants your presence at the assembly at once, *Bhratashri*.'

An unmindful Shakuni turned his face slowly towards Arjak but did not seem much interested. 'Hmm... What is the matter?'

'You have attended the assembly very rarely since your return from Mathura. What's wrong with you, *Bhratashri*?' Arjak looked anxious.

His anxiety was well founded. No one had ever mattered more in Gandhara than Shakuni, thanks to his extraordinary mental ability. And he had been behaving rather strangely ever since he had come back from Mathura about a month back. Nobody had ever seen such a lost, pensive, absent-minded Shakuni—for such a long period at that.

'Nothing, let's go. We should not keep *Pitashri* waiting,' Shakuni got up with a casual shrug and got into Arjak's chariot. Arjak curiously looked on at Shakuni's face to understand his illustrious brother's mood, though he could not decipher much. He did not dare ask further questions either. His relationship with his brother was never easy due to an issue that was too sensitive for both of them to overcome.

Their father, Subal, the king of Gandhara, was sitting majestically on his royal throne, eagerly waiting for Shakuni. The king as well as his ministers looked worried. It seemed an unexpected predicament had befallen them and they were completely clueless about how to deal with it.

Shakuni's entrance to the assembly created quite a stir among the courtiers. All stood up—more in a spontaneous excitement of having in their midst Shakuni, the mastermind, than to merely comply with the official protocol. Evidently relieved, Subal too reclined in his seat, as if Shakuni's very presence was by itself a solution to his problem.

'What bothers you, *Maharaj*?' asked Shakuni.

Subal did not reply immediately. Rather, he inspected his son's face carefully in order to find if anything was amiss, for Shakuni's absent-mindedness was something Subal could neither digest nor afford. He tried to understand the case in a roundabout way.

'I heard something went wrong in Mathura during Devaki's *swayamvara* ceremony. But you did not tell me anything. What happened?'

Shakuni frowned. His heart pounded. What had Subal heard?

'What did you hear, *Pitashri*?'

'That there was a fight, apparently...Shini and Somadatta fought....'

Shakuni felt relieved. He said quickly, 'Oh! That was a mere tiff, rather. Shini actually tried to abduct Devaki as he wanted her to get married to his nephew Vasudeva. Somadatta protested. Shini gave him a sound thrashing and went away with the girl.'

Subal stared at Shakuni suspiciously. He got a feeling that his son was not being completely honest with him. He decided to be more direct. 'Do you know it is you that is bothering me most nowadays? Since your return from Mathura you are not yourself. What's the matter, *Putra* Shakuni? You are not taking much interest in official matters either. I heard you have even stopped playing *pasha*! You without your dice in hand—unthinkable! No, no, something must be wrong. Tell me.'

Shakuni got seriously annoyed this time. Why were these people after him so desperately? Why were they so inquisitive? Was not Shakuni entitled to any personal space? The state needed him no doubt and he always felt honoured to be of such importance but at the end of the day he was a complex human being rather than a public property. These people must learn to respect his privacy.

Surprising his father, Shakuni's reply was uncharacteristically stern, 'Please, tell me if you have anything more important to discuss than wasting your precious time on a petty issue like my mental state that should concern you in no way!'

The repartee crashed on King Subal who himself was a temperamental man. There was complete silence in the assembly. Subal's face reddened but he chose not to reprimand his son at this hour as a much graver threat was looming over Gandhara.

Without wasting any more time, Subal came to the point, 'Okay, let's talk business. A good number of Vahik soldiers headed by Bahlik and Devavrata have suddenly occupied the territory we had taken over from the Sakas. There was no provocation from our side. Our border guards covering that area have been driven away by the Vahik force.'

Shakuni smiled slightly. *So, Bahlik is at it, already. My spy is absolutely correct.*

Subal did not miss that sly smirk. 'It seems it is not much unexpected to you. Did you have any inkling of this?'

'Yes *Maharaj*. I knew it. I have my undercover agents inside all our neighbouring states. One of them informed of such a possibility a fortnight ago.'

'A fortnight ago! And you did not care to inform me! What was the exact information, tell me.' A livid Subal stood up.

Shakuni said with a casual shrug, 'I did not tell you because we don't have anything to do.'

'They are occupying our land and we don't have anything to do? We must prepare our army right now. We have a fight at our hands!'

'No we don't, *Pitashri*. They are not exactly coming for a fight. They are actually coming with a marriage proposal that we have to accept under duress.'

There were astonished exclamations from all over the hall. Shakuni explained it a little further, 'They are actually coming for your daughter. They want her for Dhritarashtra, the prince of Hastinapur.'

Nobody could immediately react. Shakuni had stunned everyone into complete silence.

King Subal was the first to break free from the stupor of surprise.

'But...but...Dhritarashtra is blind! How can I marry off my darling Gandhari to a blind man? Never!'

'Do you think you have many options, O venerable *Maharaj*?' Shakuni asked mocking. 'We would still have had some chance against Bahlik and Somadatta; but once Devavrata has been seen upfront, we should better surrender than suffer obvious casualties.'

'I cannot be so cruel to my daughter. How can I destroy her life like this?' Subal clamped his hair with his fingers. Deep in his heart, a doting father and a responsible king were locked in a desperate fight.

Shakuni understood the struggle within his father and his eyes moistened. He too loved his sister very much. A tempest was raging in his mind. But his internal strife happened to be slightly different from his father's.

The secret conversation between Bahlik and his son Somadatta had been leaked out to Shakuni almost immediately, thanks to the good work of Rochaman, his most trusted accomplice posted as a guard at Somadatta's private accommodation.

Nobody knew that Shakuni too had his very own reason to settle scores with the Vrishni Yadavas. Ironically, Bahlik's motive turned out to be perfectly in agreement with Shakuni's. Bahlik and his son did not know that Shakuni too wanted to destroy the Vrishnis—something he could only achieve with Hastinapur's support. Bahlik's stratagem was likely to serve Shakuni the best. He would leave no stones unturned to fit in the role of that 'foreign agent' who would apparently split the Kuru house, as Devapi had forewarned. If the Vrishnis were really to fight a war against Hastinapur at all in a near or distant future, Shakuni would certainly ally his Gandhara with Hastinapur against the Vrishni Yadavas. And in order to forge a fast alliance with Hastinapur, Gandhari needed to get married to the blind Dhritarashtra. Poor Gandhari! Shakuni felt sad for his dear sister.

The poor girl will have to be sacrificed at my altar of revenge! She will be a collateral damage of my war! But no one should get an inkling of this. It must be kept a secret never to come out in the open. It is good that Gandhara has no other option than to submit to Hastinapur's demand.

'Say something, Shakuni. Why are you speechless now?' Subal cried in a distorted voice.

Shakuni's web of thought was torn.

'*Maharaj*, I think this is an issue of dire importance and should be placed before your esteemed Cabinet for discussion,' said Shakuni, hiding a smile.

Of the sixteen ministers of the royal Cabinet, twelve were unambiguously in favour of Gandhari's marriage to Dhritarashtra and four supported a war. One senior minister, named Virupaksh, said, '*Maharaj*, I think we should better forego that disputed land. That way we could be able to avoid both—the war and Gandhari's marriage!'

Shakuni silently cursed Virupaksh. *That old bat is about to ruin my plot!* Before anybody else could react, he hastily quipped in for damage control and bantered at the aged minister, 'So *Mahamantri,* you think that the invading army will go back happy with a barren piece of land? The entire crisis seems just as simple to you, right? And my father depends so blindly on you people! Let me tell you, old man, that neither Hastinapur nor Vahik has any serious interest in that hilly land. Even if we concede that land to them, they will want Gandhari all the same—as per the input of my most reliable spy.'

Virupaksh's wrinkled face fell. Never had Shakuni spoken to him like that. A mature and wise person, he preferred to digest the insult for the time being.

'But, what if my daughter refuses? Should we force her?' Subal was almost on the verge of tears.

Shakuni cleared his throat and said, 'She'd never refuse, *Pitashri*. I know my sister quite well—perhaps better than anyone else. Once she understands that her refusal can land us in trouble, she will never let that happen. She is an angel, you know. If you allow, I can talk to her about this.'

The situation was not easy for Subal to handle. Never had he felt so helpless before. He felt relieved to let Shakuni handle the situation. He nodded in approval and dismissed the court for the day.

Shakuni chose to walk to his sister's apartment, instead of riding a chariot. He was putting his thoughts in order and needed some time to prepare himself for a potentially difficult meeting with Gandhari. He was readying himself to put on an act to give her an impression that they were courageous enough to go to war, rather than give in to the enemy's demand. In all likelihood, Gandhari herself would put her foot down and insist on getting married to Dhritarashtra, in order to ensure safety to her beloved countrymen. Throughout the long walk towards Gandhari's chamber, Shakuni was struggling hard to prepare himself well for playing the cruel trick on his innocent sister.

The brother and the sister were sitting face-to-face. Shakuni had just broken the news that their kingdom was under serious threat and Gandhari was the matter of contention.

'But don't worry, Panna[1], we shall fight to death rather than let you fall into the hands of a blind man!' Shakuni tried to sound as courageous as he could.

'Have they sent any formal missive, *Bhrata*?' Gandhari asked calmly.

'Not yet. But they will. My spies are never wrong.'

'Hmm...,' Gandhari stood up and walked towards a corner of the room where a beautiful idol of Lord Shiva was kept. Shakuni was watching her reactions carefully.

'Don't worry, *Bhrata*. If they are here just for me, as per your information, let them have me. I want no bloodshed, especially when it can so easily be avoided,' Gandhari's voice sounded like a solemn chant.

Exactly what Shakuni had expected! But he needed to extend the drama a little more. 'Never! We can never do this to you. We shall rather die fighting!' He mixed emotion, determination and anger in right proportion to create the desired effect.

---

[1] Panna was the pet name endearingly given to Gandhari by Shakuni, influenced by the emerald colour of her eyes.

'No, *Bhrata,* no! Not a single man must die because of me. A woman can live happily with a blind person if he is a good man. And Dhritarashtra is a good man, so I have heard. Trust me, I shall adjust,' Gandhari implored with folded hands.

Shakuni lowered his eyes. It was too much even for him. Everything was going his way thus far, yet he felt a blob choking his throat. He said softly, 'Let us have a communication from them first. We can decide then. I just came to inform you of the possibility.'

'Let it come. I am completely ready for the marriage. I can easily do this much for my own country.' Gandhari sounded firm and determined, though her face was turned away from her brother.

His mission was completely successful. Yet, a thorn was pricking at his heart. He was feeling guilty.

After his departure, Gandhari sat on her favourite settee and looked at the enormous mirror that covered more than half of the left wall. Her room was dimly lit. She always loved the mystic embrace of light and shade. In that subdued light, the mirror returned a surreal reflection of her eyes that were glowing like two green emeralds seemingly embedded on the mirror's glass.

Gandhari smiled wryly. She knew her eyes were special. The eyes seemed to have mystical powers of their own. They could see many more things than they were supposed to. They had just discovered Shakuni's histrionic attempts beneath his pretentious show of courage. They could clearly see thin lines of relief on Shakuni's face when Gandhari herself offered to marry Dhritarashtra. Thanks to those eyes, Gandhari was a master of reading the minds of others. Nobody knew that—not even her prodigious brother.

But Gandhari could never understand one thing. Why did this preternatural vision always introduce her only to the dark secrets of reality? Why had these special eyes never presented any unexpected happiness to her ever? Even today, when her brother's brave words should have made her happy and proud, her eyes incorrigibly found out the bitter truth that was better left unknown.

She felt severely let down. Heaving a depressed sigh, Gandhari concluded that her eyes were actually a curse. They would never let her be happy in her life. It seemed that she must learn to live without her vision, should she have to find happiness. The idea of getting married to a blind man did not seem too bad to her anymore. This man could at least teach her to survive in eternal darkness. She brought herself to believe that she would be able to love this poor, blind man some day.

Gandhari decided to wear a strip of cloth to cover her eyes after her marriage, for she desperately wanted to be happy—even if that would cost her the sight of this apparently beautiful world. And without her vision, she would be able to become a perfect companion of her would-be husband.

Gandhari, unknown to herself, had fallen in love with darkness.

4

'O Gandhara-raj Subal,

Please accept our regards and greetings. Our uninvited arrival at your doorstep is not an invasion, at least it is not intended to be one unless the situation so demands. In fact, whether it will be an invasion or not depends entirely upon you. If it sounds strange, please do go through our appeal carefully.

We have understood that both our ancestors acted unwisely by ignoring each other and thereby missed a good opportunity of building a great bilateral relationship between the Gandharas and the Kauravas. To amend the past mistakes, we have come this far to extend our hand of friendship to you.

The segment of land we have just occupied by defeating your ill-equipped and unskilled soldiers does not interest us. Rather, we, with some degree of humility, express our sincere intention of forging a blissful marital alliance between your charming daughter Gandhari and the eldest Kuru prince Dhritarashtra who, as people say, is as powerful as a few elephants put together.

Please be assured that we shall not return empty-handed. If we do not secure your friendship, we will have to take your enmity. Should we not receive your daughter's hand in alliance, we shall have to march into your kingdom. Allow us to inform you about your vulnerability from three sides to the Hastinapur, Vahik and Madra forces. We are hopeful that given Prince Shakuni's extraordinary intelligence, you are well-advised of the realistic chances of defending your kingdom against such an assault—God forbid should it occur.

In deference to the importance of your time and ours, we have spelled out your options and set a timeline. We expect your messengers to reach us with your consent for the alliance within two days of the receipt of this communication. If they don't reach us by the specified time, it will be deemed a rejection and our army will enter your kingdom to achieve yet another conquest.

The future of Gandhara rests on your decision.

May God bless you, your family and your subjects.

Respectfully,
Bahlik Pratipeya, Vahik Desh
Devavrata Gangeya 'Bheeshma', Hastinapur'

The letter had just reached King Subal's assembly and Virupaksh was reading it aloud in front of the king and other Cabinet members, including Prince Shakuni. The cocky messenger from Vahik *Desh* was standing beside Virupaksh with a posture slightly less than courteous.

There was no immediate response when Virupaksh finished reading. Everybody was trying to come to terms with the humiliating tone of the letter. Subal looked severely pinched. Even Shakuni's lips were trembling. Though he knew it was coming, he had not expected that the proposal would be made in such an irreverent manner under the flimsy garb of politeness, especially when Devavrata was widely respected both as a warrior and a man of ethics.

All the bloody Kshatriyas of Aryavarta are equally mean, Shakuni thought. He was also afraid of his father Subal. The letter might not please the old man very much and he could try to retaliate. It would do no good to Shakuni's secret plan.

Shakuni's fear almost came true.

Subal stood up from his seat with a grim face and clenched fists. This was too much for him. He would never digest such insult!

With an irritated wave of his hand, Subal dismissed the messenger first. He then addressed the assembly, his voice unsteady with anger, 'Gandhara will never bow down to such arrogance! Had they approached me with adequate humility, I could have considered the proposal. But now, it is simply not possible. The bloody Kauravas have left us with no other option! We have only two days' time. *Yuvraj* Shakuni, hold an emergency meeting with our military commanders by the day-break and prepare the army.'

Shakuni bit his lip in disgust. His father was poised to spoil his plans. But he did not have to say anything.

'Prepare the army for what, *Maharaj*?' Pat asked Virupaksh to Shakuni's surprise.

'Why the hell are you asking such a stupid question, *Mahamantri* Virupaksh? We need to prepare for their assault after the deadline, what else?' Subal said indignantly.

'They don't need to attack Gandhara—at least not immediately. Pardon me *Raja*, you have not yet understood their strategy. They have already encircled you from three sides and cut you off from the east, the north-east and the south. Very soon, we shall run out of our supply of necessary items that we import from *Aryavarta*. The war has already started and we are the side that is going to lose because we do not keep enough reserves. We cannot resist them for long, nor can we break off the encirclement with our modest forces,' Virupaksh explained.

For the first time, Shakuni found the old minister of some merit. He secretly thanked Virupaksh.

'And this morning, the Kambojas have also started deploying soldiers along the border. The Kauravas have roped them in too,' Virupaksh remarked with a straight face.

'So, you have accepted that we have to kneel down before them and let my girl fall free into their hands?' Subal said in a peculiar voice that seemed to have flown in from faraway. His words were overlapping and he suddenly burst into tears.

Everyone present in the hall lowered their heads as the broken king cried like a helpless child. A deathly silence, punctuated by Subal's sobs, reigned over the assembly for quite some time.

Suddenly, Subal's snuffles stopped. He was slowly falling down from the throne with his right palm pressed against the left side of his chest. Shakuni ran towards his father as fast as he could. Subal's eyes were bulging and he was trying desperately to say something with slurring words. Shakuni did not fail to make out what he was saying, 'Take revenge, *Putra*...destroy them...only you can do it....'

Subal fell unconscious in his son's arms. It was a stroke.

A pandemonium ensued inside the assembly hall. Everybody rushed to the aid of the fallen king. Shakuni kept his calm and shouted, 'A doctor! A doctor, at once!'

'The throne is waiting for you, Prince Shakuni. It's high time you took over. Our Gandhara is in serious crisis,' said Virupaksh, pointing at the empty royal seat.

Two days had elapsed since Subal suffered the stroke. Fortunately, it was not massive and he survived. But although he recovered quickly, it seemed highly unlikely that he would ever be fit enough to carry on as the king again. Subal's natural composure was seriously disrupted and his self-confidence lay completely shattered.

'I can assure you, *Yuvraj* Shakuni, there is complete unanimity among our council of ministers, the royal family members and other esteemed aristocrats about your immediate succession. Please, take over without further delay, *Yuvraj*. Gandhara needs you at this hour of grave crisis.' Virupaksh conjured again, with folded hands and genuine tears in his eyes.

'He is right, *Yuvraj,* it is you, only you who can bail us out of this trouble,' the ministers, courtiers and Shakuni's brothers cried in unison.

As everybody stared at him expectantly, Shakuni looked at the throne his father had been occupying until just two days ago. As the eldest son, he was always expected to succeed his father and had been preparing himself for that.

Too many thoughts were jostling in Shakuni's mind. This world had never been too simple for him. Perhaps, extraordinary people are always swarmed with complexities that spare lesser beings. Nobody would be able to imagine how necessary it was for him to settle scores with the Vrishnis. Even the Vrishnis themselves were not aware of his hatred and how they had incurred it. Since that bitter evening which had inflicted an incurable wound on him, Shakuni's every breath fired curses at the Vrishnis. But, it would not be possible for him to get even with them should he become the king.

Shakuni knew very well that a king is not a free entity—a king is actually a captive inasmuch as his status does not allow him to do many things that a commoner can. Shakuni had understood that without any apparent official authority or responsibility, he could use his devious intellect more effectively. In order to put his plan into action, he would need to accompany his sister to Hastinapur with a sinister design to create a war-like situation between the Kauravas and the Vrishnis.

And there was another good reason for him to stay away from Gandhara. He would not have to live with his wife Arshi anymore!

Shakuni's marriage had been his greatest pain. Even after four years of their marriage and the birth of their son, Uluk, three years ago, their relationship had never been easy. Shakuni could never forget that Arshi had had a pre-marital affair—and that too with his own brother, Arjak! Though Arshi put in sincere efforts to make the marriage work, Shakuni always suspected her loyalty and did not let the past be buried. All these four years, he carried out a silent, yet gruelling emotional battle against his wife and relished it!

Shakuni was a sadist. He was cruel and unforgiving. But this battle was taking its toll on him as well. He himself was getting increasingly tired from within. He had been fed up with his ruptured conjugal life and wanted to pack a decisive emotional blow to his wife.

I must go to Hastinapur. That is final. This is the only way I can break free from this stifling marriage. I know this will break Arshi. Her tears will bring me a sense of victory. She will never be able to look at Arjak again. She will burn with a scorching feeling of guilt. How dare she even think of any other man! Wasn't it enough of a blessing for her to be Shakuni's wife? And either of the twins—Achal or Vrishak—can take care of Gandhara in my absence. Both are smart and capable. My only dream now is to get the Kauravas to fight a devastating war against the Vrishnis—as foretold by Devapi.

Shakuni's lust for revenge outweighed his concern for Gandhara which had been dearer to him than his own life once upon a time. One fateful incident had turned his world upside down, dramatically changing his priorities.

Fortunately, he had a good excuse. Before falling ill, his father had asked him to take revenge against the Kauravas. Shakuni would use this as a suitable subterfuge. He felt sorry for his father for a moment for he knew he was cheating Subal. While Subal wanted revenge against the Kauravas, Shakuni's actual target were the Vrishnis for a reason too private to disclose to anyone.

Shakuni cleared his throat and addressed the courtiers with carefully chosen words, 'Dear all, it's an absolute honour that you wish me to ascend the Gandhara throne. But, I am sorry I cannot fulfil your wish. Have you all forgotten what King Subal had said to me just before falling ill? He wanted me to punish the Kauravas who humiliated every Gandhara citizen. They are about to destroy my sister's life and we are helpless. It is the Kauravas who are responsible for what my father has been reduced to today. No, no, I can never pardon them!' Shakuni blended some contrived emotion very cautiously in his speech.

'But you can do that much better as the king of Gandhara, *Yuvraj* Shakuni!' Virupaksh cried anxiously, completely unable to understand Shakuni's game.

Shakuni had expected this question. 'No. A king remains shackled by his *dharma.* A king has to look after his kingdom killing his own emotions. Being a king, I cannot fulfill my father's wish. But as a free man, I can go to any extent, do anything, stoop to any lows. I shall make inroads into the very family of the Kauravas and conspire from within. That is the only way to destroy the formidable Vrishnis—sorry, I mean the Kauravas.'

A slip of tongue! But Shakuni managed quickly. Nobody had the brainpower to suspect his motive from that little goof-up.

Shakuni continued, 'For the sake of Gandhara, I propose that my younger brother Achal be the new king, being moments older than his twin brother Vrishak. Let him be anointed as the regent for the time being, as long as *Pitashri* is alive. And let me be on the pursuit to achieve what *Pitashri* wished. Bless me, please.'

The assembly was shocked. A Gandhara without Shakuni was much like a night without the moon. Everyone tried to pursuade Shakuni to stay back in Gandhara. But as usual, Shakuni prevailed over all of them.They had to accept his decision with teary eyes.

Unable to change his mind, the council of ministers and courtiers unanimously decided to confer on Shakuni the title of 'Gandhara *Ratna'*—the highest civilian honour for any Gandhara citizen or any one of Gandhara ethnicity. It would be a befitting tribute to their dear Shakuni before sending him off on a deadly mission. Shakuni would be the youngest recipient of the award.

Shakuni went a little numb. His eyes became moist. This beautiful kingdom and the unsuspecting people loved him so much. Did he deserve this? Was he not going to cheat his wife, sister, father, country and countrymen alike?

He was faced with a dilemma. He looked at the gold-plated, bejewelled badge of 'Gandhara *Ratna*' that was kept inside a precious crystal casket on a marble rostrum at one corner of the court for public display. It would be presented to him in a formal ceremony shortly. He felt as if the badge was mocking at him.

Gandhara Ratna? Me? On the contrary, I am the worst enemy of Gandhara! I played an ugly game with my sister, used my sick father's wish as a convenient alibi, ran away from a difficult marriage without making any meaningful efforts to make it work, deceived my own country and countrymen when they needed me the most—and all this for a trivial and personal cause. Yes, I am the greatest enemy of Gandhara!

Should he change his mind now before it was too late? Was he being destructively selfish? Was he becoming a completely different man, unrecogniseably mangled by a particularly private insult?

Shakuni looked around helplessly. There were many people inside the royal court. Everybody was looking at him. But Shakuni knew that none could be of any help. These people were unable to understand his crisis. Once more, Shakuni became aware of his loneliness. He was admired, respected, feared—but never understood. He had no real friends or peers. He was never successful with women either. Perhaps women found him too intense to love. His loneliness was sickening to him.

Suddenly, an exquisite face popped up in his mind. Shakuni remembered a particular person. He felt his ears were becoming warm. He was blushing. His breath was becoming noisy.

Shakuni's dilemma was gone, once and for all.

Who can ignore my contribution to the making of this Gandhara kingdom of today? I perfectly deserve the award of 'Gaṇdhara Ratna'. I have done nothing wrong with my sister. She is being married into a famous house; so what if her husband is blind? I have not deceived my father. The uncomplicated old man does not understand many things. And I am not cheating Arshi either. My marriage has been dysfunctional. It is better to leave her alone as she always had someone else in her mind.

Shakuni felt relieved and justified. He was now completely sure why he was doing all this. It became clear to his own self that nothing was more meaningful than the indelible image of that face he had just envisaged.

Shakuni confidently took a bow to the assembly and left the hall amidst boisterous salutations and laudatory remarks from all over.

Nevertheless, his eyes were moist. He himself could not make out why.

5

Devavrata Bheeshma finished reading the message that had arrived from Gandhara in reply and handed it over to Bahlik, giving him a cunning stare. They were sitting inside a luxurious tent. Along with a unit of their army, they were camped just outside the Gandhara border.

Bahlik hurriedly read through the note. Surprised, he looked at his nephew Devavrata. He had never expected that the Gandharas—the gritty tribe notorious for their stubbornness—would give in to their demand so meekly.

The Gandharas had conveyed that they were ready to give away their favourite princess Gandhari to a blind Dhritarashtra. Had Subal's sudden illness demoralised the Gandharas? Or, did they have any hidden design?

Bahlik became little pensive. He was wary of Shakuni. *This man should never be trusted. He is like a serpent,* Bahlik mused.

'Why do you look so worried, *Tatshri*?' Devavrata asked. He must know what was going on in his uncle's mind.

'Don't you think the Gandharas behaved rather strangely? Don't they really have the strength to engage us at least in a semblance of a fight?'

'What do you mean exactly?'

'I suspect those filthy rats may be plotting something. Have you gone through the last line of their message?'

Devavrata had already read it and he knew that his uncle would surely stumble there. The last sentence of the Gandhara communique was as follows:

'Although our consent to the alliance is purely unconditional, it is humbly requested that Prince Shakuni may please be allowed to accompany Princess Gandhari to Hastinapur as his presence would help the princess adjust to her new life with much ease and happiness.'

Devavrata asked, 'What do you make out of it, *Tatshri*?'

Bahlik scratched his greying beard and said, 'This could be tricky, I tell you. We cannot say no to this. That will be discourteous. But I am not at all comfortable with Shakuni's presence in Hastinapur. Why should he go to Hastinapur leaving his own kingdom, especially when he is the rightful heir to the throne of Gandhara? The excuse of accompanying his sister is not at all convincing. It may not be as simple.'

'Hmm... You have a point, *Tatshri*,' Devavrata stood up and slowly walked up towards the window of the makeshift camp. He stood before the window with his back towards Bahlik.

Bahlik continued, 'See, Hastinapur needs neither Shakuni's service nor his intelligence. There is a surfeit of sharp minds in Hastinapur. You yourself are there. Vidur is an extremely bright boy. That minister Kanik is wily, too. Your step-brother Vyasa is also available for any counsel or suggestions. What extra can that Gandhara fox give you? He can have no extra utility. But, he can do serious harm if he wants. I think Shakuni wants to go to Hastinapur to create trouble. Maybe, that is how the Gandharas want to get even with us. Their quick acceptance of our proposal may not necessarily mean that they are quite happy with it. I can....'

Bahlik had to stop as Devavrata had raised his hand. Bahlik had great regards for his illustrious nephew. No one else could have shown the gall to cut him short while he talked. But Devavrata was special.

Devavrata stopped Bahlik because he understood that his uncle's line of thoughts was similar to his. He had just wanted to check what Bahlik thought. He must now sort out a few things within himself—and for this, he did not need his uncle's help any more.

Many thoughts were crowding Devavrata's mind. He was thinking about the extremely complicated situation in his family. His father Shantanu's marriage with Satyavati had turned his world upside down. He could not become the king, nor could he take a wife and father children. Without sitting on the throne, he steered the kingdom to prosperity and glory just as an administrator working on behalf of the monarch. He was feeling suffocated in Hastinapur. He wanted to run away from everything that was royal, but was tied to the empty throne of Hastinapur due to his goddamned commitment to the great kingdom. He had watched unworthy youths ascend the throne right in front of his eyes. What was more, he had to let his fervent manhood go waste. Though he was almost middle-aged by now, he had never known women. Sometimes, he felt he would explode like a volcano!

He could still remember, when he had seen Satyavati for the first time, he flinched. She was about his age, if not younger. And she was going to become his step-mother! He had bowed down to touch her feet with some difficulty. She touched his headgear and bare shoulders delicately. Although the touch was appropriate, it seemed to him anything but motherly. He looked at Satyavati's face. Their eyes met for a moment. Devavrata felt goosebumps all over his body. Feeling guilty, he quickly lowered his eyes. Since that moment, he never looked up at Satyavati's face again—actually, he never dared. He could never tell anyone how every single day in Hastinapur had been like a gruelling test for him.

Then that amazing woman Amba[1] stormed into his life and left a blistering trail of memories that still disturbed his sleep every night. Amba's sisters Ambika and Ambalika got married to Vichitraveerya but Devavrata saw manifest invitation in Ambika's eyes. It was another perilous corridor he had to pass through with extreme caution. His life had been just as difficult all along. It never changed. He continued to live the same lonely, desolate life laden with an enormous responsibility.

But why the hell were such thoughts crossing his mind now? He and his uncle had been discussing about Shakuni. How could his thoughts deviate from Shakuni to such private issues?

Bahlik's words were continuously ringing in his head: 'Shakuni wants to go to Hastinapur to create trouble….'

The smile that slowly appeared on Devavrata's face could be best described as crooked. However, when he turned around slowly to face his uncle, the smile had disappeared.

'Let Shakuni come to Hastinapur, *Tatshri*. After all, he has some rights to accompany his sister. We should welcome him gracefully. And rest assured, Shakuni cannot do any harm to us,' said Devavrata, wearing a dour look.

'Hmm… You are right, perhaps. So be it, then,' Bahlik got up from his seat. He was feeling relieved as he always had sufficient confidence in Devavrata. He was fortunate

---

[1] Princess of Kashi; abducted by Devavrata Bheeshma from her *swayamvara* for Vichitraveerya but later returned to the Shalwa king when she professed her love for him. When the Shalwa king did not accept her and Devavrata too refused her marriage proposal, Amba considered herself wasted and swore to take revenge on Devavrata. By Lord Shiva's grace, she was reborn as Shikhandi and caused Devavrata's fall.

not to have noticed that curious smile on Devavrata's face, however. He could not have felt so relieved otherwise.

Arshi was sitting morose in her room. One of her maids had brought news that Shakuni was planning to go to Hastinapur and stay there for an indefinite period. Initially, the news had caused her a feeling that was somewhat akin to relief. Her husband's constant presence around her had been very stressful. Arshi had thought that a temporary separation might be helpful for both of them to work on their relationship with patience. But now, she was feeling insecure.

Was Shakuni planning to leave her for good? Was he trying to cut off all ties with her? What would be her future then? Was this the virtual end of their tense, grim cohabitation? What went wrong between them? Was it her failure to forget Arjak, or was it her husband's inability to forget his wife's first love? Who was to blame?

God knew that Arshi had always tried her best to stand true to her marital responsibilities but whenever Arshi tried to love Shakuni as desperately as she could, she would find Arjak's face emerging from nowhere between them obstructing Shakuni's, just as the moon screens the sun from the earth during a solar eclipse. Shakuni could have handled the situation with some kindness and compassion, but he did not. On the contrary, he would subtly remind Arshi of her infidelity every now and then, making their relationship perpetually gloomy.

But right now, the prospect of losing her husband was hurting her badly. She could not understand what to do now.

Just then, footsteps were heard outside the room. Arshi stood up. Was it Shakuni?

Yes, it was.

He looked slightly different today. Usually, Shakuni would wear a dour, glum look in front of Arshi. But now, although he was not smiling, there was a solemn expression on his face.

Shakuni slowly walked towards Arshi and stood very close to her. They were looking straight into each other's eyes. Some tense, speechless moments breezed past.

Arshi's heart was pounding. What did Shakuni have in his mind? He opened his mouth to say something. But Arshi did not let him talk. Her anxiety hurriedly slithered out of her mouth, 'Are you planning to leave me for good, *Aryaputra*?'

Although she was anxious, her voice was unexpectedly steady and calm. She had done well to hide her tension and insecurity from a husband who had never been a friend to her. Sympathy was the last thing Arshi wanted now—and from Shakuni at that. Arshi understood that the moment of her tryst with the inevitable was come.

Shakuni fumbled a little. It was not easy even for him to answer. 'We need to talk. Be seated, first,' he himself took a seat and pointed at a nearby couch to his wife.

'*Pitashri* has given me a great responsibility. He wants me to avenge the insult the Kauravas have inflicted on us. Our dear Gandhari is going to be married to their blind prince. Those rogues have made us kneel down before them although we had always been friendly to them. We have to hit back. I will have to do that. My plan is to plant myself within the Kauravas and cause Hastinapur's fall.'

'And me?' Arshi asked sharply, with her neck slightly bent and one eyebrow shot up.

Shakuni took some time to respond. That old wound started smarting again. His reply to this question could not be straight. On the contrary, the reply was toxic.

'You will stay here and raise Uluk. Isn't that fine for you? You shouldn't mind me staying away from you, I suppose? In my absence, you won't have to pretend anything. You shall be able to breathe freely and be left completely undisturbed to think about only the man who lives in your heart. I think it's the best deal for you and as a matter of fact, for me as well. After all, you are not going to lose or miss anything, are you?'

Arshi was prepared for this. She stood still for some time with her back towards her husband and tried hard not to shed tears. Today, she would not fight. She would not try to prove her commitment to the marriage anymore. She would not make any more futile attempts to change things henceforth. She would let her husband loose. She would now learn to accept her life just the way it was.

'It is alright, *Aryaputra*. It is just alright. Please, go on your way and be happy and victorious. Have glory. Make your father and countrymen proud. Avenge your sister's unjust marriage. After all, you are the only and the last hope of the Gandharas. And forget about me, I shall be perfectly alright here in my own way.'

Arshi's dignified words surprised Shakuni and took the sting out of his bitterness. It was a classy send-off from his wife.

Shakuni was getting a little emotional. He cleared his throat and conveyed a parting message to his wife, 'Arshi, I don't know when we would meet again or whether we would ever meet again at all—because my mission is fraught with danger. I may get exposed in Hastinapur at any time. They will surely execute me if they get to understand my real intentions. So....'

Arshi shivered a little and interrupted her husband, 'Nothing will happen to you, *Aryaputra*! No one in Hastinapur will be able to beat you in a battle of wits.

Lord Shiva will protect you always. Only, take Devavrata Bheeshma by your side. That's a must. And, beware of Vidur. Albeit young, I think he is capable of spoiling your plans.'

Shakuni looked at his wife in a way as if he was looking at a completely unknown woman.

Wherefrom did she get such insight? Is it just the natural instinct of a sensitive woman? I know Devavrata is the biggest threat but even I never took Vidur much into account... Yes, Arshi must be right. Vidur can be a potential danger. But how could Arshi sense this?

For the first time ever, Shakuni was forced into admiring Arshi's wisdom. For a moment, he even thought whether this woman was too precious to lose. Then he realised it was already too late as his mind had been irreversibly diverted. Arshi was a closed chapter in his life. Period.

Shakuni's voice choked. He said almost inaudibly, 'Thank you for your advice, Arshi. I shall keep it in mind. I have a request for you....'

'And what is that?'

'You will raise my son Uluk exactly the way I want. When I need him, you will present him to me, adequately prepared and initiated. I shall need his service some day to complete my mission.'

'Rest assured, I shall do as you wish. I give you my word, your son will be your worthy successor, if not a partner in crime!' Arshi did not utter the last words consciously, however.

Shakuni did not mind the banter, if it was so. Today, he was just too impressed with his wife—and for the first time at that. He was about to take her leave and said, 'Thank you so much. Forgive me for my inability to be a good husband. You know what went wrong between us.

I don't want to rake up those issues before leaving. We have already fought enough between ourselves, haven't we? You have my best wishes, take good care of yourself. Be happy in your own way.'

Shakuni lifted his hand to place it on Arshi's head once but could not do so. There was an invisible barrier between them that his hand failed to cross. He lowered his hand. Then he turned around and took a step towards the door. But he had to stop as Arshi's question entered his ears.

'Can I ask you something, if you don't mind?'

'Carry on, please.'

'Are you in love with someone?'

The question stabbed Shakuni like a dart. He had absolutely no idea how to react. Never had he felt so utterly helpless before. He mumbled meaninglessly, 'I…me? No….'

'For the first time I see guilt in your eyes, *Aryaputra*. And that is not just caused by your decision to leave me—but by something more serious. A woman understands… Goodbye and Godspeed!' Arshi finished with a lopsided smile.

A muddled Shakuni left the room quietly.

6

Gandhari and Dhritarashtra were standing face-to-face. They were dressed up gorgeously as the bride and the groom. The beautiful Gandhara princess was getting married to the mighty Kaurava scion. The occasion was grand and momentous.

Sacred chants and wishes were being uttered from all around. Everybody was blessing the young couple wholeheartedly. Gandhari's face was still covered with a veil. As a part of the Aryan marriage custom, the boy and the girl were to see each other's face for the first time in an auspicious moment during the wedding ritual. The event was of no significance for Dhritarashtra, for he was blind. Yet, everybody was waiting with a pleasant curiosity for Gandhari to see her husband's face for the first time.

The moment was come. With the royal priest's solemn announcement, Gandhari slowly removed the veil from over her face.

A furore rose in the hall. Though it was a loud cheer initially, it soon turned into a chaotic hubbub. Astonished exclamations were flying off from all sides. What the large number of people had just seen was completely unexpected for them.

The bride's eyes were covered with a white strip of cloth!

No one present at the venue had ever come across such a situation during an auspicious social function. What did it mean? Did the bride refuse to see her husband's face? Was she expressing her unhappiness over the marriage? Was it a rebellion of sorts? Some stood baffled, some voiced confused reactions.

Biting his lip, Devavrata held himself back from exploding. He wanted to take time, as usual, before giving his reactions. But Bahlik shouted at the Gandhara contingent rather indignantly, 'What nonsense is this, O Saubalas?[1] What's going on here? Is this girl ridiculing the marriage? Why isn't she willing to see *Kumar* Dhritarashtra's face?'

Gandhari's action had stunned the Kauravas and the Gandharas alike. Shakuni was watching his sister with unblinking, vacant eyes. Bahlik's irate words shook him out of the trance. Instead of responding to Bahlik, Shakuni himself screamed at his sister angrily. His brothers and relatives also yelled at Gandhari. They were feeling severely let down.

'What is this, Panna? Is it some sort of a prank you're playing on us?' Shakuni shouted at the top of his voice.

'If it really is a prank, don't you think it could have been better timed?' Gavaksha, a brother of Shakuni, hissed like an angry snake, gnashing his teeth.

'What's the matter, *Kanya* Gandhari? Why this transgression? Please explain, for it is extremely embarrassing for your own people,' Virupaksh, the minister, cajoled in a compassionate tone.

The gorgeous looking bride slowly lifted her head. She seemed to have been prepared for all this. As she spoke, each word was distinct, sophisticatedly dictioned, meaningful and full of conviction.

'O the venerable Gandhara and Kaurava nobles! With due humility, I must make it absolutely clear that I am quite happy with this marriage. I cannot even think of showing any kind of disrespect to my elders. My upbringing would not allow that. Kindly allow me to explain why I have taken this step,' Gandhari paused briefly here before resuming.

---

[1] The sons of King Subal, including Shakuni.

'When I was told that I was to be married to a blind man, I was shocked at first. But then wisdom dawned upon me. I made myself understand that it is actually an alliance between two noble houses that only a soulful bond between two hearts can make possible. It does not matter to me anymore whether my husband is sightless or sighted. I only need a good man I can grow old with. As a most loyal and devoted wife, I want to submit fully to my husband. I don't want to surpass him in any way. If he is fated to live a sightless life, I shall give myself a similar one. In this way I can understand him and his crisis better and become a true soul mate. He will not feel inferior to me, either. Let me hold his hand with care and let us walk abreast pushing through darkness. Please, give us your blessings.'

There was pin-drop silence after Gandhari's speech. Dhritarashtra was still standing with his head lowered. Nobody could see his expressions. Shakuni and Bahlik both opened their mouths to say something but could not utter a single word.

Devavrata was scratching his beard, clueless. Since his encounter with Amba, he had learnt to see women as a peculiar species only good at confusing men with their unintelligible emotions.

The much-revered *Kulguru* of Hastinapur, Kripacharya, had a twinge of discomfort writ large on his face. Pandu, the younger brother of Dhritarashtra, was looking at his would-be sister-in-law with admiration-filled eyes. Her words had clearly left a strong impression on the youthful Pandu. In fact, it was Pandu who broke the silence first.

'I don't know what our wise elders will decide but please let me speak my mind ahead of them. I find the attitude of *Devi* Gandhari commendable. What she has decided and is going to maintain is well beyond the ability and thought of an ordinary human being. Just to become an ideal partner of my visually impaired brother, she has decided to forsake her own vision. This shows the merit and spirit of the lady. I think we must welcome and take her home with due honour.'

Gandhari turned her face towards Pandu. For a moment, she wished she could have seen the face of the young man whose voice was so manly and words so refined.

Devavrata chipped in to bring Kripacharya into action, sensing that this emotional puff might precariously override logic and practicability, 'What does our *Kulguru* have in mind? We look forward to his opinion.'

Kripacharya clearly needed some more time to give his reaction but prodded by Devavrata, he was forced to speak his mind now. With a little hum and haw, he found his eloquence back, 'The matter is very tricky. It has to be looked at from two contrasting angles. A girl's refusal to see her would-be husband's face can be straightaway interpreted as her deep abhorrence for the alliance. The gesture is utterly inauspicious, moreover. At the same time, what the girl has just said reveals her sincerity, devotion and seriousness that the relationship requires. We need to respect that too. However, taking everything into account, I still suggest that *Kumari* Gandhari should remove the cloth from her eyes and go by the tradition. We expect a completely able bride for our *Kumar*.'

A debate followed. Shakuni was feeling increasingly restless. He needed the marriage to happen, at any cost. He removed his diadem and started ruffling the unkempt tresses.

A deep, rounded masculine voice silenced all murmurs. Finally, spoke the man whose opinion now mattered the most—Dhritarashtra, the bridegroom.

'I want to accept her exactly the way she likes to present herself to me. I feel obliged and beholden that she wants to share my blindness—by her own choice at that. I feel we can lead a visionless yet happy life together, seeing this world with our mind's eyes,' said Dhritarashtra with his head still lowered.

Gandhari smiled at Dhritarashtra with manifest happiness. The blind boy and the blindfolded girl were just meant for each other.

'*Sadhu...sadhu...*that's exactly what I expected from my brother,' shouted Pandu throwing a fistful of flowers at Dhritarashtra and Gandhari.

The Gandharas broke into a loud cheer. The enormous marriage hall got filled with praises and salutations for the noble Kaurava princes.

Shakuni felt relieved and muttered, 'Emotional fools!' However, he was certainly not complaining. His eyes quickly roamed over to notice the expressions of the eminent Kauravas. To his delight, he found contentment in almost all faces, as if everybody subconsciously wanted the tradition to be beaten by emotion for once.

But Shakuni did not fail to observe a deep frown on one young man's forehead. A very sharp looking bearded youth, Vidur.

Shakuni and Devavrata were in the same chariot. In front of them was an exquisitely decorated chariot that was being pulled by four milky-white horses with the newlyweds inside. They were being escorted by Pandu and Vidur, driving their respective chariots on the either side. All of them were part of a big, royal cavalcade that was proceeding towards Hastinapur from Gandhara, subsequent to the fairy-tale marriage between Dhritarashtra and Gandhari a week ago.

Shakuni was looking at Devavrata Bheeshma from the corner of his eyes. He had heard so much about this illustrious Kaurava regent. Shakuni had often doubted whether whatever he heard about Devavrata was really true or not. But today, seeing him from so close, Shakuni was getting increasingly convinced that this man could be anything but ordinary. The imposing personality, the physique, the appearance, the stare, the deportment, the voice, the gait—everything about the man was special. Shakuni never admired anybody much—not even in private but he simply could not help taking to this man.

Shakuni, however, was not sure what Devavrata thought of him. Although he had generously asked Shakuni to travel with him in the same chariot, it was important for Shakuni to know whether Devavrata would accept him in Hastinapur. After all, Devavrata mattered.

The royal palace of Hastinapur, the home to the great Kauravas, became visible from quite a distance. Shakuni's jaw dropped. What a mind-boggling construction it was! The golden javelin placed on top of the central dome-shaped palace roof seemed to be piercing through the clouds. One had to seriously trouble his neck to see the both sides of the building—even from a distance. It was an architectural marvel. The colossal residence quite aptly showcased the famous Kuru dynasty's glory.

The convoy entered the city, creating quite a commotion among the assembled multitude. The people of Hastinapur gave an exuberant welcome to the newlyweds. They were dancing, singing, performing tricks, showering flowers, screaming, laughing...the entire city seemed to have erupted in insane revels.

As soon as the fleet of vehicles arrived at the enormous palace gate, a team of doorkeepers rushed in urgently and started pulling at the monstrous metal gate. The gate opened slowly, with an ear-piercing squeal. A thrill crawled down Shakuni's spine. The scraping noise of the gate sounded ominous to him.

Behind the open door, there was a magnificent set. On the right side there was a large, beautiful garden. A round, picturesque pond with crystal clear water was on the left side. In the middle of the garden, there was a gigantic monolithic statue of King Hasti—the eponymous founder of Hastinapur.

The garden and the pond were separated by a broad stretch of lush green lawn. A tall flight of stairs rose gently from the lawn to reach up to a wide terrace.

On the topmost step stood three elderly women, clad in expensive, white *saris* that completely covered them just leaving their faces and the forearms out. Each of them was holding a golden tray that carried items like lamp, paddy, grass, curd, sugar, sandalwood paste and so on. Evidently, the three ladies were waiting to formally welcome the new bride into the family.

The chariots had stopped at the gates and everyone dismounted, including the newlyweds. Devavrata stretched his right hand and courteously gestured Shakuni to get down first. Shakuni, with a polite nod, placed his feet on the ground of Hastinapur for the first time.

Kulguru Kripacharya started climbing up the steps slowly, followed by the couple. They reached up to the trio at the palace threshold where Kripacharya reverentially folded his hands and bowed to the eldest of them. Then he asked the couple to touch their feet. They obeyed him. The three ladies started the formalities one by one.

'The grand queen *Maharani* Satyavati, and the widows of King Vichitraveerya, queen mothers *Rani* Ambika and *Rani* Ambalika,' Devavrata informed Shakuni in a low voice. 'You have to pay them due obeisance,' he added with a little smile.

'Sure, sure,' Shakuni said.

After the formal welcome by the queens was complete, Dhritarashtra and Gandhari were taken inside.

'Come along,' Devavrata started climbing the steps. Shakuni followed him.

On reaching up, Devavrata bent down to touch Satyavati's feet. Shakuni noticed that Devavrata's palms perfunctorily hovered around her knees only, instead of reaching down to her feet. Then Devavrata just smiled at the two queens without saying anything.

'*Matashri,* we welcome our honoured guest, *Shriman* Shakuni, who will accompany his dear sister here,' Devavrata introduced Shakuni to Satyavati.

Shakuni could hear his heart beat, for once. How would she react? Would she object?

Shakuni gave most respectful salutations to the three ladies. He had been getting a very pleasant scent right since he stepped into the palace premise. That delightful smell was getting more and more distinct here. He could understand now that it was coming from nowhere else other than from the grand queen Satyavati herself. Though all the three dowagers were beautiful, Satyavati was special. The vintage woman had a dominant personality that even her calm demeanour could betray. Her eyes were not particularly large but they were fluid and could cast a glance as sharp as a well-honed dagger.

The two comely queen mothers, Ambika and Ambalika smiled heartily and said, 'Come, *Putra*. This is your palace as well. Make yourself at home, please.' One of them even placed a hand on Shakuni's shoulder dotedly.

Shakuni flashed an obliged grin and looked at Satyavati's face. He immediately realised that his mission might not exactly be a cakewalk as it had seemed so far.

There was a curious look in her eyes. Though there was no overt disapproval, Shakuni understood that the woman was not convinced yet. And it would not be too easy to accomplish that.

'It's endearing that you are so fond of your sister that you couldn't part with her—even after her marriage! We always wanted a girl from such a close-knit family. But *Putra* Shakuni, what'd happen to *your* country in your absence?' Satyavati gave a piece of her mind right at the first meeting itself, although her words sounded sweet.

Shakuni bit his lip. He could not immediately reply. Devavrata, however, came to his rescue and chipped in, 'Gandhara is in safe hands, *Matashri*. Don't worry. And his presence will strengthen us in all respects, I am sure.'

'Who told you I am worried, Gangeya? My late husband and two sons have left behind a Hastinapur too strong to be brought down by any force other than the divine.'

The old woman's repartee completely unsettled Shakuni. The sudden truculence seemed quite uncalled for, if not astonishing. Nervous, he looked at Devavrata. Devavrata's face had flushed, probably less for embarrassment and more for the insult that Satyavati deliberately meant by distinctly mentioning her 'husband' and 'sons' as the 'cause' behind a 'strong' Hastinapur while even a child knew that it was none but Devavrata who made the kingdom what it was today.

Shakuni, even before entering the palace, became aware of the tension inside the family. He smiled within himself and thought, *Hastinapur seems to be a fertile field for me to sow exactly the kind of seeds I need. Good, very good....*

Satyavati turned to Shakuni. Her eyes were soft and expression gracious now. Her words were generous this time, even sounding almost motherly.

'Welcome to Hastinapur, Gandhara *Rajkumar* Shakuni. As my daughters-in-law have just said, this palace is yours as well. Come on in, *Putra*.'

7

'You sent for me, *Tatshri*?' Vidur asked, entering Devavrata Bheeshma's chamber. Devavrata was listening to an absorbing *veena* recital by a young and beautiful girl—probably the daughter of some minister. The music was so enthralling that Vidur did not feel like disturbing. He stood still without making any more noise following his question.

Devavrata beckoned him to sit on a chair. Vidur silently occupied the seat. He noticed Devavrata was keeping rhythm with his fingers on the hand rest. That was a little uncharacteristic, for Devavrata had never been much of a music connoisseur. Vidur understood that Devavrata was disturbed.

The music ended. With a gentle smile, Devavrata asked the girl to leave. She stood up, picked up the *veena* with great care and left, taking a courteous bow to Devavrata and Vidur.

'Are you worried for some reason, *Tatshri*?' Vidur asked with genuine concern.

'No *Putra*, I am not. But I know you are. And that's precisely why I sent for you.'

'I am not exactly worried. Confused is a better word,' Vidur replied, looking straight into Devavrata's eyes.

'Confused? You? And what makes you so, may I know?' Devavrata asked.

'The marriage of *Bhrata* Dhritarashtra,' Vidur said matter-of-factly.

'Why? Aren't you happy with the marriage?'

'I know I should be but I need to be sure of a few things first to be happy.'

'Will you come clear, Vidur? You are making *me* anxious now.'

'Why did King Bahlik, your venerable uncle, advise you to set up this alliance at a faraway Gandhara while a few neighbouring kings were interested to give their daughters to Dhritarashtra? Why did the Gandharas accept the offer so readily? Why does Princess Gandhari cover her vision? And, how long will this Shakuni stay here in our Hastinapur, leaving his own country behind?'

'Hmm...Uncle Bahlik suggested Gandhari's name thinking of a political alliance. Truly, we did not have many allies in the west. Moreover, the nearby states were trying to bargain out some concessions from us that Gandhara never did. As regards your second question, we had the Gandharas on the ropes and they were left with no other options than to accept our demand. And though I myself am not very sure why Gandhari wears the strip impairing her vision, and why Shakuni wants to stay here—I am not much bothered about these either.' Devavrata shrugged.

Vidur stood a little muddled. He realised one thing. He might be exceptionally brilliant, yet he was still just too young to understand a person like Devavrata Bheeshma. It was a good lesson for him. Vidur flashed an obliged smile, 'I think I should have been less cynical.'

'Hmm...with so much worry, you'll grey too soon,' Devavrata let out a good-natured laughter.

Vidur too joined him. 'Good night then, *Tatshri*.'

'Good night, *Putra*. I think we can do better without unnecessary strains on our imaginations. See you in the morning.'

Vidur left the palace and started walking towards the garden. It was already dark. A gust of cold wind was blowing from the north. Somewhere nearby it was raining, perhaps. The sentries on duty outside the garden were surprised to see Prince Vidur come here at such an odd time. Vidur walked past them. He did not find it necessary to explain his untimely visit. The guards did not dare ask, either. Vidur entered the garden and walked across to reach the other side of it.

Vidur stopped in front of an enormous stable. A number of armed guards and horse-tenders were on duty there. They were sitting relaxed, expecting no calls or visits from their royal masters at this hour. Seeing Vidur, they jumped up and stood at attention.

With a slight smile, Vidur walked up to a robust young man and said in a low voice, 'Bring my horse, Prasen.'

With a quick bow, Prasen rushed inside the stable and came out with a magnificent, brown-coloured steed.

Suddenly, the dark sky was lit up with a flash of thunder, followed by a rumbling sound. The steed started fidgeting. Prasen humbly asked Vidur, 'The weather is getting worse. Should I come with you, *Prabhu*?'

'No, relax.'

Vidur jumped on to the horse's back and rode away outside the city of Hastinapur towards the dense jungle. As soon as they got inside the jungle, it started raining.

Vidur was happy. The weather was just about perfect. His horse was now ambling through wild bushes and plants.

They reached a makeshift, dilapidated hut. A faint, unsteady ray of light was coming out of the hut. Vidur dismounted quietly and walked up to the hut, tying the horse to a tree.

'Are you home, *Pitashri*?' Vidur asked in a low voice.

'Come in. I knew you would come,' out came a gruff voice.

It was drizzling lightly. Vidur knew the person inside the hut was particularly fond of such weather. He entered the hovel.

A middle-aged, slovenly man was sitting inside the dingy room. The man was profusely bearded. His unruly tresses were loosely bound in a top knot. His hirsute body was unwashed and rather ill-maintained. He was carelessly covered with a whitish cloth diagonally placed over his torso and a worn-out dhoti took care of the lower half of his body. He was holding a pen made of a crane-feather and had a pile of *bhurjapatras* kept in front of him. Evidently, he had been writing something.

Vidur touched the man's feet. The man raised his right hand a little.

'Leave this habit of calling me *Pita*. Though it is not a secret that I am your biological father, it may sound uncomfortable to some. I have told you so many times,' the man chided Vidur very softly.

'Sorry, *Maharshi* Vyasa. I actually can't resist calling you so,' Vidur replied with a grin.

Vyasa smiled and said with a manifest indulgence, 'You are the only person on earth capable of giving me a distraction.'

'What about Shuka[1]?' Vidur asked naughtily.

'He is my soul. He is far greater than me…Anyway, tell me what brings you here at this hour?'

'I think you know that better than me, *Maharshi*!'

'Hmm…you are confused.'

---

[1] Shuka was another son and the worthiest disciple of *Maharshi* Vyasa. It is said that he was born out of Vyasa's body.

'Yes.'

'Good. That's important too—sometimes.'

'Actually, I'm a little uncomfortable with the marriage of *Bhrata* Dhritarashtra and Gandhari. My intuition....'

'Gandhari will make a perfect wife to Dhritarashtra, don't worry,' Vyasa cut him short.

'Oh! You think so? Then my fear is baseless. I am really relieved...,' Vidur said with a genuine happiness.

'Still, you did well coming to me. You need to know and understand some other things. It was Bahlik's idea to set up the alliance with Gandhara, you know that. What you don't know and should know is what made him get this idea.'

'Exactly! That's precisely what I asked Uncle Devavrata but his reply seemed too facile and simplistic,' Vidur said excitedly.

Vyasa smirked and said cryptically, 'From now onwards, you shall get many such superficial replies from your Uncle Devavrata, count on that!'

'I don't understand, *Maharshi*.'

'You'll understand it yourself... Anyway, listen carefully now. Bahlik was influenced by a prediction of Devapi. You've heard about Devapi, I am sure.'

'Yes...the eldest brother of King Shantanu who never became the king.'

'Devapi predicted about a great war between the Kauravas and the Vrishni Yadavas over the throne of Hastinapur. The Vrishnis would be supported by an estranged branch of the Kuru house itself. The war would ostensibly be won more on cerebral abilities than military skill. As Shakuni of Gandhara is renowned for his intelligence, Bahlik wanted to rope him in to ensure victory in that anticipated battle. He convinced Devavrata also.'

'Okay...,' Vidur was trying to come to terms with the input.

'But Bahlik could not take Devapi's prediction in the right spirit. I had also met Devapi many years ago. What Devapi actually said was that there will be a clash between two estranged Kaurava factions. One of them will apparently have the support of the Vrishnis. Bahlik has started manoeuvring straight away assuming many things on his own. Are you getting me?' Vyasa paused.

'Perfectly, *Maharshi*. Please, do carry on.'

'Most importantly, Bahlik is setting equations keeping in mind only the contemporary characters. It has not occurred to him that many new personalities will come into being in the near or distant future. What if a genius arrives in the future surpassing everyone in intelligence and abilities, sides with the other faction and wins them the war? You can't control everything falling on the passage from the present to the future. If it is pre-ordained, it will happen, by any means.'

'I think Bahlik*ji* is trying to make preparations for an eventuality. What's wrong in it? Had I been in his place, I would have probably done the same.'

'See, being far-sighted is good but that does not mean you have to destroy your present for a distant, unclear future. As per the prediction, two inimical factions will emerge inside the Kuru house, right? If you are so hell-bent on controlling the future, why shouldn't you first try to anticipate or understand the issues that can cause disputes in the time ahead and try to nip them in the bud? It is difficult, but not impossible if you claim to see far into the future. Is Bahlik doing that? He is only interested in forging alliances taking a war for granted for his own benefit, not knowing the least when or how it will break out and what factors will cause it.'

A sudden burst of wet wind flung open the shaky door and put off the lone lamp. Vyasa stood up and shut the door. Then he placed a heavy stone just behind the door to prevent it from opening. Vidur, meanwhile, relit the lamp. They resumed the discussion in that eerie atmosphere.

Vyasa continued, 'You said you are uncomfortable with the marriage. *So am I.* Though the boy and the girl are good for each other, it is not enough. I don't appreciate the culture of these far-westerners like the Gandharas or the Kambojas. They have too much of the *Mlecchha* influence. Though I am not essentially a purist, I somehow feel Hastinapur would have been better off without these Gandharas as an ally.'

Vidur asked, 'But *Pita*...sorry, *Maharshi,* exactly what was *Tatshri* Bheeshma's stand? I can't understand him properly. Does he know about Devapi's predictions?'

'Devavrata knows everything.'

'That means he intentionally allowed Bahlik*ji* to go ahead with his plan?'

'Bahlik is a very ordinary person. He is nothing in comparison to Devavrata.'

'I don't believe that *Tatshri* Devavrata happily allowed the entry of a problematic element like Shakuni unless... unless he had...'

'...his own reasons. That's what you wanted to say, isn't it?' Vyasa smiled. It was a queer, enigmatic smile.

'Exactly! *Maharshi,* I need to know what's going on in his mind.' Vidur sounded impatient.

'Yes, but understanding Devavrata is not that easy. And I don't want to make any loose comment about a person of his stature. Let me observe more.'

Vidur was getting more confused.

'Go home, *Putra*. It's getting late. Just remember one thing. A human can be noble, but he is still a human, never a god,' Vyasa sat leaning against the wall, with eyes half-closed.

Vidur got up, touched Vyasa's feet and took his leave. The last comment of Vyasa kept bugging him.

Was it about Devavrata? Vidur felt he was getting the drift of that cryptic remark slowly, albeit surely. The meeting with Vyasadeva, his mentor, had been satisfactory. Vidur got out of the hut and mounted his horse. The weather had improved remarkably. The darkness had faded too, with the prospect of an imminent dawn.

Vidur rode away towards Hastinapur.

Vyasa had come up to the door to see off Vidur. He kept looking at Vidur riding his horse for as long as he was visible. This bright, young Vidur had been his weakness. He was what could be called a lovechild of Vyasa. Vidur's mother, albeit a *Shudrani*, had come to Vyasa's life like an oasis in the midst of an arid desert. She was the only woman who had looked at an unsightly Vyasa with admiration in her eyes. Vidur was her gift to him. Vyasa shut the door softly and sat inside the hut reflecting on a very delicate chapter of his own life.

If Shuka is my salvation, Vidur is my debt to this earth. Shuka does not need me anymore, for he has risen to a far higher spiritual echelon than I myself could. But Vidur needs me—and I too need him. Though I forbid him to address me as father, only I know how I crave to hear that from him. It melts me. I am not a boundless sage that people think I am....

Devapi had told me the same thing that he had told Bahlik—Hastinapur is doomed. But he did not tell why. But, I know why

Hastinapur is doomed. Too many sins have accumulated beneath the coveted throne of the kingdom, beyond anybody's notice. Many secret sighs have overcast the fortune of the Kauravas. I can smell the imminent disaster that has been invited by the limitless ambition of my mother, Satyavati. Yes. Now have I realised that she is the real nemesis of Hastinapur.

Satyavati, the illegitimate child of the king of Chedi, had been abandoned by her biological parents and grew up in the modest household of a petty fisherman. She never did fit in there, for she was an extraordinary girl—extremely attractive and intelligent. The petty fisherman always tried his best to pamper this godsend. The girl grew up to be a fascinating damsel. Men would find her irresistible, in spite of her tattered clothes.

One day, *Rishi* Parashar fell for her charm and soon Satyavati gave birth to Vyasa. Krishnadwaipayan Vyasa was the son of Rishi Parashar and Satyawati. However, they never lived together and separated immediately after Vyasa's birth. It was never clear to him whether the relationship between his parents was purely physical or more than that. However, Vyasa would be cast in his father's mould and showed ascetic tendencies right from his childhood. Satyavati was not much of a mother material either. So, Vyasa was raised by his father and became his truest disciple. But he kept in touch with Satyavati also.

Vyasa had a complicated relationship with his mother. He always detested Satyavati's ambition. At the same time he loved her, too. Satyavati was his concern, because he knew his mother would not be happy in her life and would eventually cause her own undoing.

When Vyasa came to know of Satyavati's manoeuvres to gain entry into the Kuru house by marrying a much older Shantanu and usurping Devavrata's legitimate rights, he felt severely let down. Though it was Satyavati's adoptive father who did all the bargains from the fore, Vyasa suspected that it might be Satyavati's brainwork. Without her shrewd influence, an ordinary fisherman could not have mustered that much courage to strike such a crooked deal with a Kaurava royal so confidently.

Vyasa could never admire this manipulative side of his mother. He had had in his mind a benevolent image of an ideal woman and shockingly found his own mother failing to match it. He had decided that he would never take anything from this woman though he would stand beside her in her crisis.

That's why he could not say no to that grotesque request of Satyavati.

'You have to father sons through the widows of my late Vichitraveerya! Take it easy, *Putra* Vyasa. They are still young, beautiful. . . .'

Yes, Satyavati had said exactly this, that day. And she had made Vyasa do what she wanted, completely ignoring his shocked protests.

I can remember that singular moment as clearly as if it happened just yesterday. I can still feel the freshness of the wound as bitterly as if I received it just now.

But was not I myself tempted? Did not the thought of two beautiful princesses arouse me at all?

Vyasa himself was not very sure of that. The indelible memory of that mortal humiliation still churned out bitterness from somewhere very deep in his heart.

At Satyavati's behest, Vyasa had entered the bedroom of Ambika—the elder queen of Vichitraveerya—with his heart ablaze with lust. The lady was sitting shyly on the other side of an enormous bed with her back to the door. Vyasa shut the door behind him. He was breathing fast, feeling extremely excited. His manhood was in for a test, for the first time ever!

The lady had heard the door shut. She turned back sharply and stood up. The moment her eyes fell on Vyasa, she had shut her eyes as firmly as she could. Her beautiful face was distorted with an intense repugnance. Evidently, she was not at all impressed by Vyasa.

The humiliation was unthinkable. I can still remember that seeing her reaction, my head automatically turned towards a mirror. I found a dark, ugly, untidy, dirty man staring back at me from the other side of the glass! For the first time in my life, I hated myself. I regretted that I never took enough care of myself and never tried to look presentable. I had learnt many things in life, but the importance of looks was hitherto unknown to me. That dumb woman's reaction made me feel that despite being wise and erudite, probably no woman would ever desire me. Appearance-wise, I was just repulsive!

The princess was mumbling something with closed eyes. Unfortunately, Vyasa could hear what she muttered.

'Ohhh...Devavrata, why not you? Why this man?'

Vyasa became insane with anger. He wished he could strangle this woman. She was thinking of Devavrata in her mind.

I could not immediately decide what to do. Should I go away like a kicked dog? Or, should I fill the princess with my hatred, instead?

He chose the latter. He forced himself on Ambika. The woman's eyes remained shut and face turned away during the extremely unpleasant session. Completing the job, a panting Vyasa got up from the bed and said to the lying Ambika contemptuously, 'You turned a blind eye to me! My hateful semen will give you a blind son, Ambika. That's what you deserved!' Vyasa turned back in disgust and left the room, surprising himself with his own cruelty.

But that was not the end of his humiliation. Satyavati would send him to Ambalika, the younger wife of Vichitraveerya as a blind son was not good enough.

Vyasa readily agreed this time. Following his painful experience with Ambika, he wanted to meet another woman who could help his male ego get over the dishonour. But Ambalika proved no better. Seeing him, she became pale with horror and started trembling. After another vexatious union, Vyasa, quite sadly this time, predicted, 'Ambalika, your son will be as pale as you are now and will have physical weaknesses thanks to a weak mother that you are!'

Satyavati pushed Vyasa again. But Vyasa had had enough of these noblewomen. He had already understood how they were like. He wanted to have the company of an ordinary woman this time. So, a beautiful *Shudra* maid of Ambika was brought to him. The *Shudrani*—a low-caste servile woman—treated Vyasa with great care and respect and introduced him to a delightful chapter of man-woman relationship.

Urmila made me realise why a man needs a woman and what a woman is capable of giving to a man. The moments I spent with her were unforgettable. That memory is like a secret treasure for me.

Greatly impressed and completely satisfied, Vyasa embraced Urmila and whispered into her ears, 'You will bear a gem in your womb, my love. Your son will be *Dharma* himself—he will be an icon of righteousness and wisdom. That's my gift to you,' Vyasa planted an affectionate kiss on her forehead and left.

Vidur was that dear son of Vyasa. He was charming and exceptionally bright right from his childhood, inheriting the best traits of his parents. Vyasa realised that Vidur needed to be guided properly to prevail in the storm that was surreptitiously gathering in Hastinapur's sky.

But he had forgotten one important thing today. He should have sensitised Vidur about the importance of Pandu's marriage now.

Dhritarashtra's association with the Gandharas, Devavrata's ambiguous attitude and Shakuni's presence in Hastinapur seem to be going against Pandu's interest. What Pandu needs now is a powerful clique around him. For this, he first needs to have a wife from a formidable family.

'*Tch!*' Vyasa nodded impatiently. He needed to see Vidur again for some consultation.

8

Two factors were in Shakuni's favour in Hastinapur. First, Devavrata was not opposing him, at least not openly. He was treating him cordially enough. It never seemed that he was in any way uncomfortable with Shakuni's stay in Hastinapur.

Second, he managed to form a good friendship with Dhritarashtra, who had been very lonely before his arrival. Dhritarashtra had grown quite fond of Shakuni and the feeling was somewhat mutual. They were increasingly becoming inseparable. Shakuni knew a fast friendship with Dhritarashtra would definitely make his base stronger. He had noticed one trait of Dhritarashtra which he found quite easy to exploit. Dhritarashtra could not digest any opinion different from his. Shakuni understood it quickly and started filling Dhritarashtra's ears with exactly what he wanted to hear. They thus became very close.

One morning, Shakuni entered Dhritarashtra's chamber at breakfast time. Dhritarashtra was sitting glum, unmindfully gnawing at a *pishtak*. Shakuni was surprised to see him in such mood so early in the morning.

'What's the matter, *Jijashri*?'

Dhritarashtra did not smile and just beckoned him to the seat nearby. Shakuni sat on the chair and repeated the question.

'Weren't you present in the court yesterday?' Dhritarashtra asked.

'No. I visited Makandi to hold a meeting with the local governor regarding that taxation issue. Anyway, what happened?'

'They have decided to anoint Pandu as the king!'

Shakuni took some time to digest the information.

'What? But...but why him? You are elder!'

'Because I am blind! That has been my disqualification,' Dhritarashtra said in a voice almost unrecognisable.

Shakuni became silent. *Pandu was going to be crowned!* Webs of thoughts covered Shakuni's mind. Suddenly, he heard snuffles. He looked at Dhritarashtra and found him weeping with his face buried into his palms. Shakuni felt pity for the poor prince. Dhritarashtra continued weeping uninterrupted.

Shakuni's stare was fixed at his toes now. His eyes were shining like pearls. He was no longer feeling bad for Dhritarashtra. Rather, he smelled an opportunity.

Shakuni placed his hand on his shoulder gently. There was no genuine compassion in the touch. But the blind prince did not mind that. He was simply inconsolable.

'Tell me...tell me, Shakuni, why has God played this cruel joke on me? He gave me the strength of a hundred elephants, and simply forgot to give me vision? Why, why? What was my fault?' Even Shakuni's eyes moistened seeing Dhritarashtra's anguish. He quickly rubbed his knuckles once over the eyes. He was feeling an excitement, too. He would now have to exploit Dhritarashtra's resentment to the fullest.

Shakuni started doing his work.

'But this is sheer injustice, *Yuvraj* Dhritarashtra! You are the seniormost and have the first right to the throne. So what if you are visually impaired? That should not preclude one from being a king. A king rules over his land through the ever alert eyes of his ministers and officials. And for that matter, how can Pandu sit on the throne with that peculiar, pallid complexion and a rickety body? Will not people laugh at him?' Shakuni poked at Dhritarashtra, purposefully.

'Nobody here has the good sense that you have, *Bhrata* Shakuni. These people are just mindless. I shall never pardon these damned Kaurava nobles!' Dhritarashtra snarled in a distorted voice.

'You should not even try to pardon them, either. Exactly how did it transpire that they want Pandu as the king? Who started the discussion and how did the others react—tell me everything.'

'The issue was raised rather abruptly. *Tatshri* Devavrata was discussing the upcoming death anniversary of King Shantanu and was planning an elaborate arrangement for the celebration. Just then, *Kulguru* Kripacharya expressed that it was high time the next king was coronated as we had grown old enough to take over the kingdom. *Tatshri* mentioned my name and everybody became silent all of a sudden.'

'Who suggested Pandu's name first?'

'That precocious Vidur, who else! That much pampered son of the petty *Shudrani*. He is always jealous of me. Do you know why? His mother was my mother's maid. You heard me—*maid!* That's why Vidur can't stand me. He said Pandu should be made the king because he can see. I wished I could strangle him to death!' Dhritarashtra pummelled the handles of his seat with his fists repeatedly.

'Then?' Shakuni was trying to extricate as much details as possible from him. It would be helpful for him to understand the characters in proper light.

'Taking the cue, *Kulguru* started blabbering on the damned scriptures and the *shastras* in Vidur's support. King Bahlik too supported him.'

'What did Devavrata say?' It was most important for Shakuni to know.

'He evidently felt bad for me but ultimately supported them. *Mahamantri* Kanik too was on their side. Pandu remained silent all along.'

'Why would he speak when everything was in his favour!' Shakuni said mockingly.

'Exactly! He must be feeling ecstatic but did not show it off. I know all of them very well. Everybody thinks ill of me here,' Dhritarashtra complained like a child.

'No *Jijashri*, not everyone. Someone is here who is ready to give his best to you, always—*me*!' Shakuni announced his allegiance to the troubled prince little theatrically, knocking his chest with his thumb.

Dhritarashtra turned towards Shakuni. He wished he could see his face properly, for once. No one had sounded to Dhritarashtra as reliable before.

Shakuni remembered Devapi's words. He wondered, *I came here with the design of creating two inimical factions within the house to make the war happen. But there is already a readymade rift within the family. Now, this hairline crack has to be broadened into a gaping divide. The job seems simpler. I shall only have to fan Dhritarashtra's anguish adequately. It will cause a serious enmity bringing the war upon Hastinapur. The war will give me the opportunity to settle scores with the Vrishnis—at the cost of these bloody Kauravas!*

Shakuni embraced Dhritarashtra and whispered into his ear, 'Wipe your tears away, *Yuvraj*. I swear by Lord Shiva, the crown will sit on *your* head. Just have patience.'

'But how?' Dhritarashtra was surprised.

'Leave all that to me. Rest assured, you have Shakuni's friendship now. And one thing—Gandhari must not know anything about it.'

'Why?'

'Keep her out of politics, please. She may not like me getting involved in Hastinapur's internal affairs.'

'Hmm...okay. But what shall you do?' Dhritarashtra was curious.

'It is too early in the day to ask Shakuni that. But I need one thing in return.'

'Tell me, *Bhrata,* what is it?' Dhritarashtra stood up from his chair to hold Shakuni's hand.

'You may get to hear many things against me from now on because I shall have to play games for your sake. Don't pay heed to any of those,' Shakuni's voice sounded steely.

'I give you my word,' Dhritarashtra promised.

Shakuni hugged Dhritarashtra tight. Dhritarashtra grasped him even tighter. The embrace of the two men was long, passionate and purposeful. That very moment, a bond was forged that would survive the challenges of time. Shakuni's first meaningful step towards his mission was taken.

The god of destiny smiled wryly—unnoticed, up above behind the clouds.

Shakuni got out of Dhritarshtra's room, completely winning over the sentimental, blind prince. He was walking down the long corridor.

The day was a pleasant one. He was looking at the garden nearby which seemed to be laughing with the bright sunshine and the lovely breeze. The jubilant flowers were giving out the wonderful smell that lolled in the air. Shakuni slowed down. The garden was inviting him.

He heard footsteps from the other side of the corridor. A lean, lanky man was approaching. The passage was so long that his face could not be clearly seen by Shakuni. But his pale white complexion was enough to tell Shakuni that he was Pandu. Evidently, he was coming to meet Dhritarashtra.

Shakuni's idyllic mood changed. Something in him told him that Pandu must not be allowed to meet Dhritarashtra right now. Pandu had already come closer and it was evident from his troubled expression that he was coming hastily to sort out with his elder brother any misunderstanding over the coronation issue. And that was exactly what Shakuni did not want. The misunderstanding must prevail. Shakuni could not afford to let the two brothers unite.

He stopped Pandu. 'Why so busy, *Kumar* Pandu? Is something the matter?'

Pandu smiled politely and said, 'Not busy, actually. I need to discuss something with *Bhrata* Dhritarashtra.'

'Err...is it something really urgent? I mean, he is a little upset now,' Shakuni carefully made his words sound provocative.

Pandu frowned. How dare an outsider advise him when to meet his brother and when not to? Shakuni understood how Pandu was feeling at that moment. He smiled in his mind as he had wanted exactly that. Pandu's slightly brusque reply confirmed his impression. 'Let me see it myself,' saying this, Pandu started walking past Shakuni.

'*Kumar* Pandu, please listen to me once...please,' Shakuni almost ran after him and held his hand. 'I am completely aware that I am no one here to come between you and your brother. But still, being your well-wisher, I need to tell you something.'

Pandu fell for Shakuni's trick. 'What's the matter, Shakuni*ji*?'

'Don't mind me saying, your brother seems to be very upset with the talks about your coronation tomorrow. He is depressed and feeling deprived.'

'I know. That's why I need to talk to him now. I must console him.'

'I think you should not meet him, at least now. Sorry to say, your brother seems to have developed some complexes,' said Shakuni while carefully examining Pandu's reactions.

Pandu was taken aback. He knew Dhritarashtra was disappointed obviously. If he were in Dhritarashtra's place, he too would have possibly felt the same. But what did Shakuni want to say?

Shakuni rolled his dice very cautiously, 'Dhritarashtra seems to be thinking that *you* have plotted against him.'

'What?' Pandu could not believe his ears. 'What...what did he say?'

The arrow had struck just at the right place.

Shakuni put up a hopeless expression and said, 'Well... he didn't say much but gave out such an impression. And....'

'And?'

'...he believes you will come to meet him anytime now as you feel guilty for whatever you did behind his back,' Shakuni said in a low voice. 'That's why, I ask you not to meet him now for it will prove him right.'

Pandu was stunned. How could Dhritarashtra think so nasty of him? Had he taken leave of his senses? Did not Dhritarashtra realise how bad Pandu himself felt to supersede his elder brother? Did not Dhritarashtra know how deeply Pandu loved him? Strangely, Pandu did not think of verifying the authenticity of Shakuni's statement even for once. Perhaps, it was Shakuni's mastery that he could sound so convincing and look so genuine while telling an unmitigated lie.

Shakuni thought, *if winning Dhritarashtra's complete trust was my first victory, then preventing Pandu from sorting this dispute must be the second.*

Shakuni and Pandu walked towards the garden and sat face-to-face on two marble seats.

'You know what, your brother is extremely jealous of you. He was quite obsessed with the throne of Hastinapur. That's why he is so devastated and so spiteful against you now. Very sad! He should have realised that a visually impaired person can never head a state. My friendly suggestion to you is that you better keep some distance from him—at least for some time.'

Pandu remained quiet. He realised what Shakuni just said was not entirely wrong. He himself had noticed how Dhritarshtra's mood had changed when the talk of coronation was going on.

Shakuni's efforts to pollute Pandu's mind against his brother had been successful already to a good extent. Dhritarashtra and Pandu both proved too credulous to see through Shakuni's guiles and gave in easily.

But it was not enough for Shakuni. The clash between Dhritarashtra and Pandu was not yet useful enough to cause a serious enmity within the house. While Dhritarashtra had sympathy, he had no support and he was not much of an impactful person, either. On the other hand, Pandu was clearly in a much stronger position but he was decent, demure and lacked swagger. Unless the dispute affected the next generation more viciously, it would not be of much significance. Shakuni was feeling impatient. Dhritarashtra and Pandu were useless. He would have to experiment with their children, instead, for a better result!

The thought slipped out of Shakuni's mouth in form of a suggestion that surprised Pandu, 'You must not take too long to get married, *Yuvraj* Pandu.'

'Why are you saying this now?' Pandu asked with a surprised smile and raised eyebrows.

'Your brother is already married and may have children in due time, hopefully. He may well transmit his bitterness to his children. You may soon find yourself in the midst of a pack of inimical nephews. To counter that, you need your own band of offspring guarding your interest. Understand?'

Pandu burst into a good-natured laughter. 'You have a very long foresight, I see! Ha ha ha....'

'But don't take it lightly anyway...,' Shakuni too laughed.

'By the way, this is the second advice of the day urging me to get married,' Pandu said with an uncomplicated laugh. 'It seems my marriage is going to be the only important issue in Hastinapur...ha ha ha....'

'Oh, really? Everybody says so to an eligible bachelor like you. Who was it giving you such a good advice apart from me, anyway?' Shakuni asked.

'It was Vidur. He came to me early in the morning itself and quite seriously said that I must get married soon. I laughed at him, saying he must think of his own marriage,' Pandu replied, standing up from his seat.

Shakuni's smile vanished abruptly. He knew Vidur's interest in Pandu's marriage was not merely a run-of-the-mill concern for the older half-brother. Vidur must be thinking along the same line as Shakuni was. But what could be Vidur's interest?

Shakuni recognised Vidur as his opposite number in Hastinapur. Arshi's parting words came to his mind, for once.

9

A year went by. Shakuni had meanwhile adjusted himself quite well at Hastinapur. He presented himself as a reasonably likeable personality and had become acceptable to all. Of late, he was even taking part in discussions on state matters and politics without letting anybody feel that he was a stranger. Slowly, unobtrusively but surely, he was creating a space for himself among the Kauravas.

Meanwhile, King Subal had died in Gandhara. Shakuni was declared the absentee king while his brother Achal was ruling over Gandhara as his regent. Shakuni had no interest to return to Gandhara, however. The throne of Gandhara meant nothing for 'Gandhara *Ratna*' Shakuni.

But he was missing his son Uluk dearly. He was also feeling a peculiar unrest from within. He himself was not able to identify exactly what caused it. Was it a kind of impatience? Possibly it was nothing but a fear of being exposed with a single false step. The Kauravas were a proud race—even to a fault sometimes but they were not fools.

Or, he might be subconsciously missing Arshi— although he did not want to acknowledge that even to himself. It might as well have been his smarting pride that he had to live like a rodent in an apparently unsuspecting foreign land with a mean motive, while his own country and people wanted and needed him badly. Shakuni sometimes asked himself what the hell he was doing here, leaving his whole life behind. Was his mission worth this much at all?

Besides, there was a typical male issue that was disturbing him. Ever since he had left Gandhara, he had not touched a woman. In Hastinapur, there was a bevy of beautiful maids and slave girls to attend to him always but strangely, none could trouble the man in him. He looked at those attractive young girls quite indifferently although he was not that impassive at all. He was actually in need of a particular woman—to satisfy needs that were not only physical. He had become obsessed with the sublime face that always haunted him. This infatuation was but a result of his inexorable longing for a compatible female that Arshi never was.

One morning, Shakuni felt he must see Devavrata immediately. At first, he could not understand why he was feeling so. He realised later that it was his subconscious mind that suggested him to meet Devavrata—the man who had been fighting an incredible battle against desire all his life. Shakuni needed Devavrata for solace and inspiration. It brought a wry smile on Shakuni's face thinking how strangely he and Devavrata had been forced to live womanless lives for reasons so strikingly dissimilar!

Shakuni got up from the bed, wrapped himself with a shawl and hurriedly went to meet Devavrata.

'He is not home, *Prabhu,*' the guard on duty outside Devavrata's room informed politely.

'Where is he, so early in the morning?'

'Probably in the museum.'

The museum of Hastinapur had a great collection of exceptionally valuable heirlooms and antique belongings of the Kauravas and the legendary Pauravas[1]. It was under Devavrata's supervision. Everybody knew how passionate and possessive he was about the collection. This museum was his most favourite place. But what was he doing there so early in the morning?

---

[1] The Pauravas were the descendants of the legendary Puru (the youngest son of Yayati). The Kauravas were actually a sub-clan of the Pauravas.

Curious, Shakuni started walking towards the museum. Devavrata Bheeshma remained the only person in Hastinapur he was yet to understand properly. Devavrata appeared quite moody and very complex. But Shakuni knew for sure that this enigmatic man was the last word in Hastinapur. Shakuni had noticed another interesting thing. Devavrata had an outstanding power of controlling the thoughts of others without being too expressive.

The museum was a large, impressive, one-storeyed building with around twenty differently sized rooms. It was guarded day and night by armed sentries. Seeing Shakuni, the guards lowered their lances and saluted him.

'Is the Grand Regent inside?' Shakuni asked.

'Yes. He is in the sculpture room.'

Shakuni quietly entered the building and passed through a number of rooms to reach the hall where many life-size statues, clay models, bronze and stone sculptures of many famous ancestors and almost all present members of the family were kept.

Though the room was adequately lit, shadows cast by the randomly positioned statues had created a weird mesh of light and shade. Shakuni squinted a bit to get his eyes set, and found a strapping Devavrata doing something with his back to the door.

Shakuni mildly coughed. Devavrata turned around and looked little surprised to see Shakuni.

'Good morning!' Shakuni said softly.

'Good morning, Saubala! What brings you here, at this time?' Devavrata responded with a smile and walked towards Shakuni, cleaning his hands with a towel.

Meanwhile, Shakuni had entered the room and saw an unfinished life-size clay effigy that Devavrata had been working on. He was quite surprised. He never knew Devavrata was a sculptor.

'*Oho*...I never knew you are such a great artist, *Kurushrestha*!' Shakuni exclaimed.

Devavrata smiled shyly, 'Sometimes I feel like creating something...just playing with clay....'

'But what is this you are making?' Shakuni asked standing in front of the model. Though it was far from being complete, it was evidently taking shape of a strange looking human with muscular limbs, broad shoulders, waist-length tresses, slender waistline, heavy bosom and feminine pelvic portion. The face was not yet created. Shakuni felt he was looking at the wonderful creation of a maverick artist who was on his way to create a marvel with both male and female attributes fused together.

Shakuni looked at Devavrata with astonished eyes and repeated his question pointing at the model.

'Well...just a random experiment,' Devavrata said evasively.

'No *Kurushrestha,* it just can't be as simple. Please tell me what it is actually, I feel very curious.' Shakuni implored with a broad smile.

Devavrata's face suddenly turned serious. His eyes became fierce, voice grim.

'Why should I tell you about it unless there is a fair exchange?' Devavrata's eyes sparkled.

Shakuni had never seen such an expression before in Devavrata's comely face. But he did not lose his calm.

'What do you mean?' he asked.

'Why on earth did you have to come to Hastinapur leaving your kingdom and family behind? You must have a design. Don't you try to befool me,' Devavrata asked, looking him straight in the eyes.

Shakuni knew that he could not evade this question for long. He had wanted to divulge it to only Devavrata and take him on board by any means. The moment was come.

'You are right, *Kurushrestha*. I do have a design. I need your help, in fact.'

'Oh, really? What kind of help do you expect from me?' Devavrata asked dryly, without betraying curiosity.

'Let me talk frankly. I have a personal grudge against the Vrishnis and want to settle scores with them. But it is not possible for me to take on the mighty Vrishnis with our meagre Gandhara force. Therefore, I need the help of your people—the Kauravas!' Shakuni, revealing his secret to Devavrata, felt quite tense.

How will Devavrata react? What shall I do should he refuse to help me straightaway?

Devavrata looked surprised.

'But how can we help you against the Vrishnis? We have no enmity with them. In fact, we have cordial relations with all the Yadava clans,' said Devavrata.

Shakuni smiled and said, 'You are friends today. Are you sure you will remain so tomorrow?'

'What do you mean?'

'Please don't mind me reminding you of some old facts. The Kurus descended from the legendary king Puru, while the Yadavas came from the legendary Yadu. Yadu and Puru were step-brothers[2]. They did not get along, due to their father Yayati's preference for Puru. It is mentioned in some ancient scriptures that their descendants will fight each other towards the end of the *Dwapara yuga* and that

---

[2] Yadu and Puru were two sons of Yayati by different women. Yadu's mother was Devayani while Puru's mother was Sharmishtha.

will pave the onset of the *Kali yuga*. So, you cannot rest assured with your present friendship with the Vrishnis!' Shakuni felt it would not be right to discuss about Devapi's prophecy right now and carefully refrained from it.

Devavrata was hearing with rapt attention. 'But... but...how can you be sure that the end of Dwapara will happen in your lifetime? It can still be quite far away in the future,' he asked.

'Have you forgotten the case of Nala—the Nishadha king? He was so many generations before us and still he was believed to be under the influence of the imminent *Kali yuga*! If *Kali* was "imminent" at that time, it must be just around the corner and breathing down our neck today! I don't know whether you'd believe it or not, but long before my birth, the venerable *Rishi* Druhyu apparently forewarned my ancestors about me saying that I will incarnate the *Dwapara yuga*, bodying forth all its essential characteristics and the end of this *yuga* will roughly coincide with my lifetime.' Shakuni rattled it off in a single breath and flashed a laconic smile.

'Wait...wait! Let me understand it clearly first,' Devavrata raised his hand. 'You want to say that in the near future, the Kauravas and the Yadavas will become enemies and they will fight each other. But how does it relate to your personal enmity with the Vrishnis?'

'Simple, I want to take part in that war and fight the Vrishni Yadavas. I want to destroy them with the help of the Kauravas. That's my only chance to avenge myself.'

'But you could have done that by staying in Gandhara as well. How was it necessary for you to stay in Hastinapur for that? Your Gandhara has a marital alliance with us now and you are our natural ally. Should there really be any war with the Vrishnis, you shall be definitely on our side, isn't it?'

'Sorry *Kurushrestha*, you have not yet understood my character. I don't want to defeat the Vrishnis as a mere sidekick of the Kauravas and bask in a reflected glory. That will not give me any satisfaction. I plucked myself up from Gandhara and settled here to render more meaningful contribution to the preparation of the war. To put it simply, I want to be a major factor behind the Kaurava victory over the Vrishnis. Only then my ego will be satisfied and I shall feel avenged!'

Devavrata wondered*, the boy actually wants to cause and catalyse the war. For this, his staying at Hastinapur is but an imperative. Hmm...He needs us, but do we need him?*

'But, do you seriously think we need you?' Devavrata brought out the thought to his lip.

'Shakuni can be an asset to any kingdom. It is not a hollow boast, trust me. I am pretty useful, you'll see it for yourself,' Shakuni said with a confident smirk.

Devavrata opened his mouth to say something but chose not to. What Shakuni had said made sense to him.

This cocky young man from Gandhara seems to be really useful. But I must keep a close watch on him. And I must know why he is so vengeful against the Vrishnis.

Devavrata asked, 'Tell me, Saubala, what is your problem with the Vrishnis?'

Shakuni's smile evaporated. *No, even Devavrata has no right to know this. He does not need to.*

'Sorry! I don't think it is necessary for you to know. It is too private to divulge and discuss,' Shakuni's reply slashed through the air like a swishing whip.

Devavrata did not say anything. *This Shakuni has to be handled cautiously*. Devavrata quickly remembered his uncle Devapi's words. If Shakuni was to be believed, Devapi's predictions were coming true.

Shakuni's question broke his web of thoughts. 'Now can I know about the mysterious idol you have been making? Fair exchange!' Shakuni laughed.

Devavrata hesitated a little. Should he take this foreigner in confidence? He felt he needed to unburden himself to someone. No one in Hastinapur had ever shown any concern for his mental health. He had no friends to confide in. He had no woman to surrender to. His loneliness was strangulating at times. He could have discussed it with Vidur. But one problem with Vidur was that he was under the influence of Vyasa and Devavrata did not want his secret to travel to Vyasa. Out of desperation, he decided to share his secret with Shakuni today.

'Yes, now you have some right to know. But keep it between us, strictly,' Devavrata placed his hand on Shakuni's shoulder softly. They walked together towards a rostrum and sat on it. Devavrata had never conversed with anyone as candidly as he was doing now with Shakuni.

'Every night I see a strange dream. I am running and running through a hilly road. I am panting and extremely exhausted. But still I am not falling. Suddenly, a strange figure appears on my way. He is bizarre. His face is blurred. He is very muscular, has a cascading shock of hair, robust shoulders, bulging bosom, tiny waist and roundish buttock—he can be both a male and a female. I run into him/her. The strange human embraces and wraps me with an *uttariya*. For a moment it feels as if many thorns are pricking at me all over my body, as if I have been assaulted by a porcupine. But the feeling is short-lived, fortunately. Soon after, I have a sublime, blissful feeling. Then I fall free into a peaceful slumber…,' Devavrata Bheeshma paused to take some breath before resuming, 'This is a regular phenomenon. Some days ago, I decided to create an effigy of that mysterious person. Every morning I come here and try to add new details to it to make it look exactly like that dream figure.'

They sat speechless for a while. Then Devavrata asked in a choked voice, 'You are the only person whom I have told about it. Can you analyse dreams?'

Shakuni happened to be a master of parapsychology. He had some perception about Devavrata's dream which he explained hesitantly, 'Don't mind but I think you have a sub-conscious craving for women that you consciously decline to acknowledge. The figure you see is going to play a very vital role in your life and you yourself want to surrender to it completely. Due to your secret obsession with women, you want that person to be a woman. But due to your conscious rejection of the fairer sex, a male image gets seated immediately on the figure, resulting in a character with both male and female traits. And that porcupine feeling is nothing but your suppressed libido that gives you pinpricks!'

Devavrata looked completely nonplussed. He did not know how to react to Shakuni's explanation. At first, he was extremely cross at the temerity of the young man who dared impugn his devotion to celibacy. But he could not muster enough strength to explode. Perhaps, Shakuni had touched the right chord. But he still needed to get a good measure of the young man's mettle.

To bring out what more he had in his mind, Devavrata poked Shakuni further. 'Tell me what more could you understand today.'

Shakuni looked around the room. He had gotten a little carried away with the spurious attention Devavrata was giving him. Shakuni's prodigious intellect was slightly blunted by a youthful overconfidence. To impress Devavrata with his observation, he said something he shouldn't have. 'In this room, there are many statues of your family members, some living and some dead. The sculptures were made at different times—from the recent to the ancient. Yet, thanks to your excellent care and supervision, all of these effigies are well-dusted and almost impeccably curated—except one! It is standing at that far corner covered with dust and cobwebs, almost beyond recognition. That is the model of Lady Satyavati, if I am not mistaken.' Shakuni gave a meaningful pause, with a leering grin.

'And what do you infer from this?' Devavrata's voice was icy.

'I don't exactly infer but can suspect, at least. Please don't mind me saying, you could never pardon your step-mother, Lady Satyavati, for usurping everything that was yours. You have vented your hatred on the clay model of your step-mother. You could possibly never accept that your step-brother Vichitraveerya occupied the throne that was yours! Anyway, *Shri* Gangeya, it does not reduce my respect for you even by a little measure. It is but too human,' Shakuni said with some compassion and gently put his palm on Devavrata's rock-hard knuckles. There was no sign of his youthful frivolity now that had been irking Devavrata just a little ago.

'But what made you disclose everything to me, Saubala? What will you do if I ask you to leave Hastinapur after knowing your thoughts?'

'You shall never do that, I know.'

'And may I ask why you believe so?'

'I know that no one in Hastinapur was happy to have me here. Everybody suspects that I may have a secret plan. They must have told you not to allow me to stay here this long. Still, why did you allow me to stay without even showing any discomfort? Are you so naïve? I can't buy that!'

'What do you want to say? Come straight!'

'There may be two possibilities. First, you may be very confident that whatever I do is not going to be harmful for Hastinapur and so my presence here is in no way a threat. And second....'

'Yes, second?' Devavrata asked, wiping away beads of sweat from his forehead.

Shakuni sat closer to him. An impish expression appeared on his face. He said in a low voice, 'Probably, my presence will benefit you.'

'Benefit *me*?'

'Maybe I can serve some ulterior motive of yours.'

Devavrata's jaws jutted out. His long, battle-scarred fingers clenched into a tight ball. *This precocious Gandhara youth is crossing limits now!* But surprisingly, his anger subsided quickly.

'Is that all you want to say, Saubala? I have much work to do,' Devavrata stood up as he felt the need to restrain Shakuni now. This morning had been very interesting. It was amazing that the young foreigner could gauge him so correctly despite such brief familiarity. Though Shakuni took some liberties with him and even behaved somewhat cockily, Devavrata could not actually hate him.

'I should now take your leave, *Kurushrestha*. Sorry, for spoiling your morning,' a smiling Shakuni left the room gently, taking a bow.

Devavrata sat down on the rostrum again. He needed to be alone now—to put his jumbled-up thoughts in some order.

This Shakuni is exceptionally brilliant, but too oversmart. He has exposed himself too early. His face blushed when I asked him why he hates the Vrishnis...hmm...it must be a romantic issue. Did the lad fall in love with any Vrishni woman? But, he is already married. Is that why he is separated from his wife and is living here? Interesting...very interesting....

Devavrata stood up and started pacing. No one was aware how he himself bore a grudge against this damned Kuru family that had exploited him to the hilt. He had to hopelessly watch Satyavati's descendants flourish on his sacrifice. Shakuni's arrival now raked up a strange thought in his mind.

Shakuni has rightly guessed that his presence can benefit me. Yes, I shall now hire his service to settle my own scores. Shakuni's craving for war is likely to invite disaster for Hastinapur. A serious crisis is about to befall the Kauravas. Good! That greedy woman has taken away everything from me. Now let her suffer a bit! Let me see how her grandsons tackle the crisis. I should not interrupt Shakuni. Let him do whatever he can....

He was too absorbed to notice the long shadow cast on the floor through the doorway.

Pandu's chariot was racing at a breakneck speed. The four horses, frothing at the mouths, were lugging the vehicle desperately through the dense jungle. The charioteer's merciless whipping was not letting them slow down even for a moment.

Pandu did not know where he was going, nor did it matter to him. He was not even aware exactly how far they had gone away from Hastinapur. He left Hastinapur early in the morning after breakfast, and had been travelling non-stop since then.

Often Pandu found himself gripped by such madness. Whenever he felt down, he went out on a long drive with his most trusted charioteer Suseem towards any direction he liked. He was cautioned countless times by elders against such adventures and was advised to take a competent bodyguard with him but he never listened. This sport had been his anti-depressant.

Pandu was in a very bad mood today. Although full-scale efforts were going on to find a suitable match for him, no positive response had come as yet from any side. Pandu knew why. No girl was willing to marry him. All of them found him repulsive due to his repugnant, pigment-deficient skin. His intense eyes, chiselled face, dimpled smile, lithe physique—nothing ever mattered to anybody. No one had ever cared to appreciate his mastery with the bow and arrow, his sublime skill with the sword and the javelin, his proficiency in music and fine arts, his knowledge of the Vedas, his acumen in statecraft or even his generous nature. He never could take pride in himself—not even for a short moment. He never had any friends. Everyone would keep him at an arm's length, as if he was suffering from a contagious skin disease. He always kept himself away from women. He never felt any desire either. But now it hurt him severely because these rejections from all over almost made it official that he was an undesirable, unpleasant, uncouth man with absolutely no appeal to the opposite sex!

But he had been feeling quite upbeat since a few days when he was officially declared as the heir to the throne. Unfortunately, that good spirit was short-lived. He was stunned by Dhritarashtra's malicious reactions following the formal announcement. Pandu was basically an uncomplicated man. Dhritarashtra's behaviour was quite unexpected for him. Since then, again that intense melancholic feeling had creeped into him.

Desperately, he had been off to play his favourite sport that morning and asked Suseem to drive away towards the north-east as fast as he could. He had never visited that side before.

By noon, they had already come quite far away from Hastinapur. They were seeing a meandering river from a distance.

'Which river is that, Suseem?' asked Pandu.

'It is river Parushni, *Yuvraj*. It seems we are near the boundary of southern Madra. At the far west, there is Martikavat, I think.'

'Oh, really? We have come that far!' Pandu exclaimed.

Suseem could not react to Pandu because just then a strange looking human came out of the bushes and stood on their way. The dark brown-complexioned man was unkempt, unwashed, had bounteous beards and was clad in a peculiar armour made of animal hide. An enormous, crescent-shaped scabbard with a wooden hilt hung from his waistband. He did not appear to be friendly at all.

Suseem stopped the chariot.

The man opened his mouth and some loud, hoarse and unintelligible sounds came out, 'CHER BIRMANRE RUKH MA TIGULISI...RUKH MA LEHOT...RA! RA!'

As soon as he shouted, at least twenty similar looking men appeared from nowhere and rushed towards Pandu's chariot brandishing their weapons.

'*Aratta* bandits! We're in trouble, *Kumar*!' Suseem's voice trembled.

Pandu knew well what to do now. He strung his large bow in the wink of an eye and fired a volley of arrows in a flash. A number of bandits fell dead. A second round of firing got rid of another good number of them. But from the depth of the dense jungle, emerged a big horde of the bandits. They attacked Pandu from three sides.

Pandu was an accomplished bowman. He was fighting valiantly but was running short of arrows. Suseem, in the meantime, was struck on the head and was knocked out cold.

Pandu's arrows were now all spent. He was desperately trying to fend off the swarming enemies using the unstrung bow as a stick. He was tiring down. It was becoming certain that the marauding outlaws would soon get the better of him.

Suddenly, another group of men were seen at a distance. They were ironclad soldiers—evidently a division from a king's army. They were led by an accoutred man with a stylish helmet. He was riding a luxe chariot. The man shouted a command for attack, throwing his right hand into the air. The soldiers ferociously charged headlong at the robbers.

The robbers were outnumbered by at least one to three and were much less equipped. The soldiers routed them in no time. Almost all of them were killed and the survivors were held captive. They were tied with the cavalry vehicles by long chains and were dragged along.

An exhausted Pandu was watching the defeat of the hoodlums, sitting on his haunches inside the chariot. The robust commander of the victorious force came towards him and dismounted from his chariot. He was a little older than Pandu, very well-built and had a regal demeanour. His charioteer too got down. Pandu stepped down from his chariot and greeted the imposing man with folded hands.

'I am Shalya, the king of Madra *Desh*. I watched you fight from a distance. You are a top class warrior. Who are you, young man?' Shalya asked Pandu in a cheerful voice.

But Pandu could not immediately answer, nor could he offer proper salutation to King Shalya because his eyes and all attention had fallen on Shalya's charioteer.

The charioteer was a beautiful, young woman! Pandu had never seen a woman more gorgeous, more stunning than her. He had never seen a woman drive a chariot either. She looked so breathtaking in the armour, yet so very feminine. Pandu was unabashedly ogling at her, forgetting to bat his eyelids.

Shalya noticed Pandu's bewilderment and found it quite funny. He introduced the woman to Pandu, hiding a naughty smile, 'She is my beloved sister Madri—the priceless gift that God gave away to our Madra *Desh*. She is our pride.'

The woman removed her helmet revealing shiny black hair, tightly tied in a top-knot. She flashed a smile brighter than a thousand lamps put together.

'But who are you, man?' Shalya asked again.

Pandu came out of the spell and quickly replied, '*Maharaj,* I am Pandu, the *Yuvraj* of Hastinapur.'

'Oh really? I guessed something like that.'

Shalya lavished praises on him and said, 'You don't know what you've done. Those scoundrels were planning a rebellion against Madra and were hiding like rats at this place which is quite remote from my capital city. We had not been able to find them. We were on a regular patrol at a distance. The din of your fight attracted us to this side and we could find them. But you did not leave much for us to do! Ha ha ha....'

'You are so brave and skilled. Your arrows were so fast—like torrents of rain...those barbarians were simply clueless...remarkable shooting. Wasn't it, *Bhrata*?' Madri cried out, genuinely impressed by Pandu's heroic efforts.

'Absolutely, truly remarkable,' Shalya nodded in complete agreement.

Pandu had goosebumps. He was used to praises about his weapon skills but what was new to him was this infatuated look in a woman's eyes! Pandu quickly looked down at his hands to check whether his ashy complexion had turned into a glowing, radiant colour by some miracle. Madri was the first woman to whom Pandu's colour did not matter. She seemed to have seen through his off-putting appearance to find the real merit of the person. Pandu suddenly felt special. Madri had done wonders to his self-esteem. This was unquestionably the best day in his life that made him feel like a man. Pandu fell deep in love with the woman then and there.

Shalya was carefully watching the expressions of both Pandu and Madri. Things were just to his liking. The sister's budding romance seemed to be convenient for the brother's politics. Shalya was thinking that discounting the youth's uninviting looks, Pandu was definitely a suitable match for Madri, given his illustrious descent. Although Madra was already an ally of Hastinapur with Vahik as the common friend, it was a golden opportunity to forge direct friendship with the formidable Kauravas. It would put Madra in good stead.

10

'*Mahamahim* Bheeshma seems to be too worried,' asked Kanik, entering into the sculpture room somewhat hesitantly. He was the Prime Minister of Hastinapur.

Devavrata was in no mood to discuss state matters now. He asked rather indolently, 'Anything important?'

'I think it is, *Mahamahim.* We have just received a marriage proposal for Prince Pandu. King Kuntibhoja, the king of the Bhojas has offered his daughter's hand for our Prince Pandu.'

'Oh really?' The information was quite unexpected and surprised Devavrata. He looked on at Kanik's face blankly for some moments.

But...but...why on earth should a mighty warlord like Kuntibhoja want our Pandu for his daughter? He could have any day found a better match for his girl. Something must be amiss here.

Kanik was looking at Devavrata with sharp eyes. He was clever like a wily fox. It was an obvious requisite for his job, however. He said softly yet purposefully, '*Prabhu,* if I get to know what bothers you, I may be of some help.'

Devavrata looked Kanik in his eyes. His words sounded relaxed, despite the tension within, 'No Kanik, I was just thinking whether we should immediately accept Kuntibhoja's proposal or buy some time to look for a better match.'

'If you allow me, I must say that the latter is a better idea.'

'Why do you say so?'

Kanik coughed to clear his throat, as was his habit. Measuring every single word, he said very cautiously, 'In fact, if I were you, I would have rejected it straightaway. We can do well without such a girl.'

Devavrata became very curious. 'What do you mean by "such a girl"? Tell me clearly.'

Kanik said little uncertainly, 'Actually, I have heard a strange rumour about that girl. If that is to be believed, we should reject the proposal summarily without any second thought. Apparently, the girl became pregnant a couple of years ago. No one knows who her secret lover was. Some say she accidentally got impregnated through a rare divine phenomenon. But in spite of such dishonour, people claim that the girl was actually innocent. I don't know the exact truth. All I know is that the girl is tainted. She shouldn't be considered as *Yuvraj* Pandu's consort, anyway.'

Devavrata was listening, all agog with curiosity. Kanik continued, 'King Kuntibhoja did well to hush up the scandal but despite all his efforts, the matter could not be suppressed entirely.'

'What happened to the baby?' Devavrata asked.

'I don't know. Some say she aborted the pregnancy, some say she delivered the baby and gave it away to a childless couple.'

Devavrata's face became red with anger. *How dare that Bhoja chieftain even think of passing his defiled daughter to a Kaurava prince*?

He angrily stood up and instructed Kanik, 'Draft a letter to Kuntibhoja rejecting the proposal immediately. Make it terse yet polite. No need to cite any reason in the letter. And no need to tell *Mata* Satyavati anything about this. You may go.' He dismissed Kanik with a gesture of his right hand.

'As you wish, *Prabhu*,' Kanik bowed humbly and took a step towards the doorway before he remembered something.

'*Oho*, I forgot to tell you another interesting thing about this girl you may like to know before closing this chapter once and for all.' Kanik turned around sharply. He looked as enthusiastic as a gossipmongering village woman.

'What is it? Say quickly. The morning has already been wasted enough.'

'The girl is not Kuntibhoja's biological daughter either. Kuntibhoja apparently adopted her when she was an infant and raised her with utmost care, love and indulgence. But when....'

'Do you know who her real father is?' Devavrata's question darted like a deadly missile.

'The late King Shurasen, the Vrishni great who ruled Mathura before Ugrasen. He was Kuntibhoja's bosom friend. As Kuntibhoja was childless, Shurasen gave his daughter to him. Her birth name was Pritha. Kuntibhoja changed her name to Kunti after himself and....'

'Stop!' Devavrata's excited scream cut a startled Kanik short. His eyes were glowering. Kanik shook a little seeing Devavrata's suddenly changed mood.

'What did you say? She is Shurasen's biological daughter? That means she is a Vrishni girl? Are you sure? Are you?' Devavrata asked frenziedly, training his index finger at Kanik.

Kanik was utterly baffled. Why did this little piece of information make Devavrata—a famously temperate man—behave this unnaturally?

'Yes, *Prabhu*. Though raised in a Bhoja family, Kunti is actually of Vrishni descent,' he said sheepishly.

Kanik's information had caused Devavrata a brainwave. A 'brilliant' idea crossed his mind.

This is a great opportunity to turn Shakuni's hatred against Hastinapur. Shakuni can't tolerate the Vrishnis. He will be livid if a Vrishni woman enters our family. I shall somehow let him know that Pandu's wife is actually a Vrishni, not a Bhoja. He will most certainly try to create troubles inside our house. Lady Satyavati, now watch out! Fun...it will be fun....

'Great!' Devavrata slammed his clenched right fist into the palm of the left hand, 'Exactly what I needed!'

'Sorry?'

'No...I mean the Vrishnis are a very cultured and advanced people. Among the Yadava clans, they are by far the best. I always wanted to have a Vrishni girl in our family. We must accept the marriage proposal. Kunti will be our Pandu's wife and they will make a brilliant couple, I am sure.'

'So, we shall send them a message accepting the proposal, right?' Kanik was smart enough to go with the wind.

'Yes. Do it as urgently as you can. Our Pandu can't have a better alliance than this. And don't forget to inform the old lady but only after sending the letter.'

'As you wish, *Prabhu*,' Kanik turned back.

'And another thing, Kanik!' Devavrata had something more to say.

'Yes, please.'

'Send your most efficient spy to Mathura immediately. Task him to find out whether Shakuni was present there during Devaki's *swayamvara* and whether he got embroiled in any controversy there. It has to be done very discreetly.'

Like a true politician that he was, Kanik did not betray any curiosity or surprise. With a formal bow, he took Devavrata's leave to carry out the order.

Devavrata suspected that Shakuni had probably been enamoured of a Vrishni woman who spurned his advances causing the deadly malice in his heart. But how had he come in touch with the Vrishni girl? Usually, the Gandharas did not get much chance to mix with the Vrishnis either politically or socially. He might have visited Mathura during Devaki's *swayamvara* and met that girl there.

Devavrata had another strong hunch.

Is Kunti the very same girl Shakuni had probably fallen for? Being a childhood friend of Devaki, Kunti must have visited Mathura to attend the swayamvara ceremony[1]*. Shakuni met her, possibly. He probably does not know that she was adopted into the Bhoja clan. If it really turns out to be so, and Kunti steps into this family, Shakuni will just go mad. All his hatred will be diverted towards the Kuru family. Perfect!*

The feedback from the spy was now very important.

Pandu was staring at the ceiling of his bedchamber, sitting languorously on an armchair and resting his head on both palms. There were exquisite engravings on the plafond—most of them being vignettes of immortal love stories featuring legendary couples like Harishchandra-Shaibya, Shakuntala-Dushyanta, Kacha-Devyani, Rama-Sita, Savitri-Satyavan, Nala-Damayanti and so on. Pandu's mind was filled with romantic thoughts. He was seeing Madri's images everywhere. A pleasant air was wafting in the room. He was slipping into a delightful reverie.

The dwam was suddenly broken by the voice of the guard who announced in a peculiar accent that Prince Vidur wanted to meet him.

---

1 Devaki's father and uncle (Devak and Ugrasen respectively) were close friends of Kunti's biological father Shurasen and even her adoptive father Kuntibhoja. Kunti would become Devaki's sister-in-law after Devaki's marriage to Vasudeva—Kunti's elder brother (son of Shurasen).

Had it been anyone else other than Vidur, Pandu would not have entertained him now. But Vidur was more of a friend than a half-brother. Vidur understood Pandu better than anybody else. Although younger, Vidur's wisdom and maturity always came to Pandu's aid. He got up from his seat to greet Vidur.

Vidur entered the room with a broad grin and hugged Pandu straightaway.

'What happened, Vidur? You look quite happy today,' Pandu asked with a laugh.

'I am, indeed. I am very very happy today, *Bhrata* Pandu!' Vidur released Pandu from his hold and punched the air.

Pandu was very surprised to see a usually reserved Vidur in such a light mood. He never knew Vidur could be so fulsome in his expressions.

'I am dying to know what happened. Tell me quickly.'

'Congratulations, *Bhrata*...many congratulations! Kuntibhoja, the great Bhoja king wants to have you as his son-in-law! He wants you to marry his beautiful daughter, Kunti,' Vidur announced gleefully, spreading his arms in delight.

Pandu stood stunned. He could not believe what was happening to him. The last few days had been incredible. He thought, *I am not actually that undesirable. Even the Bhojas want me! Pity I wasted so many days of my precious life wallowing in unnecessary self-pity! But Madri? How can I ever forget her? That's impossible!*

'What troubles you, *Bhrata*? You seem to be quite tensed,' Vidur asked. Vidur had expected the information to boost Pandu's self-esteem. But why was he looking so perturbed instead?

Pandu was in two minds, unable to immediately decide whether he should take Vidur in confidence and tell him about his infatuation for Madri. However, he finally overcame his hesitation and told Vidur at length about his encounter with Shalya and Madri a few days back.

Vidur clearly understood that Pandu had been smitten with Madri. But Vidur considered Kunti as the better choice as she would bring in supports of two mighty Yadava clans—the Vrishnis and the Bhojas. Madra, on the other hand, was already Hastinapur's ally, regardless of Pandu's relation with Madri.

'I won't be able to forget Madri, Vidur,' said Pandu with a sad face.

'You don't need to,' Vidur said. He had already sorted his thoughts and knew very well how to resolve the crisis.

'What do you mean?'

'Simple. You can have both,' pat came Vidur's reply. He knew his brother wanted to hear exactly this and added, 'But first Kunti, then Madri, mind it!'

'Why so?'

'Because we can afford to keep the Madrakas waiting but not the Bhojas.' Vidur explained.

Pandu felt relieved. He secretly admired Vidur for finding exactly the solution he himself wanted. Pandu sat back in his seat with dreamy eyes. His heart was set on fire by two beautiful women.

Vidur noticed the expressions of a lovestruck Pandu but did not want to waste time with him anymore. He must meet his mentor Vyasadeva immediately and inform him about the developments around Pandu's marriage. Vyasa would be able to analyse the situation better. Hurriedly, Vidur took Pandu's leave and got out of the room.

Vidur went to the stable and rode his favourite steed directing it towards Vyasa's hut in the jungle. As he reached near the western boundary of Hastinapur, he found another horse-rider galloping towards him from the opposite direction. As they came closer to each other, Vidur recognised him as Shakuni. Both stopped their horses on seeing each other and dismounted out of courtesy.

'Namaskar, Shakuni*ji*!' Vidur greeted him politely.

'Namaskar, Vidur*ji*!' Shakuni returned the courtesy and walked towards Vidur with longish strides.

The two extremely intelligent young men stood face-to-face with complicated smiles on their faces. They were almost the same age, yet less than comfortable in each other's company.

Shakuni asked Vidur, '*Kumar* Vidur, have you seen that old man seated under the great banyan tree there?' He pointed westwards.

'Which old man are you talking about?'

'Come, I'll show you,' said Shakuni. They mounted their horses and rode away.

Just outside the limits of Hastinapur, there stood an ancient banyan tree like a watchful guard. A man was sitting beneath it, leaning against the trunk. He had covered his body with a black blanket and his face was mostly covered with an anarchic beard that seemed to have not been trimmed for years. His long tresses drooped over his face. There were very few black strands in his beard and hair. The man was very old and by no means ordinary as his facial features suggested. A robust stick was laid on the ground beside him.

Vidur and Shakuni got down from their horses and walked towards the man. He seemed to be dozing. The approaching footsteps broke his slumber. He lifted his head a little and looked at the duo.

Shakuni and Vidur slowed down because the stare of the man was withering. They looked at each other with much less confidence than before. Who or what could be that man? An ascetic? An outcast? A fugitive? A madman? A *Mleccha* rebel in disguise?

The man grinned. His teeth were squeaky clean, surprisingly. He muttered something in a low voice. In spite of the drawl, the words were clearly understandable and were intoned like a verse:

'The Future is lying low
Soon it shall rouse the Past,
The Present is a moving shadow
Wheeling around us fast,

Eight years from now
Shall there be Light,
Grab the Lamp away
Or perish in the Fight…'

'Who are you, old man? You want to tell us something?' asked Vidur.

'Go away, you fools! Don't disturb me!' The strange man snarled, waving his hand irately.

Pinched, Shakuni took a step forward angrily but was stopped by Vidur.

'Better leave him alone for now. Let's not waste time over him as we have other things to do,' Vidur said impatiently as he was in a hurry to meet Vyasa.

They mounted their horses and rode towards opposite directions—Vidur towards the forest and Shakuni back to the city.

They were unaware that almost similar thoughts were pricking them at the same time. The old man's face appeared familiarish to both. Both had a feeling that they had seen a similar face somewhere before but none could recall when and where.

'The daughter of Kuntibhoja!'

Vyasa lifted his head with a start. Vidur's information was clearly unexpected, if not surprising to the great sage. Vidur became a little nervous seeing his mentor's reaction. He had been very anxious to know whether Kunti would make the right match for his beloved brother Pandu. Now Vyasa's reaction simply scared him.

'W-why *Pitashri*—I mean, *Maharshi*? Isn't she a good choice?'

'Kunti is actually a Vrishni girl, Kuntibhoja took her in adoption. Her real father is Shurasen.'

'You know everything, *Maharshi*!' Vidur flashed an impressed smile. 'But how is the girl?'

Vyasa did not immediately answer. Pensive, he lowered his head and started scratching his beard. He sank in deep, complicated thoughts. He had met the girl once at Kuntibhoja's place. He liked her very much. She was beautiful, intelligent and very well-mannered. Vyasa was aware of the scandal around her and he also knew that she was actually innocent. He was so impressed by her that he even thought of her as his dear Vidur's bride. It was his secret desire to see Vidur and Kunti holding each other's hands. But he was too late. She was now being considered for Pandu, instead!

He did not reveal this to Vidur. A sigh breezed out of Vyasa's nostrils.

'Is there any problem with her?' Vidur asked again, anxiously.

'Better ask whether Pandu is good enough for her!' Vyasa said with a flat smile this time.

'Sorry?'

'I mean, she is a wonderful girl. I know her. I like the Vrishni people very much, you know. Your brother cannot have a better alliance, trust me,' Vyasa said with his eyes closed. He knew that the best way to hide the mind was to shut eyes.

'Oh great! I came just to hear this. *Pranaam, Maharshi,'* Vidur laughed like a child.

'But very soon, I shall find another Vrishni girl for you, I swear,' saying this, Vyasa bared his mind inadvertently.

His words sounded awkward and untimely to an intelligent Vidur. Walking towards the door of Vyasa's hut, Vidur was trying to understand the real purport of Vyasa's strange last comment.

Why did he say that he would find 'another Vrishni girl' for me? What did he mean? It seems the girl was already in Maharshi's mind. Did he actually want Kunti for ME, instead of Pandu? Oh no!

Vidur blushed. He felt a strong curiosity for Kunti. For the first time in his life, he felt drawn to a woman, that too without seeing her.

As soon as he crossed the threshold of the door, he remembered something. He turned back and entered the hut again, 'Oh *Maharshi*, I forgot to tell you something.'

'What is it, again?' Vyasa asked without looking at him.

Vidur told him about the strange old man who was sitting under the banyan tree. Hearing this, a deep frown appeared on Vyasa's forehead.

'That man was reciting a peculiar verse.' Vidur informed.

'What was he saying?'

'The Future is lying low, soon it shall rouse the Past...,' Vidur recited it perfectly, retrieving from his outstanding memory.

Vyasa looked grim and asked in a low voice, 'Tell me exactly how he looked.'

'He is very old—probably the oldest man I ever saw. But he is still quite strapping—it seems he had a massive build in his youth. Although mostly covered with white beard and unruly shock of white hair, his face clearly has very sharp features with a hooked nose, thin lips and large rectangular eyes. He seemed to have had a golden complexion once upon a time that has now tanned into deep brownish. And yes, he is cat-eyed!'

He noticed an ominous darkness descend over Vyasa's face. Vyasa was suddenly sweating.

'You may go now, *Putra*. Don't forget to report to me immediately if you meet the man again,' Vyasa dismissed him for the day.

At the very same time in Hastinapur, there was a very similar kind of gloom on Devavrata Bheeshma's face, when Shakuni was giving him the account of their meeting with that mysterious old man.

II

The pretty morning turned sour for Kunti. King Kuntibhoja had suddenly come to her room after quite a long time. She was surprised to see him today at her doorstep. Kunti's relation with her adoptive father had lately become somewhat uncomfortable following an unfortunate incident. But she knew Kuntibhoja genuinely loved her—even today, although it was difficult for him to express the love cutting across many social taboos.

When she had been a child, her father Shurasen gave her away on adoption to his bosom friend Kuntibhoja—the Bhoja ruler of Kunti kingdom. Born a Vrishni princess, she changed into a Bhoja princess overnight. The jolly and chirpy Pritha became a graceful and classy Kunti. She often thought why Shurasen did not give her elder brother Vasudeva on adoption. Why did he part with his daughter? Was it because she was a female child and hence less desired? Or, was it simply because her father did not love her as much as he loved her brother? Although she had a wonderful upbringing and comfortable life in Kunti kingdom, she often felt a scalding humiliation beneath her skin. What had made her so redundant to her biological father? Her gender or something else?

Kuntibhoja looked grim as he stood at the threshold of Kunti's room. Kunti stood up and politely said, 'Please, do come in, *Pitashri.*' There was a perfunctory formality in her voice that was quite unusual in a father-daughter conversation.

Kuntibhoja responded with a dour face, 'It's alright. I have no business inside your room. I only came to inform that I have set up an excellent alliance for you—Prince

Pandu of Hastinapur. They have accepted our proposal too. I want to organise a *swayamvara* ceremony before the marriage. I would like you to choose Pandu as your life partner in the *swayamvara*. Everything has been settled. Be mentally prepared for the marriage. I hope you shall not let me down again. I don't think you can have a better match in this situation.'

Saying this, Kuntibhoja turned around and walked away without waiting for Kunti's response or reaction. His strident footsteps died down gradually.

Although Kunti did not have anything against the alliance in particular, Kuntibhoja's last three words—'in this situation'—fell upon her like a whiplash.

Kunti could never understand why nobody had ever cared for her opinions even on matters that concerned her own life. She felt a dolorous wave of tears breaking upon her from within. She curled her fingers and clutched her hair in a fit of despair. Then she started scratching her own face and arms as if she was trying to peel her skin off.

Why do these cruel men dig up that gravest mistake of my life over and over again? Don't they realise that I have never been able to shake off that memory even for a split moment ever since? How can I ever forget that angelic face of the newborn?

That innocent, ethereal baby happened to be a part of her own body! The baby was so beautiful. He was so big. His eyes shone like diamonds. His unibrow looked like an eagle afloat in the sky. His complexion was like the blazing sun. His cries were ear-splitting. And his face was exactly hers!

When she was placing that beautifully decorated basket on the river's surface, tears blinded her. The baby was inside the basket. He was laughing, believing it to be a new kind of a game. He was holding her bangles and pulling at them. He wanted her to be with him. But she softly freed her bangles from the baby's clutch and gave a mild push to the basket that started drifting down the gentle flow of river. Kunti surprised herself with her own cruelty that she never knew to have existed at all. Since that moment, she knew her eyes would perpetually remain wet till they were closed for good.

Kunti could never understand that man—*Rishi* Durbasa. He had given her a boon that would eventually turn out to be the biggest curse in her life. Was it *his* fault to bestow such a great power on an immature little girl who was unprepared to handle it? Or was *she* herself to be blamed for misusing the power so frivolously? Whatever be it, Kunti was sure of one thing. She could have done well in her life without that boon and the man who had given it to her.

When Kunti was just a teenager, *Rishi* Durbasa had paid a visit to Kuntibhoja and sought hospitality. The celebrated sage was notorious for his combustible temper. Kuntibhoja tried his level best to play the good host and specially tasked Kunti to take good care of him. Kuntibhoja always had much confidence in Kunti and her ability to handle tricky situations well. Although very intelligent, she had a disarming sweetness too.

Durbasa took a strong liking to Kunti. Her innocence and pleasant manners left a deep impression on the moody sage. Before taking leave finally, he decided to reward her. He summoned her in his room. She turned up almost immediately with a delightful smile.

'Kunti, you have made me happy with your devotion and sincere efforts. You have looked after me very well. Now, I want to give you a boon,' said the sage with an expressionless face.

'Oh, really? Thank you so much, *Deva*! But *Pitashri* said it was my duty only…,' said Kunti, smiling.

'What you have done was far more than duty. You won't understand now. I shall grant you a power that will make any woman envy you.'

Kunti probably expected it to be something like a doll or expensive jewellery. But she could not realise why Durbasa was not smiling. She found his expressions quite odd.

'I shall teach you a very secret mantra. You shall learn it by heart. If you chant it with closed eyes and sincerely think of any god, you shall be able to see, even feel, that god. You shall be able to touch him. What is more, should you conceive a baby during chanting the mantra and musing about the god, that baby will acquire some of his qualities and will be widely regarded as that god's offspring!'

Kunti could not believe her ears. The prospect of seeing her favourite god thrilled her. She was actually too young to understand the significance of Durbasa's last sentence.

'Oh, that's great! I shall be able to see any god?' She excitedly asked, throwing her podgy arms in delight.

'Any,' there was a strange excitement in Durbasa's voice.

Then Durbasa imparted that secret knowledge to her. The girl had an extremely sharp memory. She quickly memorised the mantra and picked up the tune impeccably. Then, to test how it worked, she closed her eyes and started reciting the lines, concentrating all her thoughts on her idol—Lord Surya. Right since her puberty, she had developed a strong admiration for the Sun God, a devotion bordering on fixation.

Strangely enough, the wise Durbasa did not warn her against the perils of playing with that extremely sensitive knowledge. Rather, he allowed her!

She was slipping into a trance. The strange tune of the hymn was casting a hypnotic spell on her. To her utter delight, she envisaged a glorious figure before her. He was so dazzling yet so charming. He looked like the king of all kings. Was he Lord Surya? Was he for real or was it a figment of her self-induced imagination?

Suddenly, she felt a touch over her shoulder. The touch was very different. Nobody had ever touched her in this way. She had goosebumps. It seemed to be a hard, masculine hand that was curiously roaming over her face and body. An exciting manly smell was filling her nostrils. She felt a warm breath over her face. What was happening? She tried to open her eyes but she could not as the eyelids seemed to have been glued to each other. She seemed to be falling into a deep slumber.

When she came round and opened her eyes, she could neither see that magnificent figure nor Durbasa. She was surprised to see her clothes dishevelled. But what baffled her the most was an inexplicable feeling that she was now a completely different person. She was no more the guiltless little girl that she had been only a while ago. A mysterious magician had wielded his magic wand to turn her into a blooming woman sullied by a mortal sin. The feeling was awful.

Her pregnancy was soon revealed and the sky came crashing down on her head. She was bombarded with cruel, snide remarks from all around and subjected to frenzied dressing down from her adoptive parents and relatives. Her life became hell. Kuntibhoja stopped talking to her. She started pitying herself. She had now become mature enough to realise why her world had turned upside down. She understood she would not be able to keep or raise the baby with honour. So, she decided to abandon him.

She knew this incredibly tough decision would never cease to haunt her. She prepared for the lifelong ordeal she had invited for herself. She only wished the baby to retain Lord Surya's virtues as Durbasa had promised and become successful in life in his own right.

One thing she would never know for sure—who actually fathered her baby. Was it really Lord Surya? Or *Rishi* Durbasa? Or someone else taking advantage of her helplessness?

Entire Hastinapur was out on the streets. Spontaneous celebrations were going on all around the city besides an elaborate preparation for an official function. The much popular Prince Pandu was returning home with his bride Kunti from the Bhoja kingdom (Kunti *Rajya*).

The Kaurava nobles were all waiting at the sprawling terrace, standing on its edge from where the staircase descended to reach the ground below. Everybody was beaming with happiness. Satyavati's eyes were overflowing with tears of contentment. Her family was almost complete now. She would only have to wait for the children of Dhritarashtra and Pandu to arrive in due time.

Shakuni was happy—in a different way, nevertheless. The scope of his game had been hopelessly limited with Dhritarashtra and Pandu. Now with their wives joining the scene, soon to be followed by their children as usual, the game would undoubtedly become much more interesting. Although it was still a long way off, Shakuni's fingers were dancing in excitement on the hilt of his sword.

The big convoy entered the palace premise amidst a boisterous reception. At the centre of the convoy, there was an exquisite golden chariot that carried the bride and the groom. It stopped a little shy of the staircase.

The newlyweds slowly alighted from the chariot. Another round of applause rose from the crowd. Pandu and Kunti, holding each other's hands started ascending the steps that were covered with flowers.

The couple climbed up. The ritual of *vadhu varan* was conducted by Satyavati, Ambika and Ambalika to welcome the new bride. The procedure was much the same as in Gandhari's time although it was little less elaborate this time.

A large portion the bride's face was covered with the veil, an enormous golden nose ring and a bejewelled diadem. Her face could not be seen properly from an angle.

All of a sudden, Shakuni's heart thumped. The gait of the bride and her roundish face reminded him of someone! He was dying to see her face.

Kunti started to touch the feet of the elders one by one, according to seniority. There was a pretty long queue. Everybody was taking his or her time to bless her. Shakuni was getting mortally impatient. When would she come to him? When would he get to have a close look at her? It was urgent—very urgent for him.

Finally, his turn came.

Kunti was ambling towards him slowly. Her head was shyly lowered. She bent a little to reach out to his feet and slightly lifted her head to seek his blessings. Their eyes met. They could clearly see each other's face now.

Kunti's smile vanished. The momentary astonishment in her eyes quickly turned into a glower. Nobody could notice her quicksilver change of expressions.

Shakuni stood shell-shocked. His mouth was agape.

It is that face!

Shakuni could not believe his eyes. He was not prepared for this at all. How could this be possible? How could *his* Pritha become Pandu's wife? This very woman had been central to his every single dream. This very woman had taken his life to a completely different course. This was the woman for whom he had left everything. What crooked game of destiny it was that brought his Pritha right in front of him today with a completely different identity?

Shakuni's mind took him back to that harrowing evening at Mathura.

As a representative of his father, Shakuni had visited Mathura as a guest to attend the *swayamvara* ceremony of Devaki. There he met Devaki's best friend, Pritha, who was introduced to him as Shurasen's daughter. The delicate woman was very different from the voluptuous Gandhara girls. A love-starved Shakuni fell head over heels in love with Pritha. Finally, Shakuni planned to meet her in a secluded palace garden to convey his feelings. But by a cruel twist of fate, Pritha misunderstood him as he tried to save her from a deadly snake. She mistook his valiant effort for a molestation attempt and cruelly insulted him. Her armed bodyguards severely thrashed him. However, on Pritha's insistence his life was spared. The incident drastically changed Shakuni. His reckless love turned into a deadly animosity towards Pritha and the entire Vrishni race in general. Shakuni was completely bewildered.

I was told that Pandu is getting married to Kuntibhoja's daughter Kunti. Even the official declarations mentioned so. That means Pritha and Kunti are the same person! But how come the parentage is different then? What is happening here?

Meanwhile, Kunti recovered a little. She quickly hovered her hand around Shakuni's knees faking a *pranaam* and walked past him to the next in line.

Only two persons did not fail to take notice of the little drama between Kunti and Shakuni. One of them was obviously Devavrata, the other Vidur! Devavrata's eyes had stayed put on Shakuni and Vidur's on Kunti. Devavrata was curious to watch Shakuni's reactions on seeing her here while Vidur was dying to see the woman who could well have been *his*!

Vidur's ears were becoming warm and face red. He felt something burning inside him. He shut his eyes for a moment, but that did not help him expunge from his mind the face of Pandu's bride.

Meanwhile, Kunti alias Pritha had completed paying obeisance to all the seniors. A storm was raging in her mind too. She had not thought of seeing Shakuni here even in her creepiest nightmares.

Oh God, what have I done to face this? How come that man is here? Will he try to harm me? Will he spread bad words about me? Does he know of my secret? Will he leak it out to take revenge on me? What shall I do if my husband and in-laws get to know of my illicit son? Everybody will think I am a bad woman! Will they drive me away? But where shall I go from here? My adoptive father will not take me back. I shall never go to my Vrishni house again. Then? Why am I put to such difficult tests all my life? Shall I have to commit suicide and put an end to all this?

She was now being taken ceremoniously inside the main residential building. Everybody started following her into the palace. Only Shakuni alone kept standing there motionless.

'Any problem, *Shriman* Shakuni?'

Shakuni flinched, as the mocking tone of Devavrata entered his ear. He stared at Devavrata's face with dazed eyes.

'Not feeling well, Shakuni*ji*?' Devavrata asked again, with a more pronounced sarcasm.

'Can you tell me one thing?' Shakuni asked him in a lifeless, mechanical voice. 'Is Pandu's wife a Vrishni lady, actually?'

Devavrata smiled cunningly. He thought, *my hunch is absolutely right. Kunti is the Vrishni girl Shakuni loved! What Kanik's spy could not confirm, Shakuni's reaction did!*

'You are right. She is actually of Vrishni descent. She is the daughter of Shurasen Vrishni but was adopted by Kuntibhoja in her childhood. Her birth name was Pritha. However, she is known as Kunti now. But *how* do you know?' Devavrata tried to make his question sound as naïve as possible.

Shakuni felt as though someone was scorching him alive with a burning torch. Every single vein and artery of his seemed to be on fire. He did not care to respond to Devavrata's question. His mind was now being ravaged by a new set of evil ideas.

I have got her now! That fool Pandu cannot protect her from me. It's my turn now to pay her back. I have loved her too much to be able to forgive her! I shall have her husband and children destroyed right in front of her eyes. I shall set Dhritarashtra's sons on them. I shall make this Kuru house free from all Vrishni strains. She will be living a desolate life laden with the memories of her husband and children. Won't that be revenge enough? That's the only way I can douse my fire and rest in peace. Beware, Pritha! Your moment of redemption is come!

Well before the children of Dhritarashtra and Pandu came into being, Shakuni had started casting them as important characters in a gripping play that he was going to script and direct.

Part ii

I

Shakuni's desperation was akin to that of a caged bird uselessly fluttering its wings for revenge. Kunti was the focal point of his rage for sure but he did not intend to kill her. He rather wanted to bleed her with unendurable wounds. And for that, he had to harm Pandu as that would hit Kunti the hardest. However, it was not easy as Pandu was the king now and access to him was difficult due to tight security and protocol. All Shakuni could do was to wait for his chance.

A few years passed by; Pandu had meanwhile taken Madri as his second wife. He was smartly managing his two wives, at least apparently. Not only that, he was ruling the kingdom quite efficiently as well. As per Vyasadeva's wish, Vidur had been married to Devaki's step-sister Sulabha—another Vrishni woman. Dhritarashtra and Gandhari too, were living happily together. Gandhari seemed to have been able to alleviate Dhritarashtra's frustrations to a large extent. Everything seemed to be just fine in Hastinapur—much to Shakuni's chagrin!

But, the calm surface of the water often hides the turmoil underneath. One day, Shakuni's most favoured servant brought him an unbelievable piece of news.

'*Maharaj* Pandu would resign from kingship,' the servant muttered close to his ears.

Shakuni almost fell down from his seat. He shouted, 'What the hell are you saying?'

'You heard me, *Prabhu*.'

The servant further elaborated that Pandu had killed a Brahmin sage mistaking him for a deer during an unfortunate hunting expedition. Overwhelmed with the remorse of Brahman-*hatya,* he became hell-bent on punishing himself and decided to abdicate the throne to make way for his elder brother Dhritarashtra. Not only that, he was even determined to leave the kingdom and banish himself to the jungles for atonement.

After the news sank in, Shakuni darted a question, 'Is he going alone? What about his wives?'

'Heard they will also accompany him,' replied the servant.

Shakuni got lost in deep thought. *Pritha will accompany Pandu! She will not be there in Hastinapur anymore. If she does not stay in Hastinapur, my mission will lose all meaning. Then why should I mark time in Hastinapur any longer? Should I go back to Gandhara now?*

Shakuni felt his mind and body go numb. He felt no urge to return to Arshi again, nor could the throne of Gandhara tempt him. With a heavy sigh, Shakuni resigned himself to a painful realisation that he actually belonged nowhere now.

Pandu, accompanied by Kunti and Madri, went into a self-imposed exile. They started living in a dense jungle observing strict penance. However, Shakuni's astute mind suspected that Pandu's resignation and voluntary ostracism might have been a ruse to cover up something. But he was not being able to substantiate his doubt by any means.

Days rolled into another year. One day, Shakuni had an informal discussion with Pandu's personal doctor and ended up with a baffling piece of information. *Pandu had been apparently under medication to improve his sexual potency.*

Shakuni's doubts suddenly seemed to have found some base. Did Pandu try to hide his sexual incompetence by running away from public attention? Shakuni's instincts told him that things were going to take an interesting turn soon.

Dhritarashtra was free from any worries. The blind man was simply living his dream. In Pandu's absence, the bejewelled crown sat on his head. He was ruling over the kingdom under Devavrata's tutelage. Beside his fortuitous ascension to the throne, there was another reason for his happiness. Gandhari was pregnant and the entire kingdom was gearing up to welcome the royal baby.

Shakuni became very happy with this development. He was seeing a genuine smile on Gandhari's face nowadays. The prospect of motherhood brought back the vivacious girl that she had been once upon a time. He was even more pleased that Gandhari was going to beat both Pritha and Madri in the race of producing an heir to the throne. Dhritarashtra's line was all set to retain control over the throne without any complications.

Lately, he had observed one change in himself. He was becoming more and more absorbed in the affairs of Hastinapur. With the fire of revenge still simmering in his heart, Shakuni had gotten himself entangled in a strange love-hate relationship with the Kuru house.

However, his premonition of an imminent turn of events proved prophetic. Shakuni would never be able to forget that particular day. It could easily be considered as a watershed moment in the Kuru family's history.

Devavrata, Dhritarashtra, Vidur, Kripacharya, Kanik and Shakuni were all sitting at the assembly hall. The mood was light. Kripacharya was narrating a hilarious story about a diplomatic goof-up. Everybody was laughing.

In the midst of all this, a young boy, clad in an ochre robe, was ushered in. The boy was all smiles and carried a large basket full of fruits and sweetmeats. The boy put the basket down at Devavrata's feet very humbly and broke the explosive news.

Pandu had become a father! Kunti had given birth to a son a week ago.

Devavrata, Vidur and Kripacharya jumped up from their seats and started rejoicing. Devavrata took off his precious pearl necklace and thrust it into the palm of the boy. He accepted it shyly. Kripacharya became busy noting down the exact date and time of the baby's birth for astrological calculations. Vidur appeared the happiest—so much so that he hugged Kanik tightly with eyes moist with tears of joy.

Shakuni's head was reeling. Doubts and questions clouded his mind and assailed his thoughts. How could a man who had been under treatment for sexual impairment just until a few days ago become a father so early?

He had totally forgotten about Dhritarashtra until he heard a peculiar grunt from his direction. Shakuni looked at his face and a shiver crawled down his spine. A deadly hatred was writ large all over Dhritarashtra's face. Shakuni had seen traces of bitterness in him earlier but this expression was simply severe. Dhritarashtra had been quite confident that his son would be the eldest. But Pandu's newborn son, being the first of the next generation, was now the natural heir to the throne that he had voluntarily renounced.

Shakuni clearly foresaw a serious wrangle within the family, much to his liking. '*Finally*,' Shakuni muttered to himself with an invisible laugh.

If it was bad news for Dhritarashtra, the worse was to follow close on its heels the very same day. Gandhari unexpectedly suffered a miscarriage. She had been in an advanced stage of pregnancy. There was a critical medical emergency to save her life. Though Gandhari could ultimately be brought out of danger, she was simply inconsolable at the loss of her baby. The festive mood dramatically turned gloomy.

Vidur acted wisely in this dire crisis. He quickly called for Vyasa to Hastinapur immediately. Seeing Gandhari and Dhritarashtra in such a pathetic condition, the benevolent sage's heart melted. Vyasa collected Gandhari's discarded foetus and revived it with the power of sacred chants. He then shredded the foetus into a hundred and one pieces and placed them inside as many butter-filled pots. Then he put his palm gently on a sobbing Gandhari's head and said, 'No more tears, *Kanya*! After one year, you shall hear babies cry from inside these pots.'

Gandhari and Dhritarashtra fell at Vyasadeva's feet. The cloud of sorrow was cast away for the time being.

The deeply impressed Vidur did not say anything although his regards for Vyasa had increased manifold. But Vidur could not understand why Vyasa's wrinkled face betrayed anxiety.

On their way out, Vyasa himself placed his hand on Vidur's shoulder and said, 'Today, I have succumbed to an inescapable human weakness, *Putra*. What I have done, perhaps I should not have!'

'You want to say Gandhari's baby should have better been left unborn? But why, *Maharshi*?' Vidur shot his question like a missile. He was determined to have a straight answer from his mentor.

Vyasa too realised that it was time he took his protégé on board. With a straight face he explained, 'Dhritarashtra and Gandhari's sons will fall into evil company, I can clearly foresee. Shakuni will spoil them deliberately. They will bring a bad name to the family…they will invite doom.'

Vidur was too shocked to react.

Vyasa continued, 'You may have to start playing *your* role soon, Vidur.'

'My role? What will it be like?'

'Throw your weight behind Pandu's sons to counterbalance Shakuni's influence on the other side. Simple.'

'I understand. I shall try my level best, *Maharshi*,' Vidur said softly.

Vyasa, with a genuine fatherly affection, ruffled Vidur's hairs and said with the conviction of a clairvoyant seer, 'Don't waste your time and energy on being too self-conscious, *Putra*. You have greater things to do. There will be a devastating civil war. Posterity will learn that the sons of Dhritarashtra and Pandu fought over the throne of Hastinapur. But they will never know the real truth. They will never know that it was actually a war between Shakuni and Vidur. Everything is pre-ordained; you can't do anything about it.'

'But why should I fight Shakuni, *Maharshi*? I have no enmity towards him.'

'But he has.'

'Why?'

'Listen carefully to what I say now. I suspect Pandu is in grave danger. Shakuni will be trying to harm him, by any means. Poor Pandu does not know that he has married the woman Shakuni insanely craves for. For now, you only have to watch everything from a distance. If something happens to Pandu, God forbid, I shall be proven right. Then you have to stand behind his sons. And another thing—never disclose your thoughts to anyone, except me. In this strange house, no one is a friend to another. Understand?'

'Yes. But that does not explain why Shakuni sees me as an enemy.'

'*Putra*, I see you need every syllable to be spelt out!' Vyasa scowled in annoyance. 'I noticed Shakuni's reaction that day. He was looking sideways at you and Kunti alternately even when the others were talking. He suspects you to be Kunti's secret paramour,' Vyasa explained with a wicked twitch in the lips, whilst his eyes glinted coyly.

Vidur's face turned red. He suddenly felt as if he was being seen through. He wondered, *did Vyasadeva understand everything? But how? Have I done anything silly?*

Vidur kept quiet. His deepest concern crawled up to the surface of his mind—*if something happens to Pandu, God forbid, how will poor Kunti manage to live? I can never let her suffer....*

Vyasa was observing him. He knew very well what Vidur was thinking at the moment. He was about to say something but Vidur did not let him. For once, Vidur was less than comfortable with Vyasa's outspokenness and did not want him to comment on this particular issue any further.

Vidur silenced Vyasadeva with an unsettling quip, 'But *Maharshi*, you told me only the half-truth!'

'What do you mean?' Vyasadeva was surprised and frowned at Vidur.

'There will be two other people fighting the war from behind Shakuni and me,' Vidur said, looking Vyasa straight into his eyes.

'Really? And who are they?' Vyasa's voice was grim.

'Devavrata Bheeshma and you!'

Vidur prepared for an angry rebuff from Vyasa. But what came from him was nothing of that sort. Instead, Vyasa said in a tired and poignant tone, 'You are almost right, dear. Devavrata and I are also fighting the war, but not essentially against each other. We are just fighting our own wars. Both of us need to win badly. That's why the war will be a terrible one.'

Vyasa walked away in a huff, leaving behind his favourite son in a deep sea of thoughts.

Vyasa's promise to Gandhari came true. After a year, one hundred sons and one daughter were born in succession from the butter-filled pots. Dhritarashtra and Gandhari were over the moon. The entire kingdom was delirious. *Not one or two, but as many as one hundred and one babies at a time!*

Shakuni had come to see the newborn babies. They were kept in small, separate cots according to seniority. He stood in front of the eldest one. He remembered how he had felt seeing Uluk's face for the first time. His eyes became wet and heart numb.

The baby was quite big, with a brownish complexion, curly hair and big eyes. He suddenly stopped crying as Shakuni stood by him. What surprised Shakuni the most was his clear, steady vision. Shakuni's sixth sense told him that this boy was going to be useful—very useful!

'How do you find my cute Suyodhan, *Bhrata* Shakuni?' Dhritarashtra asked with a proud grin.

'Suyodhan?' Shakuni asked with a fun-filled laugh.

'They have named him Duryodhana. But for me, he is only Suyodhan,' said Dhritarashtra making Gandhari, Vidur, Shakuni and Sulabha laugh aloud together. Devavrata, Vyasadeva and Kripacharya only smiled.

Shakuni was feeling quite upbeat. He had been waiting for this moment. In these hundred babies, he saw an army of his own. He must ensure that he wielded complete control over them.

A week later, the very same boy who had come last year with the news of Pandu's son's birth, appeared once again with a similar basket and a similar smile. He announced, 'O Kaurava nobles! Let me inform you with great pleasure that a week back, Lady Kunti gave birth to another baby boy. The baby is unusually big and strong!'

A round of jubilation followed. Though Dhritarashtra was not particularly pleased, he managed to put up a façade of happiness and even rewarded the messenger with a precious armlet. The play-acting was little easy for him this time because he was still basking in his own happiness of being a father.

Shakuni was ravaged with suspicion now. How was Pandu being able to beget children so regularly? Was he 'hiring' someone to father the babies following the *Niyoga* tradition? The thought filled Shakuni's mind with poison. He started cursing Pandu in his mind.

Ah, now I can clearly understand why they left the kingdom. They could not have executed their dirty plans in Hastinapur with adequate secrecy. But how could Pandu deign to play with my Pritha's body? Doesn't he care a damn for his wife's chastity? Is he a pervert? I must destroy that poltroon! Such a man has no right to live. But who is the real father of these babies? Is it any hermit or sage living in the same jungle? Or, a Kshatriya from any other kingdom? Or any aborigine? Oh, wait, can it be Vidur? He travelled out of the kingdom for a month a few months after Pandu's departure, ostensibly on an official mission. Did Vidur visit them then? Quite possible...I know Vidur has a thing for Pritha... But if he is the father of the first son, who fathered the second? That cannot be Vidur. Then who?

Coming to his apartment, Shakuni picked up a *somarasa*-filled chalice and finished the entire drink in a single gulp. He stood up dazed looking at a life-sized clay model of a beautiful woman. He had a delusion that the beautiful Pritha was standing right in front of him, with her exquisite face down.

Shakuni addressed the model in an unsteady voice, 'See Pritha, see, what you have brought yourself down to! You humiliated me one day only to choose an impotent fool as the man of your life who has today made a slut of you. Huh, what have you got in life, Pritha? You are unchaste now—you are fallen. But I am still ready for you. I am still waiting. Come Pritha...come back to me....'

Shakuni saw Pritha slowly lift her head. He expected a remorseful look, but what he saw was a face fulminating with lethal contempt. He thought he could hear Pritha speak too, 'You'll never understand what I have got, Shakuni. It's always better to have a husband like Pandu than to fall into your evil hands. You are a sinner of the worst kind. And you will be punished mercilessly.'

Shakuni tried to catch the image but ended up hugging the lifeless clay model.

Trembling with rage and intoxication, he screamed at the top of his voice, 'I SHALL FINISH YOU! I SHALL FILL YOUR LIFE WITH ASHES, TRUST ME! YOU SHALL GET TO SEE WHAT THIS SHAKUNI IS CAPABLE OF!'

He hurled the chalice at the model, marring its face.

Then the inconsolable Shakuni broke into tears.

2

Kunti became a mother for the third time as another lovely boy was born to her, followed by Madri giving birth to healthy twin boys in consecutive years. Pandu was now a proud father of five sons—three from Kunti, two from Madri.

On the other end, Shakuni was losing track of time as his nephews grew up fast. He was enjoying the company of a multitude of mercurial kids. For years, he had not seen his Uluk. Arshi had sent him a recent painting of his son a few months ago. If the artist was to be believed, Uluk appeared to have grown up into a robust teenager now. The nephews would often remind Shakuni of Uluk, but he was in no mood to return to Gandhara again. He sometimes felt sad thinking how tragic his life had become. He had come here to avenge his humiliation and now it had become the only glaring truth in his life. He knew he was being wasted, yet he did not want to redeem himself. Actually, he was on his way to a kind of self-immolation. And he was aware of it.

Shakuni had noticed one thing. Dhritarashtra and Gandhari loved each other almost to a fault. They were too besotted with themselves to care for any other thing in the world—not even their children. Their love for the children was beyond question, but their parenting was flawed. They pampered the kids infinitely and could never be very strict with them. Sometimes they would involve Shakuni to take care of their children. Shakuni never knew himself to be a great father, but now, much to his own surprise, he found himself managing the kids quite well. He was, slowly but surely, becoming their real guardian.

Duryodhana, the eldest, became extremely close to Shakuni. He was a well-built, naughty and loveable boy with an extremely impressionable mind. Like a typically pampered royal scion, he was extravagant, temperamental and arrogant; albeit generous. He would often flare up at the drop of a hat and calm down almost immediately.

Nevertheless, Duryodhana was a straightforward and simple boy. He had no malice against anybody. And that was a big problem for Shakuni. It was imperative for him to create an ambience of enmity within the family. Shakuni needed Dhritarashtra's sons to destroy Pandu's sons and in turn, Pandu, then Pritha. For that he needed to plant hatred in Duryodhana's mind. But why should Duryodhana hate Pandu's sons? As the eldest son of the reigning king, he got everything he wanted. He was always unquestioned, unchallenged and uncontradicted.

Shakuni understood that if Pandu's boys stayed away from Hastinapur, Duryodhana would never learn to hate them. They must be brought to Hastinapur to make Duryodhana feel insecure. In fact, they had a greater right on Hastinapur's throne because the eldest of them, Yudhisthira, was older than Duryodhana. Duryodhana had to be reminded of it. It would be very easy for Shakuni to incite Duryodhana against them.

A terrible idea occurred to Shakuni....

If Pandu dies suddenly, two birds can be killed with one stone. The two widows of Pandu will be compelled to return to Hastinapur with the children and a tension inside the Kuru family can be created. And...and...a husbandless, unprotected Pritha will be there for the easy taking.

The prince of Gandhara had forgotten that once upon a time he had been a decent gentleman, a brave patriot, a devoted son, a loving brother and a brilliant mind. A wrong marriage had started to cripple him internally and his disastrous infatuation for Pritha finally pulled him down to this abominable low.

He was aware of his dreadful transformation but gave a damn about it. He was implacably busy plotting a devastating revenge instead.

Shakuni hired a professional goon named Parvatak to start keeping a discreet watch on Pandu's activities inside the jungle to strike at an opportune time.

Parvatak flashed a vulgar grin and said with folded hands, '*Shri* Shakuni, I usually take full payments before any risky assignments. You know, I've a family to look after. But as I am immensely honoured that I am going to be of some use to you, a little advance will do....'

Shakuni was used to handling such scums. He smiled in his mind and took out a beryl pendant hanging from his neck by a gold chain. He shoved it into Parvatak's palm very casually and said, 'Don't you worry about your honorarium. You shall get a hundred gold coins more after successful completion of the task.'

'Thank you, *Prabhu*! And this pendant is just wonderful. I shall never take it off,' a delighted Parvatak hung it from his neck and promised to do his best.

'You have to secretly keep watch on every activity of theirs to find the right moment. No one should see or know about you. The next time you come to meet me, your hands must be red with Pandu's blood. And leave no trail behind. Go!'

It was a rainy night. Parvatak busily entered Shakuni's room, completely drenched.

'Come, come. It seems you have bad news,' said Shakuni anxiously, throwing a towel at him.

'Not exactly.'

'Is the job done?'

'Yes,' Parvatak's serious expression did not match his reply.

'Tell me how you did it. And don't you dare try to feed me any concocted story. Should you do that, your pumpkin-like head will soon roll in front of the city's main gate!' Shakuni threatened in a spine-chilling tone.

'I don't need to tell you lies, *Shri* Shakuni. It's for the first time I feel some remorse after completing an assignment!'

'Oh, is it? But why?' Shakuni was genuinely taken aback by the ruffian's sombre mood.

'Pandu had been meditating, sitting under an Ashwattha tree at the bank of Bhagirathi. Though there were only a few big trees in the vicinity, the area was quite bushy. The place was little away from his accommodation inside the jungle. A beautiful woman, possibly his wife, was bathing in the river. I was hiding with a dagger in hand behind a dense bush waiting for the woman to leave. She was looking like a water nymph. She stood up and started walking through the water towards the bank. The land along the edge of the river was a little high. She tried to come up ashore but slipped. She nearly fell and probably sprained an ankle. Her painful moan alerted Pandu and he opened his eyes with a start. Seeing her struggling to come up, he quickly rushed to her and helped her find ground.

The lady and Pandu were now standing face-to-face staring at each other. She had a shy, seductive look in her eyes. Pandu was no more looking like a hermit; he looked like an aroused man ablaze with lust. Pandu held her tightly in his arms. His back was towards me. It was a good opportunity for me. I lifted my right hand to throw the dagger into his neck. I am a master of killing people this way, you know. But I did not have to do anything as Pandu suddenly started writhing on his own. His body twisted. He clutched the left side of his chest with his right hand and fell down on the ground.

It appeared he was having terrible chest pain. It was quite unexpected for me. I lowered my hand and put the dagger back in the scabbard without having to use it.

The woman was screaming for help. Pandu was flailing about. His eyes were bulging. He was gasping for air. Then, he became still forever. It was a fatal heart attack, evidently. The woman fell on his dead body and started crying crazily,' Parvatak paused and wiped his sweating face with a dirty handkerchief.

'What happened next? Tell me!' Shakuni snarled angrily.

'Hearing the lady's screams, another beautiful woman rushed in to the scene from inside the jungle, followed by five little boys and another person, evidently a Brahmin priest. The second lady shouted at the first one, "What have you done, Madri? You caused his death! Didn't you know he was unfit to bear any such strain? Why did you seduce him?" The first lady, Madri, started weeping even more loudly and with folded hands tried to convince the second lady that she did nothing wrong. Meanwhile, the priest checked Pandu's body and declared him dead. He called other people. Some hermits and tribals emerged. They made preparations to cremate Pandu's body and lit up his pyre. Then a terrible thing happened....'

'Carry on, Parvatak!' Shakuni stood up from his seat excitedly. He was shivering feverishly.

'When the pyre was burning, that woman called Madri suddenly jumped into the fire. The other lady tried her best to refrain her but failed. Madri told her loudly, "*Didi*, please look after my sons as your own. Let me atone for my mistake." The fire burnt her alive along with Pandu's dead body. Oh, what a horrible sight it was!'

Parvatak became silent.

Shakuni slowly walked up to him and took a closer look at his face. He said, 'It is really unbelievable. Parvatak,

I sent you to kill one, and two have been killed. Although you can't claim any credit for this, you shall still be rewarded.'

Parvatak smiled a little, 'Shakuni*ji*, initially I thought I'd take no rewards from you as I didn't have to do anything. But I changed my mind. The unfortunate incident has brought about a change in me. I shall henceforth try to live a decent and honest life. But for a new beginning, I shall badly need that hundred gold coins you offered. I have planned to buy some cattle and set up a dairy farm.'

'That's very good, Parvatak. I appreciate it. Here is your reward. There is much more in it than what I promised you, trust me,' said Shakuni with a hearty smile, holding a brass pitcher. The pitcher had a lid with many small holes.

'Close your eyes and put your hand in it. You won't believe what you've got!' Shakuni said joyfully.

With a curious and expectant smile, Parvatak closed his eyes and put his right hand into the pot.

The very next moment a blood-curdling scream erupted from Parvatak and he fell down on the ground holding his right hand with the left. He was contorting with excruciating pain. Blood was dripping from his hand.

'Ahh. . .my secret soldiers have kissed you, I think. My little, sweet scorpions from Gandhara! They are lethally toxic. Don't worry, you won't take long to meet Pandu and Madri again—on the other side.' Shakuni sat on his chair with a cruel smile, tightening the lid on the pitcher.

Parvatak had become still by now with a frothing mouth.

'Sorry, man. You were a witness to my wicked plan. How could have I let you live?' Shakuni muttered.

However, his alert eyes missed one little thing. The beryl pendant was not there around Parvatak's neck.

He had lost it in the jungle while hiding behind the bush. The neckpiece was lying beside that bush as a telling evidence of Shakuni's sinister plan.

What followed was exactly what Shakuni had expected. After the couple's death, a delegation led by Vidur was sent from Hastinapur to persuade Kunti to return alongwith her sons and step-sons.

'Return we must, but not because I am too weak to raise these fatherless children alone. I must return to Hastinapur to find out who killed my husband. Poor Madri gave away her life holding herself culpable. But, the actual culprit must not go unpunished,' Kunti said to Vidur in a sibilant voice. Her fervent eyes were blazing.

Vidur had already developed an intense liking for Kunti but now he felt he was facing a trampled cobra. He was surprised to witness Kunti's transition from a demure to a determined woman.

'Vidur, I need your help to find out the killer,' Kunti almost hissed, training her index finger at Vidur.

'But what makes you believe that Pandu was killed?' Vidur asked. He also had the same suspicion.

'The killer left behind a clue,' saying this, Kunti opened her palm to reveal the beryl pendant. She continued in a tired voice, 'I found it in the bush near the place where he died. It must have fallen off from the killer's neck. I am sure of this because just a little earlier I had gone for a bath in the river and put my clothes over the bush. I had not noticed the pendant there at that time. Someone must have been hiding there after I left the place and caused Pandu's death. Why would he be hiding unless he had a bad motive? Besides, ordinary *vyadhs* or bandits do not wear such expensive things. The killer or his master must be an elite Kshatriya or a rich Vaishya. But Pandu had no enmity with the Vaishyas, rather they loved him. He had excellent relations with all the neighbouring kingdoms. Only one possibility remains. He might have had a secret enemy among his own kin in Hastinapur. Probably, they feared that Pandu might return and reclaim his throne. Or, maybe they believed that Pandu would try to instate his sons as future kings.'

Vidur took the pendant from her hand and examined it closely. That particular variety of gemstone was generally mined in the Takshashila region. And Takshashila was ruled over by the Gandharas! Vidur's lips kinked faintly. His jaws stiffened.

'Any idea?' Kunti asked impatiently. She badly wanted Vidur to utter Shakuni's name to confirm her doubt while Vidur felt it was too early to take his name.

'Not yet. But let me tell you one thing. You have to be very careful in Hastinapur. If we assume any foul play behind *Bhrata* Pandu's death and if the killer or his master is indeed in Hastinapur now, he may target you and your sons. Be very careful,' Vidur sounded sincere.

'Thank you so much for your concern, Vidur. You are now the only one I can completely trust.'

Vidur suddenly felt a shiver—but was not sure what caused it. The word 'trust' seemed to have strung a chord in him. Did Kunti's 'trust', or for that matter Kunti herself, matter so much to him? But why? He was a happily married, ambitionless person. How should he now behave with his step-brother's widow who he was unstoppably being drawn to?

Vidur was exceptionally intelligent. He knew he could not control his mind and thoughts. So, he decided to control his emotions and actions instead.

'You can always trust me. I am your brother-in-law—I shall always stand by you and my nephews, rest assured. Now, please come along to Hastinapur, to your very own palace.'

Kunti's eyes moistened. She quickly rubbed her palm over the eyes and said, 'Yes, Vidur. Let's go.'

It was her second entry to Hastinapur and how different it was from the first. Years ago, she had stepped into the kingdom clad in her expensive bridal finery, forehead smeared with vermilion, heart full of happiness and dreams. Today, she was entering the same kingdom with all colours seemingly drained away from her life and a mind full of desolation and anger.

But even today, she had with her something very precious—five godlike sons. Although she would need the trust and support of someone like Vidur, her sons were her real strength now.

The city of Hastinapur was in a state of mourning. The deaths of Pandu and Madri had left everyone shell-shocked. The entry of Kunti and her sons set off a fit of wild lamentation. Even the likes of Devavrata and Kripacharya were weeping their hearts out. Gandhari stepped forward and embraced Kunti. The two women started crying deliriously, tightly holding each other.

Vidur wiped his tears as he saw Shakuni slowly emerge from behind a pillar. Vidur's cheekbones jutted out in anger. Shakuni was staring unblinkingly at Kunti. He was looking grim. But there was no sadness on his face. Vidur had expected him to pull a sorrowful face but it seemed Shakuni did not even care to pretend anything.

Vidur realised one thing. Shakuni was not just a petty conspirator—he was on a mission more sinister than what Vidur had thought.

3

Shakuni was standing on the terrace watching the children play in the playground. Duryodhana, some of his brothers and Pandu's sons were playing with a leather ball. Completely engrossed in the game, they were shouting, screaming, cheering and laughing, often even abusing each other. The most robust of the boys was Bheem, the second son of Pandu. Not only big, he was evidently the strongest too. He was dominating the game using his physical advantage. Though Duryodhana too was quite well-built, he was no match for Bheem. Duryodhana was trying to snatch the sphere away from Bheem without any success. But despite his failure, he was laughing as loudly as Bheem and the others.

A deep groove appeared on Shakuni's forehead. *These children are so bloody innocent. I think I have a job at my hand....*

Shakuni called his servant.

'Go, tell your Prince Duryodhana that I am calling him,' Shakuni commanded. The servant ran down hastily to carry out the order.

Shakuni enjoyed the fact that his importance in Hastinapur had shot up considerably. The ministers would sometimes discuss with him many sensitive state matters that they should have taken up only with the king. Dhritarashtra was also gradually becoming overly dependant on him. Even Devavrata too asked for his opinion at times. Shakuni knew he was making quite a mark in Hastinapur—too smoothly for many to notice.

Duryodhana had meanwhile climbed upstairs panting, covered with sweat and dust.

'You sent for me, *Mamashri*?' Duryodhana asked with an impatient smile, not too happy at being interrupted while playing.

'Yes, I had to,' said Shakuni, with a serious face.

'Why, *Mamashri*? Is anything wrong?' Duryodhana looked tense. He always took his maternal uncle very seriously.

'Tell me first, how do you find your cousins?'

'Oh, they are great! In fact, it is more fun playing with them than even my own brothers. My brothers don't match up to me in such games,' Duryodhana was all praise for Pandu's sons.

Shakuni made a face. *Disgusting! This boy needs a lot of tutoring.*

'That big one—what is his name, Bheem or what—was not even letting you touch the ball. You were running around him hopelessly like the third kid of a goat. And you say it is more fun playing with these boys, fool!'

Shakuni's crooked words hit him hard. Duryodhana suddenly felt humiliated twice over—once for not being equal to Bheem in the game and then being too naïve to even recognise it as a defeat. Embarrassed, he mumbled, 'But it was just a game, *Mamashri*....'

'Game! What game? Today, that fatso was repeatedly snatching the ball away from you and passing it to his eldest. Tomorrow, he will similarly snatch the throne of Hastinapur away from you and give it to his eldest. You shall be left sucking your thumb. Their attitude is not right,' Shakuni shouted at his nephew.

Duryodhana stood with his head down. His lips were pressed hard against each other. Shakuni's poison was coursing through the unfortunate boy's veins. Shakuni was watching his expressions unblinkingly. Duryodhana looked up with a confused face and asked, 'What should I do now, *Mamashri*?'

The poor boy's question sounded like music to Shakuni's ears. He had wanted exactly this—*'What should I do now, Mamashri?'* Shakuni would love to hear this particular question from his nephews over and over again.

'You are a hundred in number, they are just five. Rally your brothers against them. Use Duhshasana[1]—he can do this better. Don't let those boys dominate you. Got me?'

'Yes. Should we immediately stop playing with them?' Duryodhana was drifting with the stream.

'No, no, no. Don't make it too clear straightaway. That will make the elders intervene. Start arguing with them. Create disputes. Use your authority. Remember, it is your father who is the king now. Treat them as your subjects. If it is clear, you may leave.'

Duryodhana nodded and walked towards the staircase. Shakuni stood by the parapet and looked down at the playground. The boys were waiting impatiently for Duryodhana. Bheem was still holding the ball in his hand and fidgeting.

Meanwhile, Duryodhana had reached downstairs. He was walking towards the ground very slowly.

'Hey Duryodhana, come quickly. We are waiting, can't you see?' Bheem shouted.

Duryodhana did not reply. He took his time to reach the ground. Bheem shouted again, 'Take your position quickly. I am starting the game.'

'Wait!' Duryodhana raised his hand and said, 'I will start the game. And we must change positions. Duhshasana, you take Bheem's place and Bheem you go to that corner. As you can run faster than others, you can cover greater distance from the corner.'

---

[1] The second son of Dhritarashtra and Gandhari.

'No. I will play better from here. Send Duhshasana to the corner,' Bheem protested.

'You heard me, Bheem. Do what I tell you to do,' Duryodhana's voice was steely and firm.

'Huh! Don't you try to dominate me, I tell you. I will be wasted playing from the corner, can't you understand, you moron!' Bheem raised his voice.

'B-H-E-E-M! HOLD YOUR TONGUE! DO YOU KNOW WHO YOU ARE TALKING TO? I AM THE PRINCE OF THIS KINGDOM. HOW DARE YOU TALK TO ME LIKE THAT, YOU BLOODY UPSTART?'

An irate Duryodhana shouted at the top his voice. His face was all red; he was trembling with anger. If it was not enough, what he said next was even more offensive, 'Do you know that I can kick you out of this kingdom right now?'

Bheem had a ferocious temper. He had already been fuming and Duryodhana's last words set him on fire. He uprooted a wooden stump meant for tying cows and charged at Duryodhana like a mad bull. All the other boys kept looking at Bheem with horror-filled eyes. Duryodhana too stood perplexed with fear.

But Yudhisthira, the eldest son of Pandu, reached Bheem and hugged him as tightly as he could. Yudhisthira was dragged by Bheem to a good distance. Pandu's third son, Arjuna, too held Bheema's one thigh with two hands. Bheem had to finally stop a little short of Duryodhana. He was panting and his eyes were bloodshot with fury. Through clenched teeth, Bheem issued a frightening threat, 'Say that again and I shall break your neck! This kingdom is no less ours, if not more, than yours. Remember it always to your own benefit. Prince, my foot!'

Bheem threw the wooden stump away and stormed out of the ground, followed by his brothers.

Duryodhana, robbed of all his vanity, stood like a tree that had lost all its leaves in a sudden storm. He looked at his brothers. They were still cowering in fear. Nobody, not even Duhshasana, had had the courage to save him from Bheem's assault. Duryodhana was suddenly feeling very lonely and insecure.

Suddenly, he remembered Shakuni. *Why am I feeling helpless? I have the best uncle one can have. He will never leave me.*

He turned around and looked up. Shakuni was still leaning over the balustrade, watching everything. Duryodhana could see an unfamiliar smile on Shakuni's face. Much relieved to see his uncle smile, Duryodhana too smiled shyly and left the field. However, the true meaning of Shakuni's smile was well beyond Duryodhana's ability to comprehend.

Shakuni had never expected that his maiden advice to Duryodhana would produce such a brilliant result.

A new character had recently arrived at Hastinapur. *Acharya* Drona. Although a Brahmin, his distinction was his exceptional knowledge in warcraft, weaponry and martial arts. An honest and upright man, he was not much successful in life and was living almost like a destitute. One fine morning, he came to Hastinapur alongwith his wife and only son, Ashwatthama. Drona happened to be Kripacharya's brother-in-law and was also known to Devavrata, who immediately, appointed him as the martial trainer for the sons of Dhritarashtra and Pandu. An obliged Drona started an extensive training programme for the princes of Hastinapur, with the ambitious objective of making each prince an invincible warrior in his own right. Drona's son Ashwatthama also started training with the princes.

There was great enthusiasm among the boys. Drona was an extraordinary teacher and in a short time his pupils were acquiring skills too good for their age. The Kaurava elders were very impressed with Drona's efforts.

But soon this training became a cause of contention. Pandu's sons proved exceptionally meritorious. The eldest, Yudhisthira became an accomplished javelin thrower, Bheem a champion wrestler and mace-fighter, and the twins—Nakula and Sahadeva—outstanding swordsmen. The most exceptional among them however was the third brother, Arjuna, who turned out to be a prodigious archer. He became Drona's favourite. On the other hand, Dhritarashtra's sons were too mediocre in comparison. Only Duryodhana was showing some promise with the mace while none of his brothers seemed to have any talent.

The overwhelming superiority of Pandu's sons was making Duryodhana and his brothers markedly jealous. Shakuni's words started to seem prophetic to Duryodhana. He became absolutely sure that those boys would usurp everything he had.

One morning Duryodhana entered Shakuni's room sulking. Nowadays, Duryodhana would always meet Shakuni with various complaints against his cousins. But today, although gloomy as usual, there was something different in his demeanour.

'What happened, Su[2]? Have you fought with Bheem again?'

Instead of giving a straightforward answer, Duryodhana asked a question that sounded a little complicated to Shakuni.

'*Mamashri*, why is it so that all virtues and talents have travelled to their side, completely ignoring us?'

Shakuni opened his mouth to say something but faltered. Duryodhana's question was not merely a juvenile expression

---

[2] Short form of 'Suyodhan', which was what Dhritarashtra and Shakuni fondly called Duryodhana.

of resentment; rather there was an adult frustration in it. For a moment, Shakuni felt guilty and blamed himself for playing with this innocent boy's emotions.

Shakuni took some time to frame an appropriate reply to buck up Duryodhana.

'Have you seen puppies on the street, Su? They look so cute and loveable. And what do they grow up into? Mangy, scrawny, despicable street dogs. Pandu's boys are like those dogs—loveable now but will be dismissed when they grow up. Conversely, you are like a majestic peacock, my dear—may not be very impressive as a child but will have beautiful feathers all around you as you grow up.'

'Ah, *Mamashri*—your words always work like medicines! I am really feeling better now…ha ha ha…,' Duryodhana let out a loud laughter. A good laugh was becoming a rarity in his life nowadays.

Shakuni smiled a little, then quickly became serious and said, 'But that is about the future. As of now, you could be in trouble.' The grim statement again brought darkness back on Duryodhana's face.

'What should we do? Please advise,' Duryodhana implored with folded hands.

'You need a strong, trusted friend—one who can match your cousins in capability.'

'I understand. Can it be Ashwatthama? I am quite close to him already. And he is a very gifted archer—almost as good as Arjuna,' Duryodhana said enthusiastically.

'Hmm…no! Mind you, Ashwatthama's father favours your cousins more. He may be your good friend, but he will not give his best for you. Keep him in good humour, but he is not the kind of friend I am talking about. You need someone who is only yours—fiercely yours.'

'Who can it be, then?'

'Unfortunately, I cannot see anyone who fits the bill at this moment. Nonetheless, you need to survive and for that, do one thing—get rid of that Bheem! He is the most disturbing of the lot,' said Shakuni, with a straight face.

'W-what? What do you mean, *Mamashri*?' Duryodhana sounded shell-shocked.

Shakuni completely ignored his reaction. He mumbled, as if talking to himself, 'Iron, fire or poison? Well, iron is impossible, fire troublesome…poison… Poison is the best! The fatso loves to eat…a little dose of *kalakuta*[3] in his favourite dish… Done!'

Shakuni jumped up from his seat and started walking up and down, biting his teeth into the knuckle of his index finger. Duryodhana was following him like his shadow, breathlessly.

'Okay, fine,' Shakuni stopped abruptly and clicked his finger. 'Now, listen carefully to what you have to do. Arrange a feast outside Hastinapur. Invite your cousins cordially. While serving them food, cleverly mix the poison in Bheem's food. Then throw him into the river. Simple. And if you cannot even do this small task, stop calling yourself a Kshatriya!'

'But *Mamashri…*,' Duryodhana had many questions and confusions. His head was reeling.

'No more questions. You have to execute it yourself. Make a foolproof plan with your brothers. Take all precautionary measures and leave no clue behind. Nothing must prove your involvement, mind you. It is a test for you. All the best for your maiden kill!'

Saying this, Shakuni sent Duryodhana away without letting him ask further questions.

---

[3] (*kālakūṭa*) A poison created from the sea when Devas and Asuras churned it in order to obtain *Amrita,* the nectar of immortality.

Shakuni was in a hurry of his own, he had an early start planned for the next morning. On Dhritarashtra's request, Shakuni was scheduled to visit the uninhabited Khandav province of the kingdom. Some nomads had come inside the Kaurava territory, possibly mistakenly. Shakuni was tasked to negotiate with them first before force could be applied.

Shakuni was followed by a small contingent to Khandav. A division of the Kuru army was kept on standby. Should the nomads not comply with Shakuni's verbal orders, the Kuru army would be set on them.

Dhritarashtra had sent his private chariot for Shakuni's use—such was Shakuni's stature in Hastinapur presently. Shakuni found the charioteer quite interesting. He was a very well-built, young boy with a handsome face. He was wearing a golden cuirass—something too ostentatious for a petty charioteer. His demeanour appeared even more curious. The boy looked surprisingly serious. Evidently, he had an attitude bordering on arrogance.

Shakuni realised that the boy was a master charioteer. Shakuni had kept his curiosity in check thus far but could not do so any further.

'Who are you, *Balak*? I don't think I've ever seen you before.'

'My name is Vasusen. I am on duty in my father's place. He is not well,' replied the boy matter-of-factly.

As they entered the Khandav forest, a dreadful noise was heard. It seemed a very big animal was rushing towards them at a breakneck speed. The four horses of the chariot stopped and started neighing in fright. A big tree at a distance suddenly collapsed, crushing a bush. It was immediately clear what caused its downfall.

It was a gigantic elephant, evidently a mad one! The monstrous animal shoved the fallen tree aside with a casual push of its trunk and stood in front of Shakuni's chariot. The distance between them was about twenty yards. The great tusker was observing them with menacing eyes.

The horsemen accompanying Shakuni quickly turned their mounts back and started racing away to save their own lives. But Shakuni's vehicle was too big to turn around inside the narrow strip that ran through the jungle. Seeing him in trouble, the troopers turned back to come to his aid. But unfortunately, one advancing horse tripped over a tree root. As it fell down alongwith the rider, it caused the other horses to tumble over one another.

The elephant, meanwhile, had come dangerously close to Shakuni's chariot. Shakuni started saying his prayers.

But the boy, Vasusen, did something extraordinary. He picked up a whip-like thing from his side. Shakuni thought it was a spare whip. But he soon realised that it was a bow with its string unattached. The boy strung the bow in no time at all and took out an arrow-filled quiver from under his seat. He then rapidly shot four arrows pulling the bowstring up to his ear. Shakuni, meanwhile, had forgotten about the elephant and kept looking at the boy, agog with astonishment.

The elephant was just about to charge. The four arrows struck it on the head in quick succession. The hits were so powerful that the arrows went almost quarter-length into its head. The elephant staggered a little and then fell down dead.

Shakuni was looking at the boy wide-eyed.

'Let's go, *Prabhu*. We are getting late,' Vasusen took his position and started driving the chariot.

'H-how did you learn to shoot arrows this way?' Shakuni was stammering.

'Oh, that is my favourite sport since childhood,' the boy said rather casually.

Shakuni did not ask him anything more but kept on wondering, *this boy's archery skill is sensational. Vasusen—I have to remember the name....*

Shakuni's negotiations with the nomads were very successful. They gave in to his veiled threats easily and unconditionally agreed to vacate the place within three days. Shakuni detailed an army commander to camp there for a week to ensure their pullout and started his return journey to Hastinapur.

On his way back, Shakuni did not speak much to Vasusen. He asked him only one question, 'Why didn't you attend *Acharya* Drona's training sessions here?'

The boy's cheeks hardened. 'I did for a few days, but somehow I felt *Acharya* was not too interested to coach me—may be due to my low caste and pedigree.' There was a strange, dimpled smile on Vasusen's face that made him appear even more attractive for a moment.

That smile made Shakuni absent-minded. He felt he had seen a very similar smile on someone else's face. But...but....

Duryodhana was standing with his arms akimbo outside the city gate, looking very tense and restless. Shakuni was surprised to see him there. As their chariot approached towards the entrance, Duryodhana rushed to him. Shakuni asked Vasusen to stop the vehicle and got down.

'*Mamashri,* we have done it! We have done it!' Duryodhana whispered to Shakuni.

'What have you done?'

'We—we have killed Bheem!' Duryodhana was stammering in excitement.

'Shhh!' Shakuni put his index finger over his lips and quickly turned around to ask Vasusen to leave. With a casual salutation, Vasusen drove the chariot into the city.

'Tell me now, how did you do it?' Shakuni himself was very excited.

Duryodhana told him that they had taken Pandu's sons to a resort for a feast. Exactly as Shakuni had advised, they gave Bheem poisoned sweetmeats. The gourmand Bheem gorged on the spiked food unsuspectingly and fell unconscious. Then Duryodhana and his brothers threw him into the river.

'You are sure his brothers did not see you in the act?' Shakuni asked.

'No. They were kept busy far away.'

'Excellent. Go home now and pretend to be sad. Tell this to your brothers too.'

'Right, *Mamashri*,' Duryodhana ran towards his apartment. His face was glowing with a sense of achievement. He never knew killing someone could be so easy and amusing!

However, Bheem would not die. He was saved by the *Nagas*[4]. They rescued him from the river and treated him with mithridates to negate the poison's effect. Bheem came back from the dead even more powerful. Moreover, he became immune to poison and diseases thanks to the

---

[4] The *Nagavanshis* or the *Nagas* were a martial tribe, who worshipped serpents. They had a distinct indigenous culture. They closely mixed with the Kshatriyas and were often considered as a branch of the Suryavanshi Kshatriyas.

Naga medication. Suspicion did fall on Dhritarashtra's boys but there was no proof to implicate them. Bheem's incoherent statements made matters even more confusing. The episode was deemed an accident as no evidence of foul play was found.

The failed adventure dispirited Duryodhana and his brothers again. Surviving the scare, Bheem became more confident, aggressive and dominating. But Shakuni was not at all unhappy. Even in this apparent failure, he had found a hopeful side. Absence of any remorse in Duryodhana seemed like a good sign to Shakuni. Malice had taken full control of the young boy. Shakuni said to himself, *Su has now become like a well-strung bow from where I can shoot my arrows at Pritha's sons.*

Shakuni felt the need to cheer up Duryodhana.

'Remember, I told you once that you need a strong, formidable friend?' Shakuni asked him.

'Yes, but I have no such friend,' said Duryodhana.

'I have found one. But you have to win over his trust.'

'Who is it, *Mamashri*? Tell me,' Duryodhana suddenly seemed enthusiastic.

'That, I shall tell you later. Don't be so upset, Su. I can't stand your glum face.'

Duryodhana hugged Shakuni tightly. Shakuni too put his long arms around the boy and whispered into his ears, 'Everything will be alright, Su. Just give me some time.'

4

While the storm was gathering strength in Hastinapur, sensational developments were taking place at Mathura—the most important Yadava state traditionally ruled by the Vrishnis.

The command of Mathura had been usurped by Kansa—Ugrasen's son. He had put his father under house arrest and assumed all authority. Kansa was a wicked, cruel person. He exploited the common people to the hilt and launched ruthless persecution against the recalcitrants. The Vrishnis were living under constant fear. It was easily the darkest hour in Mathura's history.

Although Devaki and Vasudeva found love in each other, Kansa made their life miserable. Kansa feared their son might pose a challenge to his authority in the future and put the newlyweds in prison almost immediately after their marriage. Not only that, he brutally killed their seven infant children one by one in the prison itself, right in front of their eyes. Vasudeva was granted a temporary parole for a few days to meet his first wife Rohini outside the jail. During this time, Rohini conceived and moved to Gokul, a prospering village located near Mathura, to ensure her child's safety. At Gokul, she gave birth to a sturdy boy who came to be known as Balaram.

Meanwhile, Vasudeva had to return to the prison. Devaki became pregnant again and in due time, gave birth to another son.

The day of his birth was very tempestuous. Mathura had never witnessed such devastating weather before. Vasudeva was desperate to save this boy from Kansa's wrath. With the help of a prison guard, he made a daring effort to take the baby out of the prison. With the newborn carefully wrapped in his lap, he walked all the way to Gokul in the night itself defying the extremely inclement weather. Much to his astonishment, Vasudeva noticed that the baby was not at all troubled by the rain and the furious thunderstorm that was wreaking havoc all around him.

Vasudeva reached Gokul safely and handed over the boy to his cousin Nanda *Gopa*—a leader of the local cowherd community. Nanda and his wife Yashoda—a childless couple—received the boy most gladly and would raise him with uttermost love and care. Vasudeva's opportune escape and strange experience during his nocturnal journey from Mathura to Gokul led everyone to believe that the boy must have been bestowed with some supernatural power. The boy was named Krishna. Having secured the baby with Nanda and Yashoda, Vasudeva surreptitiously returned to the prison at Mathura on the same night lest Kansa should get wind of it.

Very soon it became clear that Balaram and Krishna were prodigious children. Krishna, in particular, established himself as a wonder kid—a child with miraculous abilities. As days went by, tales of Krishna's amazing feats started being bruited about relentlessly. It was quite inevitable that it would attract Kansa's attention. He correctly suspected Krishna to be the son of Vasudeva-Devaki and sent his goons to settle Krishna's case once and for all. But while some of them came back to Kansa severely punished, the rest never returned. Insane with rage, Kansa desperately kept on trying to harm Krishna without any success.

Krishna's fame had reached Hastinapur too. Shakuni was aware of this phenomenal boy but did not recognise him as an important factor in his scheme of things until Kunti entered Hastinapur. When it became clear that the little prodigy happened to be Kunti's nephew[1], Shakuni started taking serious notice of him. He did not like the connection at all as it meant that Krishna would naturally be on the side of Kunti's sons. He started to be wary of Krishna's meteoric rise.

One afternoon, Shakuni was sitting with Dhritarashtra in the latter's private chamber. Shakuni was interested in discussing some administrative issues. In the absence of Vidur, the Royal Advisor and Kanik, the Prime Minster, Shakuni would whisper ideas into Dhritarashtra's ears. But today Dhritarashtra was more interested in listening to music than a political discourse, much to Shakuni's annoyance.

Just then Vidur stormed into the room excitedly. '*Maharaj*, have you heard the news from Mathura?' Vidur asked Dhritarashtra, completely ignoring Shakuni.

'No, Vidur! What happened?' Dhritarashtra asked anxiously.

'There has been a coup! Kansa had been deposed and killed,' Vidur shouted. However, he did not appear unhappy at all, only astonished.

'What?' Dhritarashtra and Shakuni cried in unison, standing up from their seats, 'Who-who killed him? It's unbelievable!'

'Krishna! The two brothers, Krishna and Balaram had invaded Mathura and defeated Kansa's supporters. Then Krishna killed him.'

'But...but Krishna is just a boy,' Shakuni croaked like a frog.

'He is divine. He can do anything he wants. Kansa was killed inside his own palace, can you believe it? And

---

[1] Kunti was Vasudeva's sister and hence Krishna's paternal aunt.

the two boys did not have any army either,' Vidur was gushing.

'And we should feel proud too. After all, Krishna and Balaram are our relatives. And that Kansa was a bloody tyrant,' Dhritarashtra exclaimed joyfully.

Shakuni looked at his brother-in-law with disgust-filled eyes. *This man is so useless! He can't even understand that this Krishna is a relative of Pritha and her sons, not of Dhritarashtra. With this boy's support, Pritha's sons could be invincible. Then who will protect Dhritarashtra's sons? And this fool is feeling proud now. Tch, tch!*

'Let me take your leave now. I must inform *Tatshri* Devavrata immediately,' Vidur left enthusiastically.

Shakuni took this opportunity to educate Dhritarashtra a little and made him aware of the likely fallout and Krishna's possible allegiance to Pritha's sons that might tilt the scale against Dhritarashtra and his sons in the future.

Shakuni was worried, very worried.

Acharya Drona was going to organise an event to demonstrate the martial skills of his students. The training of the princes was nearing completion and *Acharya* was very proud of the way his pupils had shaped up. Through intense hard work over the years, he had spectacularly transformed those delicate princelings into brawny youths with fearsome warrior skills. But it was clear to everybody by now that Drona's real pride was Arjuna. Even the usually composed Ashwatthama was feeling jealous of his father's preference for Arjuna. Everybody knew that the exhibition would eventually turn out to be Arjuna's show only.

Shakuni noticed that as the day of the show was coming closer, Duryodhana started to look more and more tense.

'What happened, Su? You look nervous.' Shakuni poked at a sulking Duryodhana.

'Can't you really understand, *Mamashri*? Those confounded ruffians will walk away with all the honours and the whole city will witness my humiliation. It will be official now that Dhritarashtra's sons can't hold a candle to Pandu's boys!' Duryodhana was slurring his words like a semi-conscious man.

'How can you be so sure that Pandu's sons will prove better than you and your brothers? Why are you so full of self-doubt?' Shakuni provoked him further.

'What are you saying? I am any day more skilled than Bheem with the mace but haven't you seen how big he is? He will kill me with his sheer body weight. And that confounded Arjuna! *Acharya* has taught him many things secretly. Even Ashwatthama doesn't have that knowledge. Don't you know what happened to Ekalavya—that Nishadha boy? He seemed to have greater talent than Arjuna. So, *Acharya* compelled him to cut off his own thumb. An evil conspiracy is going on here to push them up, at our expense. My poor father understands nothing. *Pitamaha* Devavrata turns a blind eye deliberately. *Kulguru* Kripacharya is only a sidekick of *Acharya*. And Uncle Vidur is the real mastermind behind all this. Don't you understand? I live in constant fear...,' Duryodhana started sobbing.

Perfect! Shakuni silently exclaimed. *The boy has been prepared well.*

'You needn't be so upset, as long as I am here,' assured Shakuni.

'What more can you do, *Mamashri*? Even you can't do anything now,' Duryodhana replied without even looking at him.

It hurt Shakuni's ego. With an impish smile, he said, 'On that day, you shall have a pleasant surprise waiting for you and you must not squander it away at any cost. Remember my words, Su.'

Shakuni took a disconcerted Duryodhana's leave and came out of the palace. He started walking towards a cluster of modest-looking houses that were the quarters of the underlings. The residents were quite surprised to see him there. Shakuni was promptly mobbed by people on the street scurrying to pay their respects.

Putting them off with a polite smile, Shakuni crossed the localities and entered the hood of the *Suta* community[2]. He got a similar welcome here too.

'Can anybody tell me where Vasusen lives?' Shakuni asked the crowd that had gathered around him.

An elderly man busily broke through the crowd and fell at Shakuni's feet, completely surprising him. With folded hands, the man implored Shakuni, 'Please forgive him, *Prabhu,* if he has done anything wrong…he is a hothead… he is very good at heart but a little immature…punish me for his fault if there is any but please spare him….'

Shakuni was very much surprised, 'Who are you, old man? Where is the boy?'

'*Prabhu,* I am Adhirath. I am the charioteer of *Maharaj* Dhritarashtra. Vasu is my son… Please pardon him…,' he started whining again.

Shakuni lifted the man with two hands and said very softly, 'Don't you worry, Adhirath. He has done nothing wrong. Rather, I am quite pleased with him. I need to meet him once.'

His words changed Adhirath's mood completely. The old man got on his feet quickly and with proper salutations invited Shakuni to his house. Adhirath's family members

---

[2] The community of professional charioteers.

excitedly emerged from inside, greeted him and touched his feet. But the boy was not there. Shakuni was getting increasingly impatient. He had otherwise no interest to mingle with these people.

'Do get me Vasusen now. I am getting late,' he said a little firmly.

'Yes, yes *Prabhu*...actually he is a little reserved. I am sending for him right now,' Adhirath said.

He called a little boy and whispered something in his ear. With a nod, the boy ran out of the house, and came back with Vasusen shortly. That strange armour was on his body even now. There was no haste in his expressions. Adhirath almost ran towards him and said in a measured, civil manner, 'Vasu, see who has come. *Shri* Shakuni himself! He wants to talk to you in person.'

It seemed Adhirath looked up to his moody son with awe. Vasu looked straight at Shakuni and smiled smartly. Shakuni too smiled back.

'How're you, Vasusen?'

'I'm just fine, *Prabhu*. And you?' Vasu touched Shakuni's feet casually.

'Good. Come outside. We have to talk,' saying this, Shakuni stood up and walked straight towards the backyard followed by Vasusen. They stood at one corner of the yard.

'Just tell me one thing. I saw that day how well you can shoot arrows. I want to know whether you've had any formal training in archery or not,' asked Shakuni.

Vasusen spelt out each word of his reply with manifest pride, 'I was the most favourite disciple of *Guru* Parashurama. He has taught me almost everything he knows.'

Shakuni stood with his mouth wide open. *This boy is Parashurama's student! And no one knows of him!*

Shakuni had understood that the boy was special but did not expect this much. However, he recovered quickly and gently put his palm on Vasu's shoulder. Then he whispered something in the boy's ear.

Vasu's eyes were shining. He was vigorously nodding his head up and down. What Shakuni told him was clearly to his liking and he was excited.

'See you there,' waving his hand at Vasu, Shakuni walked away in a huff, ignoring the requests of Adhirath and his wife to stay back for a meal.

'Thank you, *Prabhu*!' Vasusen said in an obliged tone.

The exhibition day arrived. The event had been given such hype that from the very early morning itself, people started swarming into the enormous stadium that had recently been built for this particular occasion. *Acharya* was taking the main initiative, with enthusiastic support from Vidur and Kripacharya. *Acharya* had a mutually respectful relationship with Devavrata that put him in a good stead. Devavrata too was very excited to watch the progress of the boys. However, for Duryodhana and his brothers, it was nothing but an organised conspiracy to humiliate them in public. The blind Dhritarashtra had initially been interested in it, but was gradually being influenced by the negative attitude of his sons.

Duryodhana's apprehensions proved accurate. Pandu's sons were reigning supreme in the whole stadium. Yudhisthira first showed his mastery with a lofty spear. Then the twins—Nakula and Sahadeva—brilliantly fought each other with swords. In stark contrast, Duryodhana's brothers could only perform some ordinary martial tricks. Some of them even struggled during basic manoeuvres. There was a murmur of disappointment among the spectators who had clearly expected better performance from Dhritarashtra's sons. *Acharya's* broad smile at the beginning of the show was disappearing fast, thanks to the lacklustre show by Duryodhana's brothers.

The names of Duryodhana and Bheem were announced together. They were to fight each other with maces. Bheem leaped into the arena first, brandishing an enormous bludgeon in his hand. He was bubbling with enthusiasm and could not wait to start the duel. Duryodhana was still inside the pavilion. He was feeling jittery. Shakuni sensed this and quickly came to him.

'Su, why are you delaying? He is already out there in the middle. Can't you see?' Shakuni whispered to Duryodhana.

'He will kill me, *Mamashri,*' Duryodhana muttered hopelessly.

'Yes, he will—if not today, surely tomorrow,' Shakuni said fiercely.

'What are you saying, *Mamashri*?' Duryodhana almost cried in fright.

'You heard me right. And there is only one way you can save yourself—kill *him* before he can kill *you*!'

Shakuni's words shook a young Duryodhana to the core. He suddenly had goosebumps all over his body. He felt his fear slowly dissipating to make way for an intense urge to turn around. Shakuni gave him a gentle push and said, 'Go!'

The audience was getting impatient. *Acharya* Drona's angry voice was heard, 'Duryodhana, where are you? You can't keep us waiting like this.'

Bheem's loud guffaw was heard too, 'Don't you worry, Duryodhana, I won't hit you too hard. It's just a game, nothing serious—ha ha ha...bloody coward!'

'You heard what he said? And still you are crouching at the corner like a beaten rabbit. Shame on you!' Shakuni deliberately tried to make the humiliation as hard-hitting as possible.

Duryodhana could not take it anymore. He picked up his mace and rushed to the arena. He had realised that he had no other option in life than overcome his fear.

Bheem and Duryodhana faced each other amidst thundering cheers from the crowd. The duel began. Bheem was much more powerful and was towering over Duryodhana. Duryodhana was trying to get away from Bheem's reach using his nimble footwork. Their cudgels were clattering against each other—CLANG...TONK... CLONK...CLINK...THUK...CLUNK....

Bheem's relentless attacks pushed Duryodhana on the defensive. On two occasions, Bheem's mace found Duryodhana's body. The hits were really painful. Duryodhana's limbs were smarting. He was desperately trying to defend against Bheem's assaults.

Bheem was fighting with a playful spirit. He was more interested in impressing the spectators than doing his opponent any serious harm. But he did not know that his humiliating gestures were effectively doing more harm to Duryodhana than any critical physical injury.

Bheem had pinned Duryodhana against the low rampart on the edge of the arena. Duryodhana was showing remarkable defensive skills foiling Bheem's assaults. But his excellence was going unnoticed by the crowd as they seemed to be more impressed with Bheem's aggression.

Suddenly, Duryodhana leapt viciously in the air using the rampart and menacingly thrust his club right into Bheem's face. The pointed spike on top of his mace badly hurt Bheem's nose. The sudden counter-attack took Bheem by surprise and had an electric effect on the crowd. There was tremendous applause for Duryodhana—for the first time. The crowd was boisterous.

A bloody-nosed Bheem furiously gnashed his teeth and pounced on Duryodhana all out. Duryodhana quickly moved aside from under Bheem to go around him. Missing Duryodhana, Bheem was off balance. Duryodhana took this opportunity and hit him hard on the shoulder from behind. With a cry of pain, Bheem knelt down holding his injured right shoulder with the left hand. But Duryodhana squandered the opportunity. He had paused a little to catch his breath. Bheem now gave the proof of his strength and power of tolerance. He withstood the stinging pain and swooped on Duryodhana before he could take a fresh guard. Both fell down, rolled over the ground a little and stood up almost simultaneously. They fiercely looked at each other—there was murder on their minds.

Suddenly, another youth entered the arena. It was Ashwatthama who had jumped in from the gallery. *Acharya* Drona had instructed Ashwatthama to restrain the belligerents and call off the fight. Drona had correctly anticipated that the fight was going to turn deadly. Ashwatthama stood between them and with some difficulty managed to calm them down. Bheem and Duryodhana returned to the pavilion, glowering and swearing at each other.

Although the fight was inconclusive, Duryodhana had a moral victory. Not only had he overcome his obsessive phobia about Bheem, but he made everybody sit up and take notice of his true calibre as a mace fighter. Shakuni was feeling quite happy though he did not display it. Duryodhana was the only son of Dhritarashtra who could make a mark today.

But with Arjuna's entry, everything that had happened so far faded into inconsequence. Except Devavrata

Bheeshma himself, Drona and to some extent Kripacharya, no one else present in the stadium had any idea that one could put up such a magical performance with bow and arrows. Arjuna was creating intricate designs and patterns with arrows. The crowd was completely stunned. Arjuna's shooting was lightning fast and his aim impeccable. He was such a master that he could seemingly hit any target, moving or static, without even taking a proper aim. He could shoot using either hand with the same precision and proved why he was famously called '*Sabyasachi*'[3].

But this was a mere prelude. Arjuna summoned thunder-capped clouds and heavy rain using one of his weapons, then cleared the sky using another. He brought darkness all around all of a sudden, only to dispel it the very next moment. Suddenly, there was a flood of water causing serious panic. But just as a serious pandemonium was about to break out, the water vanished into thin air leaving the place absolutely dry. It was an unbelievable show!

Concluding the demonstration, Arjuna was gracefully bowing to the gallery. The crowd became delirious with joy, with deafening applause and Arjuna's name being chanted all over.

Duryodhana and his brothers were sick with jealousy. Shakuni, on the other hand, was looking towards the main entrance of the stadium. He was frowning and appeared impatient. He seemed to be waiting ardently for someone.

Suddenly, a storm broke out followed by heavy rain and lightning. It was very strange as there had been no squalls in the weather just a moment ago. More surprisingly, the storm and the rain died down abruptly—as if they were rescinded by any magic power.

---

[3] Ambidextrous.

Even Arjuna was stunned because he had not used his weapon this time. Who did it, then?

A strapping, young, armoured boy entered the arena through the main gate. It was Vasusen, the haughty son of Adhirath the charioteer!

Shakuni heaved a sigh of relief. *Ah...finally he has arrived. He will be our answer to Arjuna.*

Wrapped in an unbearable arrogance, Vasusen effortlessly emulated Arjuna's feats. That was exactly what Shakuni had expected. He had discovered Vasusen as the perfect rival of Arjuna and wanted to pit them against each other. Now, Shakuni must get Duryodhana into action. Duryodhana needed to befriend this Vasusen, by any means.

Vasusen's thrilling display had a huge impact on the spectators who were now extolling *him* instead of Arjuna. Arjuna stood sulking, feeling grossly humiliated by the uninvited entry of this insolent stranger. The elders were not feeling any better either. Especially for *Acharya* Drona, the insult was intolerable and was almost like a slap on his face. To add to the discomfort, Vasusen's conduct was quite provocative. He dared challenge Arjuna straight-away in a single combat.

Arjuna was ready to accept the challenge. He looked up to *Acharya* for permission to fight the stranger. But Drona, for reasons best known to him, was not ready to let his dearest disciple face Vasusen now. He exchanged quick glances with Vidur and Kripacharya.

Kripacharya stood up and addressed Vasusen, 'You should have introduced yourself first and sought permission from us before showing your abilities here. It is not open for all, you know. Anyway, we must know who you are before deciding whether you are qualified at all to challenge Prince Arjuna.'

The question, though sounded quite relevant for the particular moment, actually had a sly insinuation which was not lost on at least Shakuni. Drona knew Vasusen very well as he had been the *Acharya*'s student for a brief period. But still, he had Kripa demand Vasusen's introduction just to humiliate him in public.

'My name is Karna. People fondly call me Vasusen,' he replied, lowering his eyes.

'And your parentage, Karna?' Kripacharya asked.

The young man remained silent.

'Don't you hear me? Who is your father?' Kripacharya asked again, with a crooked smile this time.

'My father is *Shri* Adhirath, the chariot driver,' Vasusen said very softly.

'Chariot driver! You mean to say that our Prince Arjuna will have to accept the challenge of a petty charioteer's son?' Kripacharya cried, as if he could not believe his ears.

The Kaurava elders were stunned at the audacity of the young boy. Disparaging comments flew in from Pandu's sons lampooning Vasusen. Insults, hurled thick and fast from all over, were coming crashing down on Vasusen.

Shakuni sat close to Duryodhana and whispered into his ear, 'It's your time, Su. Rope him in now. You shall have no better opportunity than this. This boy is your only hope.'

'You're right, *Mamashri*. He is a gem. I must have him, at any cost.' For the first time, Duryodhana quickly understood what Shakuni meant to say. He jumped into the arena and shouted at the crowd, 'NO ONE SHALL DARE SAY A WORD AGAINST HIM! HE IS MY *FRIEND—MY* F-R-I-E-N-D!'

Duryodhana turned to Dhritarashtra and began in a sombre tone, 'It is a shame, *Pitashri*, that this brave hero now stands pierced with slurs and insults after putting up such a show. It will not speak well of you. Therefore, to compensate and honour him, I propose that this mighty hero be gifted our Anga *Pradesh*. He deserves nothing less.'

Dhritarashtra, much like a marionette operated by a puppeteer, moved his head up and down in approval. There was a rumbustious roar of applause from a section of the crowd.

Shakuni was looking at Duryodhana with great amazement. *Su has delivered a masterstroke. He is fast becoming my worthy disciple. Bravo, my boy!*

Vasusen and Duryodhana exchanged stares. Duryodhana flashed a sweet smile. Vasusen did not smile. Rather, he could not. His eyes were moist and lips trembling. Duryodhana walked towards him and held his hands. Vasusen broke into tears and embraced Duryodhana as tightly as a child clinging to his mother on a thunderous night.

'Here, I pledge my life to you, *Kumar* Duryodhana! Karna is all yours. . . .' He could manage to say only this.

There was a sudden turmoil in the royal section of the gallery, as if there was some emergency. Soon it became clear what happened.

Kunti had suddenly fallen down from her seat, unconscious. Gandhari and Kripi[4] were sprinkling water on her face to bring her around. The royal doctor, leading a team of physicians, rushed pell-mell towards the royal enclosure to attend to her. Everybody's anxious attention was shifted to her for that moment.

'Poor lady! It must have been too much for her to bear the scorching heat this long,' an elderly woman commented with compassion.

---

[4] Drona's wife and Kripacharya's sister.

The comment entered Shakuni's ears and set him thinking.

Scorching heat? On the contrary, today is the most pleasant day of the season. And despite her delicate looks, Pritha is a strong woman. Moreover, she has spent so many years outside royal comfort and that must have made her quite tough. But what exactly happened to her today? Is it more a mental breakdown than physical strain? But what on earth can put this much stress on her mind?

Shakuni stood with a very deep frown. He was looking unblinkingly at Vasusen's radiant face.

That cleft on the chin, that dimpled smile, those pearl-like teeth, the poignant eyes—how can that Sutaputra have features so unmistakeably similar to Pritha's?

A disturbing suspicion had been troubling Shakuni for long. It was now turning fast into a conviction.

5

Kunti knew her past would come back to haunt her some day. She had been trying to prepare herself for that. But not even in her wildest fantasy had she anticipated such a bizarre tryst with her karma. How earnestly she had yearned for years to see her abandoned firstborn. But when she finally got to see him, it was a terrible shock. She kept asking herself, *why—why does destiny have to play such cruel pranks on poor mortals?*

Karna was now friends with Duryodhana. Karna was now an enemy to Arjuna. Her two sons would surely fight each other one day. Oh! How would she be able to see one of them fall?

But even amidst this trauma, Karna's recognition had brought her some peace. She was feeling proud of him as well. When the boy was introducing himself as Vasusen alias Karna, Kunti's heart jumped to her throat. It seemed to her at the moment that the echoes of the word 'Karna' were being thrown back on her from all sides. Kunti had given him that name and embroidered it on the baby's robe before leaving him for good. Vasusen was the name given to him by his foster parents—Adhirath and Radha—later. He might have been known as Vasusen now, or even '*Radheya*'[1], but for Kunti, he would always remain Karna.

But these delicate emotions were overwhelmed by excruciating sadness. Kunti knew she would never be able to accept her firstborn. What was more, Karna was now in bad company. His friendship with Duryodhana was the

---

[1] Radha's son.

last thing she would have wanted. Fear for the safety of her other sons gripped her.

Kunti was surprised at Duryodhana's magnanimity. She never knew he was so broad-minded that he could accept a low-born *Sutaputra* as his friend that readily. She suspected that Duryodhana's kindness might have been contrived. But even if it was so, someone must have lent the cunning to him for Duryodhana was never this sharp.

Kunti knew who he was.

Shakuni! The scoundrel, I know why he is so dead against me and my sons. His love for me has now turned into a murderous hatred. Can a spurned man become so deadly? I firmly believe it's him who plotted Pandu's murder. My poor Karna does not know that he is just being used by Shakuni and Duryodhana. Oh, my God! What should I do now?

Kunti was a confident, strong, proud Vrishni woman. Yet, a mother's fear and worries were killing her now. Although the morning was exceptionally bright, Kunti was seeing no light anywhere.

Footsteps were heard outside the door. Kunti knew who it was. Apart from her sons, Gandhari and Kripi, only one other person would often meet her at her room without any formal appointment. Vidur.

'May I come in?' Vidur asked from behind the curtains.

This was the only person in Hastinapur Kunti felt somewhat comfortable with. But right now, she was hesitant to meet him, for she had something to hide. She was dithering to let him in; then thought she must not shy away from the reality.

'Come in, Vidur.'

'How are you feeling now, *Devi* Kunti? What happened during the exhibition?' Vidur asked.

'Nothing serious, Vidur…might have been caused by the heat. I had fasted the previous night, moreover,' Kunti replied, lowering her eyes.

Vidur was not convinced at all. He was too intelligent to buy such a simple explanation.

'Did you know that boy, I mean that Vasusen or Karna whatever, from before?' Vidur asked cautiously, guessing that he was entering a dangerous territory.

Kunti flinched and looked up with a jerk, 'W-why do you think so?'

Vidur pulled a chair with a haughty, squeaking sound and sat down on it facing the woman.

'*Devi,* please don't mind me saying that somehow I believe that boy has some connection with you.'

Kunti was too stunned to say anything. She had expected that Vidur might bring up some uncomfortable discussions but never thought he would be so direct. She lifted her head very slowly, looked Vidur straight into his eyes and said, 'Please, state clearly what you mean. I expect at least *you* to come straight.'

Staring at his fingers as if he was inspecting the nails, Vidur said very casually, 'Any one with good eyes could see that none of your sons has inherited your features as much as that *Sutaputra* has. Even his smile and expressions have uncanny resemblance to you. How are you going to explain this?'

'Is it in any way binding on me to explain?' Kunti's tired eyes suddenly glinted.

The woman now appeared both mysterious and difficult. But Vidur was desperate. He must know and understand what was going on around him. Vyasa had taught him to be hyper-vigilant all the time. Vidur's reply to Kunti's retort was poised and confident.

'Certainly you have your own right to keep secrets but mind you, *Devi,* I am not the only one who doubts Karna's identity. Tongues are wagging behind your back and whispers being bruited about. You may better take a firm stand and boldly accept the truth, whatever it is. Take it as a humble suggestion from a…a….'

'From a…?' Kunti asked sharply, with one eyebrow raised.

'Er…I mean…,' Vidur hovered a little to find the safest word, 'a well-wisher.'

Kunti strode up to Vidur like a leopard and stood very close to him. She was breathing heavily. Her eyes were piercing Vidur. He felt a strange heat given off by her body. He had goosebumps all over him.

'Yes, Karna is my son. You heard me? Karna-is-my-son. My illegitimate son!' Kunti cried hysterically. Overwrought with the heavy emotional stress, she reeled awkwardly. Vidur quickly held her and helped her sit on a cushion.

The tension in the room lulled into an uncomfortable silence. With heads down, they sat quietly for some time. Then Kunti spoke in a halting manner, 'He was born to me well before my marriage. I was scared of the society and kept his birth a secret. I put him in a basket and set it afloat in a river. I did not know what befell that helpless baby until the day of the exhibition. I recognised him when I saw him at the stadium. I sat completely dazed; then passed out.'

Vidur shot out the most inevitable question, 'Who is his father?'

The indecently private query ushered in another spell of uneasy silence. Kunti said to herself, *a line must be drawn somewhere.*

'Don't you think you're already bordering on your limits? Don't cross it, Vidur,' although the words were harsh, Kunti said it with a disarming softness.

Vidur did not mind the riposte. He gracefully smothered his curiosity and said, 'Forget my question, *Devi,* if you find it inappropriate. I have more important things to tell you, however. In fact, that is why I came to meet you. The exhibition has spawned dangerous amount of envy and malevolence among Dhritarashtra's sons. They may try to harm you and your sons by any means. Be cautious, I am smelling trouble.'

Kunti sat still with her eyes fixed to the floor. She was not frightened, rather extremely sad.

This is the kingdom my husband once ruled. And today, we have become unwanted outcasts here. My sons are being seen as a threat to the throne. This is what our fate has brought us to!

Before taking leave, Vidur said with a slightly unkind smile, 'And mind you, your enemies are feeling much stronger now. They now have the support of the mighty Karna—your estranged and illegitimate firstborn.'

The words assaulted Kunti's ears like some red-hot metal shafts.

'Come, *Mamashri*! We have been waiting for you for so long. I need to discuss something with you immediately,' Duryodhana enthusiastically greeted Shakuni.

Shakuni was a little surprised. He had observed a slight change in Duryodhana's attitude these days. He had suddenly become more confident and seemed to be coming of age. He knew what had caused this change. Karna's entry into Duryodhana's life had made him unduly confident. Shakuni understood he would not have to instigate Duryodhana anymore. He would only have to channelise Duryodhana's ardour the right way.

'What do you want to discuss?' Shakuni asked dryly, without showing much interest.

Duhshasana and Karna were also present in the room, besides Duryodhana. There was a sharp exchange of glances between Duryodhana and Karna.

Duryodhana began excitedly, 'We have made a grand plan. You will like it, for sure. We shall send Pandu's sons and their mother away on a vacation and have them killed there. It will be given the look of an accident and nobody will suspect us as it will happen away from Hastinapur. We shall get rid of those scums and also that witch—their scheming mother—once and for all.'

Shakuni was too stunned to say anything immediately.

Su is maturing too ominously, I see. Who is giving him these ideas in my absence? It must be Karna. That bloody Sutaputra is snatching Su away from my clutches... Wait, Karna is not a Sutaputra—he must be Pritha's base-born son, I am sure. That means he too is carrying those wicked Vrishni strains. That brat does not know that he is plotting against his own mother. But I cannot let Pritha die so easily. Without her, my very existence on this earth will be meaningless. She must live. She must live to suffer—she must live to feel the heat of my vengeance. I shall have to secretly bungle this plan. But, I must not let Su guess this.

Shakuni hid his thoughts and feigned happiness, 'Brilliant idea! You are really growing up, I see. I suggest, you better send them to Varanavat. We shall put them up at a luxurious accommodation made up of timber and inflammable substances. Make them feel at home. Then after some days, our hired goons will set that house on fire in the middle of the night, plugging all possible escape routes.'

Shakuni chose Varanavat because he knew that the place was quite familiar to Vidur. Shakuni's actual plan was to pass this information to Vidur by some means so that he could take proper measures to protect Kunti and her sons. It would be easier for Vidur to make such arrangements at Varanavat than any other place.

Duryodhana and Karna cheered gleefully, taken in by his pretence. Shakuni's crookedness was well beyond their reach. A happy Duryodhana finalised the plan then and there as per Shakuni's suggestions.

The next morning, Duryodhana had his father call the Pandavas and ask them to visit Varanavat to settle an administrative issue, which was actually a ruse. The unsuspecting Pandavas[2] took the bait and set out for Varanavat along with Kunti.

Seeing them off, Shakuni came to his own apartment hurriedly and sent for the attendant on duty. A middle-aged slave turned up. Shakuni observed him a little and asked, 'Your name is Ketak, isn't it?'

'Yes, *Prabhu*.'

'I hear you can act well. Is it right?'

Ketak did not show his astonishment but smiled shyly, lowering his head.

'Well, you have to do a little bit of acting for me today. You shall meet Vidur in the evening and tell him exactly this: "*Prabhu*, I am Prince Duryodhana's butler. I overheard his conversation with *Angaraj* Karna in the morning and came to know of a terrible conspiracy. The Pandavas are in serious danger, *Prabhu*! Duryodhana and Karna are planning to burn them to death at Varanavat. Please caution them, and try to protect them if you can." Learn your lines by heart, Ketak, and make it sound as

---

2 Pandu's sons.

convincing as possible. And don't overact,' saying this, Shakuni gave him five gold coins as a reward.

'I shall try my best, *Prabhu,*' Ketak said in a sincere tone and took his leave to carry out the order.

In the afternoon, Ketak found Vidur in the garden. He was seated pensively on the grass under the lingering shadow of a tree. Ketak introduced himself as Duryodhana's butler and repeated exactly what Shakuni had tutored him. His acting was reasonably good.

Vidur was no less sharp than Shakuni. Even though he became sufficiently worried about the safety of the Pandavas and Kunti, he found something amiss at the same time. It did not seem much believable to him that Shakuni, the mastermind was *not* apparently involved in the plot. He asked Ketak, 'Are you sure you did *not* see Shakuni*ji* in the room?'

'I am sure, *Prabhu*. In fact, he did not visit Prince Duryodhana the entire day. He was busy attending a Gandhara merchant at his own place who had arrived last night only. He was buying some items from him and was also enquiring how things are going on there. It is the idea of Prince Duryodhana and Karna only,' he replied emphatically.

'Hmm... Okay, thank you very much for your help. Let me see what I can do. You may go, Ketak. Thank you once again.'

Vidur was watching a departing Ketak from behind. After going some distance, Ketak turned his head around to see Vidur's reaction. Then he walked away fast with long strides.

A frown appeared on Vidur's forehead. *Didn't the man appear a little cocky? His eyes are shifty and insincere. How did he know so certainly what Shakuni was doing in his own room at that time?*

Vidur faintly remembered that he had probably seen that man serving at Shakuni's residence, not Duryodhana's. Did Shakuni himself send him to Vidur to convey the message?

However, it might probably be true that the Pandavas were in danger. So must be Kunti. Vidur himself had a similar hunch. He decided to send a message to the Pandavas cautioning them. The letter would be written in the *Mleccha* dialect. Only Yudhisthira and Vidur knew that language.

But Vidur failed to understand one thing. Why on earth would Shakuni try to save Kunti and her sons—if he was really trying to do so at all as Vidur guessed? A freaky thought was ambling through his mind.

Is this Shakuni really a secret paramour of Kunti? So deep is his feeling that he is even ready to sabotage his dear Duryodhana's plot for her? The present development does prove my suspicion to be correct... But...but...is the feeling mutual?

Vidur's lips twitched in contempt. He remembered the dead Pandu. He knew with certainty that Shakuni was somehow behind the deaths of Pandu and Madri. The torn necklace that had been found at the spot was surely Shakuni's. Perhaps he had sent a hired killer rewarding him in advance with the necklace. Vidur was now trembling with fury.

He noticed a strange thing about himself. Although he had always disliked Shakuni, his dislike turned into a fervent hatred as soon as he suspected Shakuni's infatuation for Kunti.

Am I being too possessive about Kunti? Am I actually seeing in Shakuni a rival fighting me over her? But why should I? Why am I turning so unfamiliar to myself?

Suddenly, his wife Sulabha came to his mind. The demure, devoted woman had already surrendered her soul to Vidur. She had impeccably blended her own priorities with Vidur's. He could not even realise when Sulabha became like a habit to him in such a quick time.

Vidur felt guilty for a moment. The very next moment, he felt ashamed.

Vidur immediately sent a secret note warning the Pandavas of the imminent danger. The letter was addressed to Yudhisthira and was written in a dialect incomprehensible to others. A trusted messenger delivered it to the Pandavas at Varanavat. The intelligent Yudhisthira quickly understood everything and calmly apprised his brothers and mother of the gravity of the situation. He neither raised hell, nor did he let others panic. Instead, they put their heads together and figured out a counter-plan.

Duryodhana had detailed one of his officers, named Purochana, to carry out the task. Purochana and his team received the Pandavas at Varanavat and gave them a rousing reception. The Pandavas feigned to be ignorant of his wicked design and behaved quite credulously. Purochana became overconfident and convinced that his job was going to be easy. Relaxed, he decided not to hurry and let the Pandavas feel at home first before getting into action. And that would prove his undoing. Before he could do anything, the Pandavas themselves set the house on fire one night and fled through an underground tunnel that Vidur's messenger had secretly dug up for them.

Purochana and some of his accomplices used to stay at a part of the same house. The sudden fire caught them by total surprise. They could not save themselves from it as the Pandavas had bolted all possible exit routes from outside. The scoundrel Purochana and his cronies received the punishment they deserved. Their burnt corpses were mistaken for the bodies of the Pandavas. Rumours about their death started being bruited about. Surprisingly, Purochana's death did not bother anyone at all and it was conveniently accepted as an unfortunate accident while discharging official duty.

The news reached Hastinapur quickly. The city was immediately plunged into inconsolable grief. Duryodhana and his brothers lamented pretentiously concealing their real happiness. Devavrata was genuinely shocked and completely withdrew himself from public glare. He rightly suspected some foul play in it. Although he had his own issues against the establishment, he was aghast at such turpitude. Much to his chagrin, malice had already been deeply embedded in the psyche of his later progeny and it was just too bitter for his comfort.

Only Vidur knew for sure that the Pandavas and Kunti were safe as his messenger had bidden them goodbye on the safe side of the tunnel.

Shakuni too guessed that they were safe. He had that much confidence in Vidur. He knew that once Vidur had been made aware of the plot, he would certainly do something.

But I must be sure and know with certainty whether Pritha and her sons are alive. But how? They must be living incognito now. Duryodhana's spies are not good enough to track them.

But as always, he did not have to wait long for a good idea.

Shakuni entered Duryodhana's room with a serious face. Duryodhana was not alone. Karna too was inside as usual and they were giggling merrily. Since the reported death of his rivals, Duryodhana had been in a high spirit constantly.

Shakuni disapproved of Duryodhana's intimacy with Karna. He had wanted Karna in a servile role, rather than as a close confidante of Duryodhana. But these two haughty young men had become intensely drawn to each other and were completely oblivious of their unequal social position.

'*Pranam, Mamashri,* come, have a seat.' It was Karna who welcomed Shakuni. Karna was no more a shy stranger, rather he had of late started behaving like a rightful insider and sometimes even dared speak to Shakuni with slight overbearance. Shakuni hated this transition of Karna but never expressed it.

Shakuni looked at him from the corner of his eyes and ignored him. He looked straight at Duryodhana and said, 'Su, are you sanguine that your enemies are really dead?'

'What do you mean, *Mamashri*?' Duryodhana asked sternly.

'Have you ever thought how your Purochana died?'

'Well, it must be due to carelessness, I think. While he was setting the house on fire, he himself got trapped inside. What else do you make out?' Duryodhana asked with a curious frown.

'I suspect the matter is not as simple. I believe it was *not* Purochana who lit the fire. Had he, he should have been able to secure himself. He actually fell victim to a Pandava ploy, I am sure. They are way smarter than you think, Su. They got wind of our plan and set the house on fire themselves while Purochana and his men were asleep. The Pandavas have fooled you, dear. They are safe and gone underground waiting for the right time to reappear.'

'Oh my God! You really do make sense. They must have taken me for a ride. I shall skin them alive!' Duryodhana barked furiously.

'For that you need to find them first, *Putra*! And I tell you, your men can never find them unless they themselves show up. They are too smart.'

'So what should I do now, *Mamashri*?' Duryodhana asked.

Duryodhana had to seek Shakuni's advice earnestly for the first time since Karna's entry into his life. A crooked smile appeared on Shakuni's face. He had always loved to hear this particular question from Duryodhana's mouth.

'Are you interested in marrying the Panchala princess Draupadi?'

Shakuni's completely unexpected question brought in a stunned silence in the room. Duryodhana and Karna exchanged stares with their mouths agape in astonishment. Before they could ask any question, Shakuni resumed talking.

'I came to know that the Panchala king Drupad is going to hold a *swayamvara* ceremony for his daughter Panchali alias Draupadi. It will not be an ordinary *swayamvara,* apparently. The suitors will be put to a very difficult archery test to win her hand. I would like you to compete, Su.'

Duryodhana was still unable to understand the real purport of this marriage talk now. He replied boastfully, 'It is beneath my dignity to take a test for a woman's hand. Duryodhana is chased after by the best girls in the country.'

Shakuni sounded tempting, 'Draupadi is a very special girl, mind you! Her beauty is extraordinary. So are her intellect and wisdom. She is a peerless woman. She is a big *trophy* to be won.'

'A trophy? She is a *trophy* for you!' Karna sharply rejoined revealing his disapproval of Shakuni's misogynist comment objectifying a woman.

Shakuni was annoyed by Karna's impertinence and glowered at him, preparing to give Karna a piece of his mind. But Duryodhana shouted impatiently, 'Oh, come to the main point. We were talking about the Pandavas. Why do you suddenly start talking about a certain Draupadi?' Shakuni gave Karna another bitter glare and swallowed his words, before turning his eyes to his nephew.

'You may have forgotten that the Panchala king Drupad had expressed his desire of getting his daughter married to Arjuna long back. I believe he is not yet convinced that Arjuna and his brothers are dead. Probably he believes that they are living in disguise. He has devised a very difficult test possibly thinking that the challenge will attract a disguised Arjuna to turn up—if not the charm of his daughter.' Shakuni explained.

'Oh, that's why you want Prince Duryodhana to be present there to identify the disguised Pandavas, I understand now,' Karna said. His eyes were shining with youthful enthusiasm.

Shakuni, for once, liked this particular mood of Karna. A strangely ambivalent, love-hate feeling towards the boy was developing in his mind.

'But what if Arjuna does not come? What will I do there? I am not going to pass the test for sure—I am not that good at archery, you know.' Duryodhana mumbled.

'You won't go alone. Karna will be with you. Remember, if Arjuna is able to pass the test, Karna can also do it. Isn't it, Karna?' Shakuni turned towards the *Sutaputra*.

Karna blushed and quickly lowered his eyes, very uncharacteristically.

Shakuni did not mind that and said to Duryodhana, 'The girl, by herself, is actually not important. I am more interested to have her father as your ally. Drupad is a powerful king. So, even if you don't find the Pandavas there, you can well try to secure Drupad's friendship by becoming his son-in-law. If Karna gets Draupadi, it will be as good as you winning her because in either case, the mighty Panchalas will be our allies. So, you people must be there at the *swayamvara*.'

'Very good, so be it. And not only us, Ashwatthama too must go there to give it a try. And of course, you too must join us—as a spectator though,' Duryodhana said flashing a broad grin.

Shakuni looked at Karna. He appeared unmindful. He was looking blankly through the open window.

Shakuni knew what distracted him. His words, 'If Karna gets Draupadi...' seemed to have brought in a deluge in Karna's heart.

And Shakuni was right, as always.

Ever since those words had come out of Shakuni's mouth, they were flying in Karna's mind like a humming swarm of honeybees.

6

Duryodhana, Karna, Ashwatthama and Shakuni were returning from Panchala, after attending Draupadi's *swayamvara*. Duryodhana and Karna were in the same chariot while Ashwatthama and Shakuni were riding their respective vehicles. None of them uttered a word. In fact, none was in the mood to say anything.

Karna's condition was especially bad. His heart was brimming over with a scalding anger. The insult he had to suffer was unbearable. He would never be able to forget the impudence of that conceited Panchala princess. She had disqualified him citing his low birth when he was all set to pass the archery test.

Duryodhana's humiliation was of a different nature. He had been booed and ridiculed by fellow competitors as he failed the test. Almost all contestants—some of them quite famous in their own rights—had cut a sorry figure and had to receive taunts from others. Duryodhana was no exception but he was too thin-skinned to digest it. He could not forget how he had fallen down to the ground while trying to string that confounded bow amidst peels of thundering laughter from all over.

Ashwatthama had missed the target by a whisker. He too had not been in complete control of that enormous bow and his aim went little haywire. However, he drew some praise for his attempt. Still, he was not at all happy. He knew he had fallen for Draupadi's inescapable charm. He would keep her in his heart until his last breath. Ashwatthama decided he would never marry and lead a celibate life. His manhood was not meant for any other woman.

Even though they were suffering from different kinds of pain, the same curiosity was pricking their minds.

Was it actually Arjuna disguised as a Brahmin youth who won away Draupadi? He had handled that bow so comfortably as if it was his own limb. He must be Arjuna. But he looked so different, so slovenly! Was it a deliberate disguise to conceal his real identity? And who was his gigantic mate? Was it Bheem? His stature was much like Bheem's but again, he looked totally different. If they were really the Pandavas, they must be very accomplished actors as well.

Shakuni did not have any doubt whatsoever. He was sure Draupadi had fallen into Arjuna's hands. He correctly surmised that the Panchala king had been in the know of everything from the beginning. He possibly knew that the Pandavas were alive and had set up this drama of the *swayamvara* to get Draupadi married off to Arjuna. The Panchalas might well have been in touch with Vidur who kept them abreast of the actual situation. Shakuni's body was taut with anger.

Now, I feel I should have let them die at Varanavat. These Pandavas are alive today just because of me. Pritha—it was only for you I had to do that. I couldn't let you burn to death, Pritha! Grimacing, Shakuni scraped his nails against the side of his chariot.

He looked at Duryodhana, Karna and Ashwatthama. Shakuni knew the young boys were brooding over that dazzling girl who eluded them all. Shakuni's concern, however, was completely different.

That concern was Krishna. Shakuni met him for the first time at Panchala and was completely convinced that this person was absolutely extraordinary. Krishna had come to Panchala as a guest, not a suitor. But his appearance, his personality, his countenance—everything exuded an inexplicable aura of brilliance. He looked every inch the very same person who was believed to have performed those legendary feats in his childhood itself. Shakuni could foresee that this man would one day control the history of the entire country.

Shakuni had observed that Krishna appeared visibly happy when that strange Brahmin youth won Draupadi. *Why?* Did he know who the man actually was? Krishna was Pritha's nephew and her sons were his cousins. He was expected to have natural weakness for Arjuna. Krishna's happiness bespoke the Brahmin youth's actual identity. And that was what bothered Shakuni. Not only the Pandavas survived the Varanavat carnage, but also had found extremely formidable allies in Krishna and King Drupad.

The day was extremely hot and humid. Shakuni took out his diadem and ran his fingers through his long hair. His head was sweating profusely. Another thought had just invaded him.

Krishna happens to be a Vrishni Yadava. And he has a clear allegiance towards the Pandavas. The Pandavas are understandably 'the estranged Kuru faction' Devapi mentioned. Are these clear indications that Devapi's prophecy is coming true?

Shakuni felt an unfamiliar excitement within himself.

It was a long journey from Panchala to Hastinapur. The sun had moved westward. Shakuni noticed the shadow of his chariot had turned to the other side. The rotating shadow suddenly called to his mind a particular line—*'The present is a moving shadow wheeling around us fast....'*

In all these years, he had completely forgotten about that old man he and Vidur had met just outside the city of Hastinapur. That man had been babbling something that sounded like doggerel. Shakuni was able to remember it perfectly, thanks to his extremely sharp memory,

'The Future is lying low
Soon it shall rouse the Past,
The Present is a moving shadow
Wheeling around us fast,

Eight years from now
Shall there be Light,
Grab the Lamp away
Or perish in the Fight.'

Something told him that it must have some deep meaning; probably it was an important message and must be taken seriously. He started making desperate efforts to crack the riddlesome lines.

The first four lines sound somewhat philosophical. The future will recollect the past and the present is like a constantly moving shadow…well…that makes some sense. But 'Eight years from now'—what had happened after eight years from that day? It must be quite an important event. What can it be? What is meant by 'Light' or the 'Lamp'? And which 'Fight' did he refer to?

Shakuni was lost in grim thought. It was now imperative for him to decipher the cryptic message—at any cost. Vidur too had been present there that day. Had he already decoded the message?

The thought made Shakuni restless. He could not afford to trail Vidur in a battle of wits.

The official announcement that came from Panchala took everybody by surprise. It stated that Princess Draupadi had been married off to all the *five sons* of Pandu, consequent upon Arjuna's success in the archery test of her *swayamvara*.

All the five brothers had taken her as their common wife! The information raised hell in Hastinapur. *Five brothers marrying a single woman*—nobody could understand why the Pandavas had to take such a bizarre decision. There was a sudden exigency to consult sacred scriptures, the *Vedas* and the *shastras* to find sanction of such a marriage. The entire kingdom was rife with frenzied discussions, speculations and rumours. Even the likes of Devavrata Bheeshma, Kripacharya and Drona were left dumbstruck.

Duryodhana and his group were initially too stunned to react; then they resorted to vulgar mudslinging. It acted as a balm to soothe their bruised egos. They tried to project this peculiar marriage as a promiscuous experiment and indulged in ridiculing it in every possible way—often stooping to distasteful lows.

Shakuni once heard Duryodhana tell Karna, 'See Karna, *this* is what Draupadi rejected you for. She is now whoring for five declassed princes....'

The mindless Duhshasana burst into an unstoppable laughter, too impressed with his eldest brother's humour. Shakuni noticed that Karna did not smile at all. Duryodhana continued saying many filthy things, encouraged by Duhshasana. Shakuni felt disgusted though he did not say anything.

Vidur was the only person in Hastinapur who was completely unperturbed by this marriage. His mentor Vyasadeva himself had been instrumental to make this marriage happen.

Vyasa had felt that all the Pandava brothers were equally smitten by the girl and it would be extremely difficult for them to accept her as a sister-in-law. Apprehensive of serious complications in the future, Vyasa decided a polyandrous settlement would be much better although it was unorthodox. He managed to convince everybody, including the Panchala king who had initially taken serious offence at it. When Vidur came to know of this from Vyasa, he too found logic in his system and accepted the arrangement.

King Dhritarashtra, obviously on the advice of Devavrata and Vidur, sent an emissary to the Panchala king requesting him to send Draupadi with her husbands to Hastinapur, calling it the bride's 'own kingdom'.

The Pandavas returned to Hastinapur in style, alongwith the gorgeous Draupadi and Kunti. Today, they were fearfully formidable. They had the entire might of the Panchalas behind them. They had Krishna by their side. In spite of all malevolent attempts to harm them, they had only emerged stronger.

Another important development had taken place in the meantime. Balaram was showing keen interest to set up an alliance between his dear sister Subhadra and Duryodhana. But one day, Subhadra, with Krishna's active support, eloped with Arjuna, taking everybody by surprise. The matter was about to cause a flare-up between the Vrishnis and the Kuru house. However, Krishna managed to placate both the sides and eased out the tension.

Duryodhana was in his worst mood these days. He was becoming extremely rude, disrespectful, abusive and irascible. He would lash out at almost everybody except his mother Gandhari on the slightest of pretexts. He would ignore Dhritarashtra, avoid Devavrata, taunt Drona and Kripacharya and severely affront Vidur. In fact, Duryodhana could not stand Vidur. He had correctly understood that his step-uncle was the chief patron of his enemies.

Vidur never tried to hide his preference for Pandu's sons either. Shakuni believed that Vidur's apparent weakness for Pandu's sons was actually a cover for his infatuation for Pritha. But Shakuni never shared this suspicion with Duryodhana or anybody else. He always wanted to keep *his* Pritha out of any discussion.

However, Shakuni's own relation with Duryodhana was straining too. When angry, Duryodhana would not even spare him. Shakuni's love for Duryodhana was receding fast. After many years of settling in Hastinapur, he was feeling lonely again.

But he realised one thing—his mission did not require him to love Duryodhana. For him, Duryodhana was only a weapon to harm Pritha's sons. The loneliness had become a habit; in fact he was quite comfortable being alone. He had prepared himself well to live off only hatred.

The re-entry of the Pandavas put Dhritarashtra in an extremely awkward situation. While Devavrata and Vidur were pressing him to anoint Yudhisthira as the crown prince, Dhritarashtra wanted Duryodhana as his heir apparent. He was frenetically looking for scriptural provisions in order to install his own son as the crown prince surpassing the older nephew.

Shakuni knew it was useless. Dhritarashtra would never be able to instate Duryodhana on the coveted seat with Yudhisthira around.

'There is only one way you can see your son as a king,' Shakuni told Dhritarashtra in a little desultory manner one day.

'What is it, Shakuni? Don't tell me again to get Yudhisthira killed. Such efforts have never paid off. If there is any other way in your mind, please tell me,' Dhritarashtra brusquely held Shakuni's palms.

Shakuni gave him a furtive glance and said, 'It's no use discussing because you won't be able to do this.'

He had successfully provoked Dhritarashtra who almost screamed, 'I can do anything for him—anything for my Suyodhan! Just you tell me what to do.'

'Divide your kingdom. Simple.'

'What?'

'You heard me. But do it with some guile. Announce that you are equally dividing the kingdom between your and Pandu's sons as you don't want to deprive anybody. Then give them the worthless Khandavprastha province and retain Hastinapur for your Suyodhan. He will be the king of Hastinapur while Pandu's boys will get to rule over some aborigines and wild beasts in that desolate land,' Shakuni winked an eye at Dhritarashtra.

Dhritarashtra was left open-mouthed. He wondered, *what a brilliant idea! Why did not it occur to me earlier? But… but…will the elders allow me to do this? How shall I convince them?*

Shakuni read Dhritarashtra's thoughts correctly. He said as if he was replying to Dhritarashtra's unspoken question, 'That's even simpler. Threaten them with the prospect of a civil war.'

Dhritarashtra again looked clueless. Shakuni elaborated, 'Just tell them that the cousins can never get along. In future, the rift will only widen. It's better to let them amicably part ways before anything untoward happens. I think this is enough to blow sense into those old bats. And mind you, you are the reigning king now. Your decision should be final.'

Dhritarashtra did not find it much difficult to send the Pandavas to Khandavprastha. However, that did not mean they happily went there. Rather, they clearly understood what Dhritarashtra actually wanted but did not resist because they knew Hastinapur had turned into an enemy state for them. Although Vidur was on their side, Devavrata and Kripacharya were often equivocal. All the other ministers and officials had been bought off by Dhritarashtra, Shakuni and Duryodhana. The Pandavas realised that it would not be wise of them to hang on to Hastinapur, given their past experiences. They accepted their share, albeit grudgingly.

On an auspicious day, they set out for Khandavprastha. Surprisingly, Kunti did not accompany her sons and daughter-in-law. She stayed back in Hastinapur.

Shakuni was surprised when he came to know about it.

Pritha will stay here alone? Why? How dare she stay back while her sons are away? Does she want to provoke me? Or, does she want to show that she gives me a damn?

Shakuni called Kanik to his room. Kanik had become his good friend these days. Shakuni asked him straightaway, 'What's the matter with Pritha—I mean Kunti? Why didn't she go to Khandavprashta? Do you know?'

With a sheepish smile, Kanik said, '*Shri* Vidur did not let her go.'

Shakuni felt as if a whip was lashed on his back.

Vidur did not let her go! Who the hell is Vidur to decide what she will do? Vidur wields so much control over her! Hmm... They want to stay close to each other, I see. That means my doubt was correct....

Kanik was sharp enough to understand what pinched Shakuni. He said softly, 'I heard Vidur tell her not to leave this palace. Hastinapur was her late husband's kingdom and unless she stayed here, Pandu would be apparently forgotten. That's how Vidur tried to persuade her. She agreed after giving it some thought. And our king did not object as Queen Gandhari herself wanted Kunti to stay here.'

Kanik's tone was enough to provoke Shakuni further. However, he did not give any immediate reaction. His mind was being ravaged by envy. He would have otherwise liked Pritha's staying in Hastinapur but he could not digest that she was here only at Vidur's bidding. Shakuni gnashed his teeth in anger. Once again, he renewed his pledge to teach her a lesson by destroying the lives of her sons.

However, that was easier said than done. Kunti's sons were smart, mighty, intelligent and most importantly, powered by Krishna himself. They did not take long to prove their mettle once again. Very quickly, they turned a god-forsaken Khandavprastha into a blossoming city.

Years passed by, the two branches of the Kuru family started growing independently without meddling in each other's affairs. One day, a sensational incident in the great Magadha kingdom drew much attraction. The invincible Jarasandha was killed in a gruesome manner by a mysterious wrestler. Jarasandha was easily the most powerful king in Bharatavarsha and the most intimidating personality in the contemporary political circle. He had built up a strong alliance of eastern states under his command which was an emerging threat against Hastinapur and the Panchalas. Jarasandha had a special enmity against the Vrishnis as well.

Dhritarashtra summoned his advisory council for an emergency meeting to discuss about the possible fallout of Jarasandha's death. Everybody was expressing astonishment at this unexpected turn of events which was being unanimously perceived as a positive development. During the session, a messenger from Khandavprastha suddenly arrived at Hastinapur with a message from Yudhisthira. The letter was addressed to Dhritarashtra and read thus:

'O Venerable Kururaj,

Kindly accept the most respectful obeisance from your nephews. Your kingship will be much pleased to know that we have settled down pretty well here at Khandavprastha. We have been able to reform and develop the place spectacularly. It gives me immense pleasure to inform you that this place has now become a bustling city with almost all civic amenities. The population in the city is rising day by day as it is attracting people from our neighbouring states. We have renamed the city as "Indraprastha". Hope you will like and approve the new name.

Let us inform you further that we have been able to eliminate the mighty Jarasandha of Magadha who was a potential danger for our united Kaurava Empire comprising of Hastinapur, Vahik Desh and Indraprastha. Bheem, Arjuna and Shriman Krishna visited Magadha in disguise. Bheem managed to kill Jarasandha in a fiercely contested wrestling duel, showing amazing physical and mental strength. The best part is that Sahadeva, Jarasandha's son and successor, has pledged allegiance to us. And all these have been possible only because of Shriman Krishna. We feel infinitely blessed to have him by our side.

It would give us unbound pleasure if you, alongwith your complete family and our beloved mother, could kindly visit us and spend a few days at our new royal residence at Indraprastha. It may be humbly mentioned in this regard that the great Mayasura—the peerless architect—has obliged us by building the palace for us.

O noble Kururaj, kindly oblige us by accepting our invitation. Besides the obvious fact that we have been missing our mother and our kin too much, there is another additional reason we request your presence here. On Shriman Krishna's astute advice, we are preparing to conduct the Rajasuya ritual which can neither be successful nor complete without your presence and blessings.

We are looking forward to receiving all of you at Indraprastha.

Most respectfully yours,

Yudhisthira Pandava'

The letter was being read aloud by the messenger in Hastinapur's royal assembly hall. Dhritarashtra and Duryodhana looked at each other. Dhritarashtra was trying hard to work up a smile. Duryodhana did not even make any such efforts. He was sitting glum.

Vidur was visibly happy and exuberantly told Dhritarashtra, 'See *Bhratashri*, see! These boys are really special. I can't believe what they have done. They have killed Jarasandha! They are simply brilliant, aren't they?'

Dhritarashtra coughed and said, 'Yes, yes. Pandu's boys have really made us proud.'

Duryodhana's face became overcast with an ominous cloud. Shakuni was enjoying the situation to the hilt. *The fire is about to spread now.*

'But...but...,' Dhritarashtra was looking around little indecisively, 'I think we must accept the invitation, isn't it?'

'Of course. We must go there to bless those fatherless boys and appreciate their achievement. They have brought glory to the entire house. Prepare for a visit immediately,' Devavrata gave his opinion that sounded more like an instruction. He left the room, looking very happy.

A beaming Vidur also left the room in a huff.

Shakuni watched him with bitter eyes. *I know why Vidur is in such hurry. He cannot wait to convey the good news to Pritha. Bloody jackal!*

Duryodhana's eyes were smouldering like live coals. He bit his lip and said, 'We must go, *Pitashri*—we must. I need to know exactly what they have achieved that we could not.'

His words were filled with hatred.

7

'You have a visitor, *Prabhu*,' informed the doorman.

'At this time?' Shakuni was surprised. Although he had not yet eaten his dinner, it was too late to meet anybody, unless there was an emergency.

'Ask him to come in the morning,' Shakuni tried to dismiss the doorman.

'I told him so. He said if he has to come tomorrow, he would rather never come. He insisted that the matter is too sensitive to be kept pending. And...,' he looked flustered.

'And?' Shakuni asked curiously.

'*Prabhu,* I find the man scary. He looks weird—strange accent, bluish-green eyes...his skin is also peculiar.'

The description of the stranger was quite intriguing. Shakuni asked him to show the man in.

Within moments, an odd specimen was brought in. The man was not pleasant, by any means. What the doorman had not mentioned was that his dress was also outlandish. He was wearing a loose, brown tunic with a hood covering his forehead and eyes. A mild burst of cold wind entered the room alongwith the stranger.

'Who are you?' Shakuni was not feeling comfortable with this untimely guest who did not appear to have come with the noblest of motives. The person had meanwhile dropped the hood. Albeit young, his greyish skin was coarse and scabrous. A fiendish smile hung on his face. His greenish eyes had a sickening gaze.

'I am Ashwasen—a *Naga* prince, son of the famous Takshaka. I hope you have heard of him,' said the stranger in a raspy tone.

Shakuni had heard Takshaka's name. He was a great leader of the *Nagas*. Shakuni asked Ashwasen to take seat.

'Let me come to the point straightaway, for I can't stay here for long.' Ashwasen said.

'That will please me too, for I have other plans for the night,' Shakuni too replied with a mischievous wink.

'I have come to offer my support for you against the Pandavas,' Ashwasen said, looking straight into Shakuni's eyes.

An astonished Shakuni too locked stares with him for some time. He noticed Ashwasen did not have eyelids.

'Who told you we are not friends with the Pandavas?'

Ashwasen chuckled, 'I have learnt from a very reliable source. Please, don't press me to disclose his identity.'

'Hmm... But what's *your* problem with the Pandavas?'

An ugly expression distorted the *Naga's* face. Grating his jagged teeth, he muttered, 'Do you know how they built up the city at Khandavprastha?'

'No, how?'

'There was a vast jungle called Khandav. Arjuna and Krishna decimated the forest and burnt it down. They did it apparently to please the Fire God. Almost all animals living in the jungle were killed. That cruel son of Pandu killed the poor, hapless animals who were trying to flee. And my mother was one of them. I could manage to escape somehow. They just spared one *Rakshasa* named Mayasur. He is a great architect. Out of gratitude, he built that city for the Pandavas. *Mitra* Shakuni, that accursed city of Indraprastha has been built over my mother's dead body, over the corpses of my relatives and friends. That jungle was like a house to me. That jungle was the cradle

I grew up in. Everything is lost today,' Ashwasen's voice was trembling with anger and grief.

His anguish touched Shakuni. He said softly, 'That means you want revenge, right?'

'In fact, that is the only thing I want now. But I know my limitations also. I cannot take them on alone. That's why I have come to you.'

'Hmm... How do you think you can help us?'

'Should the hostility between you and them precipitate a battle someday, I shall lend my most lethal weapon to Karna. It is infallible, unless divinely intercepted. Karna can easily kill Arjuna with that. I myself will be present on the battlefield, in disguise though. My army, however small, will be all yours. Don't forget, a faction of the *Nagas* will support the Pandavas too. Arjuna has married an influential *Naga* woman, Ulupi. I can infiltrate a group of my followers into that *Naga* faction. They can work as spies and can destabilise their war efforts as well,' Ashwasen said.

'I see,' Shakuni was thinking with his head sunk into his chest. *This man seems to be useful. But how can I be sure that it is not a trap laid by the Pandavas and this man is not a Pandava agent?*

'I know what you are thinking. You don't need to trust me. But you can remember me whenever in trouble and check if that helps you. And you can easily verify my antecedents too. You shall get to know that I cannot be friends with the Pandavas under any circumstance. Arjuna killed my mother. I am ready to go to any length to avenge my mother's death!' Ashwasen's solemn words sounded genuine and sincere.

'Where are you staying now? How can we connect to you?'

'Listen carefully. The Pandavas are after me. They know I can be a potential danger. I am on the run. I could have taught them a lesson had there been no Krishna. He is the only person I am afraid of. He always protects Arjuna like an impregnable armour. There is no immediate hope for me here. I have to wait for my chances. I am going towards Takshashila now. That is your area I know. My father is there. If you want to connect with me, you may ask any of your trusted men at Takshashila to meet me with the code word "Karkotaka". I will understand and communicate with him freely.'

'Good idea. It is good that you are going to Takshashila. I can arrange security for you there, if you need. By the way, what is this "Karkotaka"? What does it mean?'

Ashwasen smiled. That ugly, hideous smirk exposed the diabolical mindset of the man once more.

'"Karkotaka" is like our totem, you can say. He was a great *Naga* king. Have you heard the story of Nal, the legendary Nishadha king? Karkotaka fought against him bravely and made his life miserable. He knew of a terrible poison that can affect a human in myriad ways, depending on the dose and the variety.'

'Oh, really?'

'Yes. As a token of our friendship, I have this little gift for you,' Ashwasen put his hand in his pocket and took out a tiny glass bottle filled with a dark blue liquid.

'Take it, Shakuni*ji*. This is a very diluted sample of the "Karkotaka" poison. It is very expensive—almost worth a kingdom! A sharp man like you can use it to the deadliest effect.'

'Is it lethal?' Shakuni asked with much interest.

'Oh no! Killing your enemy is actually forgiving him. If your enemy is dead, how will your victory give him pain through the rest of his life?'

'True! What can this potion do, then?'

'It can temporarily cripple the mental resistance of a person. Under its influence, the victim will play to your hands and dance to your tunes. It can be lethal if used in higher dose or in a more concentrated form. A particular variety of this drug can even temporarily change the appearance of the victim, like it did in Nala's case. Anyway, keep it. It can be of good use.'

'Thank you, Ashwasen. Let me see what I can do with this,' Shakuni accepted the gift and carefully placed it on a shelf.

'I must take your leave now. But before I leave, I must tell you one more thing. It's not an advice, but a friendly suggestion. Enmity must not be limited to a particular generation only. If you reckon anybody as your enemy, you must count his descendants too as the same. What I want to say is that even if you fail to punish your enemy, his progeny must not escape your wrath. If you have successfully destroyed an enemy, you must annihilate his descendants too. Only then will your mission be complete. Even if his offspring are too young, show them no mercy. Not even should you spare his unborn babies. It was Arjuna's mistake that he let me go. He will have to pay for this. We must not return the favour. Good night.'

'Good night, *Kumar* Ashwasen. I shall remember your sensible words. Thank you so very much.'

'Why the hell did you have to concede Khandavprastha to Pandu's sons? Why did you break your own kingdom apart? The entire undivided kingdom should have been mine one day. Why should I be happy with only a half of it? Just see what those cunning boys have done. Cashing in on your foolish benevolence, they have built up a property greater than ours right under your nose. Why do we have to see this? WHY?' Duryodhana was screaming at his father. They were waiting for Shakuni sitting at his room. Shakuni was outside, busy talking to his gardener.

Dhritarashtra was nervously trying to pacify him, but to no avail. Shakuni, meanwhile, entered the room. Seeing him, Duryodhana started lashing out at him straightaway, 'Come *Mamashri*, come! What a brilliant idea you gave my gullible father. You had our kingdom divided and gave our enemy the advantage. *Sadhu! Sadhu!*'

Shakuni did not lose his cool. He clicked his tongue and told Duryodhana, 'Don't be so upset, Su. Let them develop that place before handing it over to us.'

'Why will they hand it over to us? Did they ever appear to you that stupid?' Duryodhana howled angrily while Dhritarashtra frowned in astonishment.

Shakuni laughed out loud. Duryodhana's expression changed. He gave a sly look at his uncle now, realising that he must have had some plans. He asked in a low voice, 'Do you mean we will snatch it away from them by force?'

Dhritarashtra shouted anxiously, 'Are you suggesting a war, Shakuni?'

Shakuni did not answer immediately. He got up and slowly walked across the room to reach the other side. He opened an iron casket kept on a marble shelf. With all the time in the world, Shakuni opened the lid of the chest.

'What the hell are you doing, *Mamashri*?'

Shakuni completely ignored Duryodhana's petulance. From the chest, he took out a pair of white dice and some exquisite looking pieces required for a *pasha* game. Then he brought out a scroll of carefully rolled cloth that, when spread out on the shelf, turned into a cross-shaped *pasha* board. The board was actually a very expensive fabric adorned with nine precious jewels—two placed at each of the four sides and one at the centre. The dice were no less beautiful, though. A little longer than the middle finger, the dice looked like hexagonal sticks dotted with golden points. The crystal pieces were actually some miniature models of dancing *apsaras* in different poses crafted with amazing artistry.

The *pasha* set had been given to him by a mysterious Brahmin ascetic named Arstisena. Shakuni never lost any game played on the board. However, everybody believed it was his outstanding skills that won him games rather than any mystical properties of the board.

His mind was cast back aeons ago to one fateful evening at Mathura. He had tried to gift the same *pasha* set to Pritha as a token of his love. But everything went haywire. He had to return to Gandhara with incurable wounds in his mind. Since then, he had kept that particular set locked in the closet as the very sight of it reminded him of that horrible evening. But today, he decided to embark on the most decisive phase of his mission using it as a weapon.

'Force is the only option for a fool. Shakuni is neither a fool, nor has he run out of options,' said Shakuni cryptically. A strange rattling sound was being heard. He was grating the dice in his left palm.

'Will you please, for God's sake, reveal what you have in your mind?' Duryodhana asked theatrically, with his hands folded.

'I've got bored of playing *pasha* with petty stakes. Now, I shall play with a higher stake.'

No one asked anything this time, for a change. They chose to let Shakuni speak uninterrupted.

'Let us accept their invitation. You see for yourself what they have achieved. Be very cordial with them.

Let everybody believe that the two branches of the Kuru family are on amicable terms. After returning from there, have your father invite them here as a return courtesy. Treat them well. Entertain them in every possible manner. Then before they leave, very casually request Yudhisthira to play a game of *pasha*. That Yudhisthira is a simpleton. Moreover, he has a weakness for dice games. He will easily accept it. And the stake of the game will be just a little hefty—for us Hastinapur and for them, Indraprastha!'

There was pin-drop silence in the room. The idea was taking time to sink in. Then Dhritarashtra asked, 'But if we lose? Duryodhana is not a very good *pasha* player either.'

'Duryodhana will not play. I shall play on his behalf. There has never been a *pasha* player greater than me. And to assure you more, let me tell you that I have never lost even a single bout played on this particular board with these dice and pieces,' Shakuni gloated.

'But, what's the guarantee that Yudhisthira will take the bait? His brothers and wife are much smarter. They will not let him be trapped any way.' Duryodhana sounded sceptical.

'My gut feeling says Yudhisthira will accept the challenge. Although naïve, he is quite stubborn. We have to exploit that. And, if I am not wrong, Yudhisthira is an unhappy man. He is vulnerable. He is the weakest link of the Pandavas. Nevertheless, being the eldest he has the last word. We should try to destroy them through him.'

Duryodhana picked up the comment that Yudhisthira was unhappy. He became curious, 'Now, what makes you believe Yudhisthira is unhappy?'

Shakuni only smirked, but did not answer. He had observed Yudhisthira when they were living in Hastinapur after their marriage. He sensed more things than what met the eyes. Draupadi's entry had not made the lives of the Pandavas any simpler. She seemed to have a special weakness for Arjuna. There was a silent competition among the brothers over the woman. Shakuni could sense that. A sardonic smile appeared on Shakuni's face.

Life seems particularly difficult for Yudhisthira now, as he is the most sensitive of them. Nobody knows better than me how a man feels when his wife is in love with his own brother!

Shakuni felt no necessity to explain this to Duryodhana.

8

Khandavprastha used to be a forbidden area. The major portion of Khandav had been covered by a dense, tangled forestland infested by wild beasts and outlaws. Since Shantanu's time, this place had been left out of civilisation. The glory and prosperity of Hastinapur had never touched this area. That's why, Yudhisthira's claim sounded so tall and surprising to many in Hastinapur.

The big retinue from Hastinapur approached the dreaded area with all sorts of security arrangements in place. Everybody was curious to know how the Pandavas managed to reform such a hopeless place. They did not know that they were in for the surprise of their lives.

As they crossed the vast field lying between Hastinapur and Khandavprastha (now Indraprastha), they found themselves at the gateway of an amazing city that dwarfed Hastinapur in every aspect. Many of them rubbed their eyes in disbelief. Kunti was crying. After years of sorrow and struggle, the widowed lady was feeling blessed. Her sons had finally brought her glory.

As a mark of courtesy, the Pandavas had appointed some high-ranked soldiers to usher the guests into the city. Duryodhana was listlessly looking around, clutching the sides of his chariot all the way and goggling at the beauty, prosperity and happiness of the great Pandava wen. He was not talking to anybody, not even to Karna or Shakuni. He kept thinking what magic had turned a forsaken land into such a magnificent city. Shakuni himself was stunned. *Pandu's boys are really special,* he was wondering.

They were escorted to the royal residence of the Pandavas. The house was phenomenal. It looked like an enormous cloud that emerged from the horizon overcasting the sky. The exterior of the mansion was deliberately given an ancient look bearing distinct imprint of the famous Kaurava culture and elegance.

The Pandavas and Draupadi gave them an emotionally loaded reception. All eyes were moist, except those of Duryodhana, Shakuni and Karna. Karna's wanton eyes were pursuing Draupadi all along while Duryodhana was looking around at everything with his mouth agape, burning with jealousy. The coruscating grandeur of Indraprastha demonstrated the superiority of his cousins too clearly for his comfort and too starkly for anybody to miss.

Duryodhana was walking inside the house like a sleepwalker. And that caused the accident. He stepped into the water of an artificial lake, failing to distinguish it from the crystal surfaces surrounding the pool. He fell into the water with a loud splash, embarrassing his friends and amusing others. A round of good-natured laughter broke out from all around. Yudhisthira himself hurriedly brought him a towel, albeit with a smile on his face. Duryodhana was almost dead with humiliation.

Shakuni was at a little distance, watching the developments with a frown. Two young slave maids ran past him giggling. They were laughing among themselves over the incident. Shakuni heard one of them say, 'Prince Duryodhana seems to be blind, just like his father!'

Shakuni was aghast. He looked around. No one else seemed to have heard the remark. He thought for a moment whether he should call the girls to tick them off or complain to the hosts against them. But he did neither. A crooked idea had rather popped up into his head.

Shakuni went to Duryodhana who was still drying himself standing at a secluded place. Shakuni placed his hand on his shoulder lightly. Duryodhana's face was dark and sullen. He did not say anything.

Shakuni whispered into his ears, 'You know what your gorgeous sister-in-law was saying about you?'

'Draupadi? What did she say?' Duryodhana's breath became faster.

Shakuni relayed the slave maid's lowly comment with a straight face and passed it off as Draupadi's without any hesitation.

Duryodhana was shivering—not out of cold, but anger. He bit into his lips so hard that they started bleeding. In a ghostly voice, he could only say, 'Let my day come, *Mamashri*. I shall return her thousand times what she gave me today.'

Even his most favourite Gandhara folk music could never give as much pleasure to Shakuni as a wounded Duryodhana's words did. His tricks were working wonders.

Despite his secret achievement, Shakuni could not return from Indraprastha without worries.

The Pandavas had announced Krishna as the guest of honour, recognising him as the most influential personality in the country. Although quite young, he was being widely regarded as divine. The majority of the invitees, including the Kaurava veterans welcomed the decision wholeheartedly. The Pandavas started preparations to felicitate Krishna to conclude the proceedings.

But there were a few detractors too. The foremost of them was Shishupal, the king of Chedi. He was a first cousin of Krishna, his mother Shrutakirti (Kunti's sister) being Krishna's paternal aunt who had been married to King Damghosh (Shishupal's father) of Chedi. Shishupal was a notorious Krishna basher and always spoke ill of him at every opportunity. Opinions were divided as to what had caused such malice in Shishupal's mind. Some attributed it to a Vrishni-Chedi feud while some believed that Shishupal had had a crush on Krishna's beloved wife Rukmini and got spurned by her.

However, Shishupal's greatest pillar of support had been Jarasandha. After Jarasandha's death, Shishupal became insanely desperate. Krishna was aware of his many evil acts but always ignored them respecting the close family tie.

But today Shishupal crossed all limits. He started affronting Krishna and other honourable guests in a language too vulgar to withstand.

Shakuni was looking at Krishna unblinkingly. Krishna's mood was changing. He looked no more like a charming and amiable youth as he normally did. Rather, he looked dreadful.

Shakuni's lips dried. Meanwhile, Shishupal had taken out his sword. *What was that lout up to? Had he taken leave of his senses completely? Had not he noticed Krishna's fearsome expression?*

Shishupal pounced on Krishna with his sword upraised. There was a frightened uproar in the hall.

Krishna was no longer unarmed now. God knew from where a dazzling discus had appeared on top of his right index finger. It was whirling around his finger. The discus was shining so much that it made many shut their eyes.

Krishna flipped off the discus with a queer movement of the finger. It reached Shishupal in no time and sliced though his throat. The severed head tumbled on the ground, followed by the decapitated trunk.

That typical smile was back on Krishna's face again. No one dared raise any voice of protest. No one was courageous enough to challenge Krishna or his status as the guest of honour anymore. The ritual was concluded without any further dispute.

On their way back to Hastinapur, the Kauravas were endlessly talking about Krishna and his amazing achievements. His deadly retaliation had left everyone awestruck and it was a kind of re-affirmation of his capabilities. Even Duryodhana was impressed. Only Shakuni was not saying anything. He was rather trying to understand Krishna's politics. He was busy analysing Krishna's recent activities.

Jarasandha was his chief enemy. So Krishna first got rid of him through Bheem. Then, he killed Shishupal himself who was the most loyal ally of Jarasandha. Meanwhile, he had already neutralised the Nishad hero Ekalavya who was loyal to Jarasandha. Krishna himself had assassinated the tyrant Kansa long back. That meant, Krishna was clinically eliminating his adversaries one by one as Jarasandha and his allies were becoming the biggest threat for Hastinapur and Dwarka.

Krishna's other activities too seemed to fit in Shakuni's theory. In order to evade Jarasandha, the Vrishnis had shifted to Dwarka. Krishna and Balaram had already pushed their kingdom's boundary up to the banks of the Sindhu river. The Gandharas were anxious that the Vrishnis might cross the Sindhu and pose a threat to them.

The game was crystal clear to Shakuni now. He thought, *Krishna cannot be our friends as our interests collide along the Sindhu river. As the Gandharas and the Kauravas are fast allies now, Krishna badly needs the support of the Pandavas. The*

Pandavas have become strong enough, after carving a separate kingdom out of Hastinapur. Krishna and Pritha's sons will always remain inseparable. Moreover, the Pandavas too are of Vrishni origin through Pritha's line. Indraprastha has actually become a Vrishni settlement now. Effectively, the Vrishnis have already made inroads into the Kuru house without any bloodshed, completely unnoticed. Brilliant!

Devapi is proving himself correct at every single turn. But no doubt, it places Duryodhana and his brothers precariously. The Pandavas are clearly far stronger than them now. They have Krishna with them. Now Duryodhana should try to become close to Balaram at any cost.

It was a fact that Balaram was fond of Duryodhana. Balaram was a genius mace fighter. He had trained both Bheem and Duryodhana briefly on Drona's request. Duryodhana's elegant, acrobatic technique of mace fighting had impressed him more than Bheem's physical, power-based style. Since then, Balaram had developed a fondness for Duryodhana. In fact, he was not at all happy with Subhadra's elopement with Arjuna as he had wanted Duryodhana to marry her. Shakuni had noticed that Balaram was often at odds with Krishna but had to give in to his charming manipulations always. Nevertheless, the bond between the two brothers was simply unbreakable.

Shakuni was so occupied with his thoughts that he did not realise they had reached Hastinapur. Before retiring into his own apartment, he held Duryodhana's hand.

Duryodhana was still pulling a long face. The humiliation he had suffered at Indraprastha was too much for him to get over so soon. He tiredly looked Shakuni in his eyes.

Shakuni whispered, 'Everything Yudhisthira has today will be yours, *Putra*. Have your father invite the Pandavas here. Get Yudhisthira to play *pasha* with me. Shakuni's dice are infallible!'

Duryodhana's placid eyes twinkled. But his voice was still tired, 'See what you can do. All our efforts have gone in vain so far. I don't expect much anymore, *Mamashri*.' Duryodhana's words sounded like the mutter of a moribund man.

'Your *Mama* Shakuni will deliver this time, I swear. I have a very old score to settle now.' The last line was but a slip of Shakuni's tongue.

Duryodhana was surprised. He came close to Shakuni and asked, 'What score do you have to settle with them, *Mamashri*?'

'Everyone has his own war to fight, my boy. Nobody fights for others. That's the law of this planet. When I play *pasha* with Yudhisthira as your proxy, I shall be fighting my own battle, not yours. However, the result will benefit you the most.'

Duryodhana had always thought of Shakuni as a selfless well-wisher who schemed and conspired just for his sake. He had never thought that Shakuni had any personal interest. In the fading light, Shakuni appeared very unfamiliar to Duryodhana. His green eyes were glinting like emeralds. He was now looking more heinous than what Duryodhana knew him to be.

९

Yudhisthira had already lost all his wealth and properties. Indraprastha too, had now been annexed to Hastinapur.

He was not losing any battle. He was just losing a *pasha* match!

He was playing *pasha* with Shakuni. Actually, he was made to.

The game had started rather innocuously, with low and petty stakes. Yudhisthira was losing every game. As the game progressed, he behaved strangely and started playing with exorbitant bets. The game was turning increasingly serious. Then, in one bout he wagered his entire kingdom and lost it away too!

Duryodhana and his cronies were rejoicing louder with each win. The Kaurava seniors soon became wary and wanted the *pasha* game to be stopped immediately. They realised that the game was going to pave way for a disaster. The matter had already become disgraceful enough. They were desperately pleading with Dhritarashtra to intervene before it was too late and annul the results.

Shakuni was playing like a wizard today. He was rolling, tossing, flipping and spinning his dice on the board with a queer twist of fingers. By some inexplicable tricks, the numbers shown up by the dice were exactly matching his calls preceding every throw. They seemed to be behaving like loyal slaves obeying their master's orders.

Was he cheating? Without deceit, no gambling game could have been so one-sided. But the fraud, if there was any, was completely undetectable. It was not for nothing Shakuni was regarded as a genius. He had the uncanny ability to play unperceivable tricks with subtle sleights of hands. No one had the intellect or the required knowledge of the game to notice that.

Unbelievably, Yudhisthira himself refused to quit the game although he had the option. Gripped by a strange madness, he was readily accepting Shakuni's every formal invitation to start the next game. His suicidal stubbornness seemed to be a greater mystery than Shakuni's incredible play. Had the eldest Pandava taken leave of all his senses?

He had, actually. The confounded 'Karkotaka' was taking its toll on the poor Yudhisthira.

Nobody except Shakuni knew that. Not even Duryodhana. Shakuni had Yudhisthira's morning drink spiked with the potion Ashwasen had given him. Completely under its influence, Yudhisthira was just playing in his hands like a puppet.

Soon, the assets dwindled. What would Yudhisthira gamble now? He had no earthly possession left with him that he could lose.

'Why don't you count your relations as your possessions? What can be more precious asset to a human being than his family?'

Shakuni's wicked words ushered a deathly silence in the hall. Everybody was taking time to understand the real purport of his comment. Duryodhana's eyes became wide and shiny. He could sense what his uncle was up to.

Yudhisthira nodded like a hypnotised man driven by someone else's will. He played on, amidst shocked protests from all over, risking his brothers and himself one by one. With a few immaculate throws of dice, Shakuni turned the illustrious Pandava brothers into slaves. But Yudhisthira did not stop there. He now pledged his wife Draupadi!

Everybody knew Shakuni was a bad influence on Hastinapur. But nobody could even imagine how diabolical his mind was. He had a crooked calculation in his mind. He had correctly expected that Yudhisthira would swallow the last bait too and continue playing with his family members. Shakuni actually wanted him to play the game with his mother at stake. What could have been a sweeter revenge for Shakuni if he could reduce Pritha to a slave woman?

But his plan was not successful due to the overenthusiasm of Duryodhana and his henchmen. Shakuni had no interest in Draupadi but Duryodhana and Karna had. They had their own scores to settle with her. As soon as Draupadi got reduced to a slave woman, they went completely overboard and crossed all limits of decency. In order to humiliate her, they plunged to an abominable depth.

On the insistence of Duryodhana and Karna, a dim-witted Duhshasana dragged Draupadi from the female quarters of the palace holding her by the plait of her hair. He brought her right into the assembly hall and tried to strip her. Duryodhana and Karna were cheering and making obscene gestures at her. Both of them were actually trying to avenge their wounded egos.

Shakuni did not like this at all. He knew that after this extremely shameful act, the game would be called off most certainly. Yudhisthira would not be allowed to play another bout. He tried to dissuade Duryodhana to no avail. A frustrated Shakuni bit his lip in disgust.

These useless fools have spoiled everything. Now this game will definitely be aborted and Pritha will be spared. Idiots!

Duhshasana was still pulling at Draupadi's *sari.* It was not coming off easily as Draupadi was desperately clinging on to it.

Then a dramatic incident took place. The enormous wooden door of the assembly hall suddenly came crashing down with a frightening sound.

Everybody stood up afraid. The floor seemed to be swaying a bit. Was it an earthquake?

A man entered the hall through the broken door. Everybody knew him. He was Krishna. But nobody had ever seen him in such a form. He was looking like a burning torch. His wide eyes were raining fire. His stormy breaths were causing uneven air movements inside the sprawling room. His dazzling entry resembled the sudden appearance of a thunderbolt ripping apart a dark, overcast sky.

Duhshasana had stopped trying to disrobe Draupadi. He was looking at Krishna with frightened eyes. Draupadi was staring at Krishna with tears of veneration and relief. She knew her saviour was come.

Krishna swept the entire room with a fervent glance. Then he walked towards Draupadi who was still kneeling on the floor with dishevelled clothes. Nobody dared stop Krishna from interfering. Reaching her, Krishna removed the yellow *uttariya* from his upper body and put it around Draupadi with great care. Draupadi looked on like a stone statue, with an unexplainable look in her eyes.

'Don't feel sad, Panchali. Your humiliation will be duly avenged one day. And don't blame your poor husbands for this mishap. They were helpless victims of the circumstance. But you have me by your side. No one shall dare do anything bad to you. Go inside with all your pride and honour.'

Krishna's lips had moved but the solemn words seemed to have come from a different universe afar, sounding like an oracle.

Everyone hung their heads in shame. Krishna single-handedly defended a helpless woman's modesty while the august assembly had been disgracefully watching her ordeal without making any meaningful efforts to stop it.

Krishna's chivalry was, in effect, a scathing rebuke to the masculine pride of some illustrious men present there.

Shakuni was staring at Krishna, forgetting to bat eyelids. A bare-bodied Krishna was now standing at the centre of the hall with arms akimbo. Shakuni had never seen such an exquisite male figure. His body was impeccably sculpted and perfectly proportioned. Although dusky, he appeared to be radiating a strange halo that made everything around look brighter.

Suddenly, something crossed Shakuni's mind. He recollected some lines of the strange poem he had heard many years ago from that very old man seated under a tree just outside the gate to Hastinapur.

'Eight years from now
Shall there be Light,
Grab the Lamp away
Or perish in the Fight.'

The meaning of the words was now clear to Shakuni. Krishna was born exactly eight years after Shakuni and Vidur had heard these lines. The 'Lamp' must be Krishna himself that seemed to have illuminated the world with an inscrutable 'Light'. The last two lines of the old man probably meant that unless Krishna's support could be secured, a certain war could never be won.

The thought darkened Shakuni's mind.

Given the present situation, Krishna will never be on our side. He is a steadfast friend of the Pandavas. That precisely means that Pandu's sons will emerge victorious in case a war breaks out, if that old man is to be believed. But who can that man be? How seriously should he be taken?

Krishna had meanwhile turned around and started walking towards the partly shattered door. He had greeted no one while entering the scene, nor did he say anything to anyone while leaving. His entry, action and exit—everything was equally dramatic. It seemed he dropped in only to save Draupadi from the humiliation. But how did he know from the faraway Dwarka what was going on in Hastinapur? And how could he make it just on time from such a distance?

Quite instinctively, Shakuni's eyes turned towards Vidur. He noticed a very faint, almost indiscernible, smile on Vidur's face. Shakuni got stung by a suspicion.

Did Vidur send any message to Krishna well in advance, anticipating such trouble? Very possible, because Vidur is the only person here who does not appear surprised to see Krishna. He seemed to be expecting Krishna. And did not Krishna give a meaningful stare to Vidur before leaving the place? But how did Vidur guess what we were planning? Probably it was our excessive interest and enthusiasm to invite the Pandavas to Hastinapur that made him suspicious. Good job, Vidur!

While Shakuni was grudgingly appreciating Vidur in his thoughts, a serious dispute had ensued in the assembly. The Kaurava seniors were severely castigating Dhritarashtra and Duryodhana. Of them, Devavrata and Vidur were particularly scathing. They were putting pressure on Dhritarashtra to declare the *pasha* game invalid and restore the pre-game status quo. Duryodhana and his brothers were hysterically protesting against this and demanded the result of the game be sustained. The ever indecisive Dhritarashtra found himself in a serious predicament.

Shakuni looked at Yudhisthira's face from the corner of his eyes. Evidently, he was still in a trance. He thought, *there is still time to recover the damage.*

He joined the debate in a raised, aggressive tone, 'O the venerable Kauravas, you people are wise and just. Don't you feel it will be grossly unfair to us if the results of the games are not officially taken into account? There was no coercion involved in it. The game was played with the consent of both the parties. And according to the ancient codes and scriptures, consensual *pasha* games played with royal witnesses are rendered legitimate and the results count. So...,' he was cut short by Vidur who snapped sharply.

'But it is also said in the same codes and scriptures that only the games played with sub-human or non-human stakes would be considered legitimate. Once Yudhisthira pledged humans, the game becomes illegitimate.'

'In that case, only the last six bouts where Yudhisthira staked his brothers, himself and wife should be discounted. The seventh last game where he lost his kingdom should stand,' Shakuni refused to yield to Vidur.

'No, the final bout sets the merit of the entire game. The last bout disqualified the whole process, in this case,' Vidur too stood his ground adamantly.

The two rivals continued crossing words and logic.

Finally, Shakuni said, 'The decision should be unbiased preserving the interests of both the sides. For that, I propose that the last six bouts be cancelled and the last legitimate round be replayed.' Saying this, he cunningly turned towards Yudhisthira and quickly asked him, 'What do you feel, King Yudhisthira? Won't that be fair enough?'

Bheem tried to put his palm on Yudhisthira's mouth but he was too late. A dazed Yudhisthira had already started talking in that mechanical, lifeless tone, '*Mama* Shakuni is right...I agree with him....'

The issue was sealed.

The last bout was replayed with the pledge that the loser would be expelled from the respective kingdom to live in jungles for twelve long years, followed by another year of '*Agyatvaas*' when they would have to remain in unrecognisable disguises. Should the loser be detected during the *'Agyatvaas'* period, another twelve years of banishment would be imposed. The victor would rule both Hastinapur and Indraprastha until the loser came back, successfully completing their exile.

There was no dramatic twist in the deciding game either. Yudhisthira was beaten again, as expected.

Draupadi and her five husbands quietly walked out of Hastinapur, leaving behind all their worldly possessions and glory to comply with the terms of the disastrous *pasha* game.

At the same time, Shakuni, Karna, Duryodhana and his brothers were exuberantly celebrating their victory and mocking the Pandavas. Shakuni was very happy. He knew that the damage he had just caused to the Kuru house was irreparable.

A pensive Devavrata was pacing the terrace of the royal residence of Hastinapur, brooding over the contrasting fortunes of the two sides. Earlier today he had witnessed the beginning of the Kuru dynasty's end. He could now see the future clearly. The aggrieved Pandavas would come back with a vengeance after thirteen years. If Duryodhana did not return them their kingdom, which he most certainly would not, the Pandavas and Krishna would destroy them. And with that, the combined Kaurava Empire would fall into the hands of the Vrishnis as the Pandavas were half-Vrishnis from their mother's line and did not have a single drop of the Kaurava blood in their veins as Pandu was not their biological father.

But should Devavrata feel sorry about the imminent extinction of the Kuru line? Rather, shouldn't he be happy and feel rather avenged?

It was becoming increasingly difficult for Devavrata nowadays to read his own mind. He was getting more and more confused. He realised that he must prepare for an unconditional surrender to the inevitability now. He was hopelessly running short of options.

Devavrata was roaming his hands over the beautifully designed marble parapet. Blackish stains had appeared on the marble caused by the wear of time. This palace had been built during his father Shantanu's time, in order to celebrate his (Devavrata's) resounding victory over the Yavanas. The entire construction process was funded by the enormous wealth Devavrata had recovered from them. He had contributed to the building of this glorious empire more than anybody else. And today, he had ceased to matter here. He heaved a sigh.

'It's difficult to sleep tonight, isn't it *Tatshri*?'

Devavrata turned back with a start.

It was Vidur. Vidur's voice was broken and face sullen. Devavrata turned his face away from him to look at the dark, moonless sky.

'Only tonight? I think I shall never be able to sleep easily again.' Devavrata cautiously tried to leave no scope for ambiguity in his reaction. He did not want Vidur to get wind of the extremely complicated thoughts that were crowding his mind.

But Vidur happened to be too sharp for Devavrata's comfort. 'I told you many times, *Tatshri*, that this Shakuni is evil. See what he has done today,' Vidur said.

Devavrata did not turn his face. He knew Vidur would say this. He also knew that Vidur must be holding him responsible for his discreet indulgence that allowed Shakuni to grow here.

'When a very big rock starts rolling downhill, no one can stop it. That is exactly what is happening now. Shakuni is not a factor,' said Devavrata grimly.

Vidur was not at all impressed by Devavrata's evasive rhetoric. Devavrata had his own course of thought that was incredibly convoluted. It would be a sheer waste of time to try understanding him. Vidur came straight to the point instead of prying into Devavrata's mind.

'*Tatshri,* I have something to tell you.'

'Carry on.'

'Many years ago, Shakuni and I met a strange old man just outside our city gates. He was sitting under a banyan tree. Although very unkempt and shabby and clad in tattered clothes, he did not look ordinary at all. His eyes, features, build—nothing was ordinary. Seeing us, the man chanted something that sounded like an ill-composed poem. Those words have been deeply embedded in my mind. I don't know why the old man has been haunting my mind again since today's shameful incident. Who could that man be, *Tatshri*?'

Devavrata's breath became faster. His muscles became taut. Vidur could only notice that his fingers clutched the parapet's edge more tightly. Devavrata asked in a tense voice, 'Do you remember his lines?'

'The Future is lying low, soon it shall rouse the Past...,' Vidur started reciting the lines.

But to his utter surprise, Devavrata sharply chipped in with the next line, '...the Present is a moving shadow, wheeling around us fast....'

Vidur stood wide-eyed. He asked, 'How do you know?'

Devavrata turned towards him now. A bitter smile appeared on his face, 'You didn't inform me that day but Shakuni did, which surprised me a lot.'

Vidur felt ashamed and lowered his head, 'I am really sorry, *Tatshri*. I should have told you about it the very same day. I was going to meet *Maharshi* Vyasa that day. I met that man on my way to the jungle where he lived. Then I told *Maharshi* about him.'

'And how did he react?' Devavrata asked with a caustic touch.

'He became serious and asked me to inform him immediately if I see that man again. But he did not tell me who that man could be, nor did he explain why he became serious. I came back with loads of curiosity, but forgot about it in some days.'

Devavrata did not say anything. He was still looking at the dark sky with his back to Vidur.

'Who was that man, *Tatshri*?'

'First, tell me what do you make out of those lines?' Devavrata asked.

Vidur could not understand whether Devavrata was trying to test him or genuinely wanted to know. He said, 'It mentioned about a "Light" that would come into being after eight years. I believe, especially after today's incident, that "Light" or the "Lamp" is none but Krishna. He was born exactly eight years after we had met that old man. I have calculated it. Whomsoever Krishna supports will win a particular dispute or battle. I think he foretold a war between Dhritarashtra's sons and the Pandavas which seems very much on the cards now. As clearly Krishna will support the Pandavas, they will win.'

'Hmm... Maybe what you are saying is right. But the first four lines....'

'I found those rather easier to comprehend, *Tatshri*. Don't they refer to the simple idea of *Kalachakra*—the wheel of Time?'

'Maybe, but what was the need to remind this? I can smell some hidden malice in those lines—it almost sounds like a warning that the past will be raked up in the future. Doesn't it sound ominous? I guess....'

'What do you guess?' Vidur asked anxiously.

'Leave it. You saw the face of the man, didn't you? Let me give you a clue. Try to notice if you find any face in our midst with similar features. Work on this. The lead may open up to what I suspect to be a shocking truth we were never aware of. Go.'

Vidur came back to his room excited. He remembered that when he had seen that man the face appeared somewhat familiar. Devavrata set his mind ablaze with bizarre suspicions now.

Why did Devavrata ask me to find a face similar to that old man? Was he actually a known person in disguise? But why would a known man do that? Who can it be? Drona? Kripacharya? Bahlik? Maharshi Vyasa? Dhritarashtra? Any minister? Or...was he Devavrata himself?

Vidur knew Devavrata would not give a clearer clue. And if he consulted Vyasa now, he would only get more confused.

Only one person could be consulted over this. He was Shakuni. And Vidur would never deign to discuss the matter with him under any circumstance.

Vidur realised that he would have to get to the bottom of this all by himself.

10

Duryodhana was all over the moon nowadays. He had now two magnificent kingdoms to play with, something he had not dreamt of even a few days ago. He was not ungrateful, however. He heaped lavish gifts and praises over Shakuni and granted special executive powers to him. Everybody knew Shakuni was the last word in Hastinapur now. He started wielding overwhelming control over Duryodhana and Dhritarashtra, much to the chagrin of Vidur, Drona, Kripacharya and the likes. Devavrata's exact attitude to Shakuni's elevation was as usual ambiguous, his public dislike for Shakuni notwithstanding.

But Shakuni himself was not much moved by the recognition and the increasing political clout. He was aware that an important section of the Kaurava nobles was dead against him. They would tear into him once any opportunity came their way. Vidur was obviously the most prominent and the most hateful among them. Like Vidur, Shakuni too was unsure of Devavrata's actual stand. Shakuni could have become far more formidable had he enjoyed Devavrata's full support.

Shakuni also did not see much of Kunti these days as she lived in a rather remote part of the palace. She had not accompanied her sons and daughter-in-law to exile. After the departure of the Pandavas, Shakuni had met Kunti only once and he would rather prefer not to remember that meeting.

They met in a lonely passage that connected the annexe to the main palace. A number of outhouses were being constructed on the other side of the passage. Shakuni would often visit the place to inspect the work in progress. One late afternoon, Shakuni was casually walking down the passage. The light was fading fast when Shakuni noticed a white-robed woman at a distance. She was leaning against a pillar, as if waiting for him.

A surprised Shakuni immediately stopped in his tracks.

Pritha here? At this time? Is she waiting for me? Does she want to tell me something?

Shakuni's heart was pounding. Kunti started coming towards him like a languorous snail. She was walking so slowly that it seemed she would take an eternity to reach Shakuni. He was sweating. She stopped at about an arm's length from Shakuni. He felt his knees were getting groggy.

You are still so beautiful, Pritha! You are greying, your skin is a little wrinkled, your eyes are sad yet you are so amazing. I have never seen a more graceful woman than you. Every movement, every demeanour, every countenance of yours is like poetry. Are you human, Pritha, or an apsara? No, you must be a human, because apsaras are laced with impurity. You had been with many men yet you look so chaste. How, Pritha? How did you manage that?

Shakuni remained lost in the reverie until Kunti's sharp voice broke it apart. In a remarkably calm tone, she said, 'Congratulations, Shakuni Saubala. Very well done!'

Shakuni looked on vacantly. Was she mocking him? But there was a surprising serenity on her face. But why would she congratulate him? On the contrary, she should have cursed him.

'Your revenge has been savage, I must admit,' Kunti said further, with a smile that could make even the most poised man lose his way.

'R-revenge?' Shakuni was left stammering.

'Wasn't it? You had my husband killed. You snatched away the kingdom of my sons. You reduced them to paupers. You had my daughter-in-law dragged into the court like a slave maid with a pack of ruffians leering at her, one of them even trying to strip her.'

With horror, Shakuni watched a beautiful face degenerate into a dreadful, witchy visage right in front of his eyes. He was almost feeling unsafe, being left alone with this scorned woman at such a remote part of the palace. Pritha looked lethal.

'And you don't even have the courage to accept what you have done. Pathetic, Shakuni,' Kunti gave him a withering look. Her next round of assault was particularly unbearable.

'I feel disgraced when I think that an obnoxious leech like you desired *me* at one time.'

The ruthless insult crashed down on Shakuni's face like a thundering slap. His head reeled. He had to touch the pillar to steady himself.

But Kunti wasn't done yet. 'Do you remember what happened at Mathura many years ago? You tried to take me by force. My guards thrashed you. They would have killed you for sure had I not intervened. Remember?'

'Do you regret that today? You should have better let me be lynched and killed, isn't it?' Shakuni asked, with a tired smile.

'On the contrary, I believe I acted very wisely that day….'

'Really, and why so?' Shakuni could not understand what she actually meant.

'…so that one day I can witness my own sons tear your limbs off and gauge out your entrails before leaving you behind in a pool of your own blood, where you shall meet your end after suffering an excruciating punishment. That day I shall be avenged. Rest assured, Shakuni, your end is coming fast.'

Kunti stormed past a bewildered Shakuni. Her mind had become like a ruined city letting out smokes of dark, sad memories. Her footsteps were hitting Shakuni's ears like iron nails.

Shakuni had been standing still with a blank look in his eyes. He smiled a little, gave a sad nod and finally, muttered to himself, '*Die* I shall. But *live* you shall not either, Pritha!'

Shakuni repeatedly cautioned Duryodhana that his happiness was only temporary. The Pandavas would return from exile and demand their kingdom back. After ruling over it for thirteen years, it would be very awkward for Duryodhana to part with Indraprastha and his reluctance to return Indraprastha to the Pandavas, would precipitate a bloody war.

A war! The very thought of a war depressed Shakuni—not because he was afraid of it, but because he thought he knew the outcome. He had a gut feeling that the war was going to spell doom for Dhritarashtra's sons. 'Grab the Lamp away or perish in the Fight'—the forbidding lines of that unidentified old man were worrying him. If Krishna was the 'Lamp' as he presumed, he had already been 'grabbed away' by the Pandavas. That meant the outcome of the war was already sealed.

Again, the disturbing thought pricked him—*who was that man*? When Shakuni had seen the man, he felt for a moment that he had seen him somewhere before. He now started scourging his memory desperately.

One night, a thought occurred to him when he was half asleep. It made him sit on the bed and wonder, *did not the man very much look like Arstisena—the Brahmin mystic who often visited my father? I was a mere child when he used to come to our place…yes…he too had strange cat-like eyes like this old man—that's why he looked so familiar at the first sight. Arstisena gave me that special pasha set. He loved me very much. Although I was still a child, he had a very high opinion about my intelligence and merit. But is Arstisena still alive? Did we see him that day? But what can be his connection with Hastinapur? Why was he reciting those strange lines? Had he become insane? But he did not appear so, eccentric nevertheless.*

The mystery deepened. Shakuni got up from his bed and started pacing up and down. Finally, he sat down on a cushion and started writing a letter to his son Uluk who was being raised by his mother in Gandhara and had now become a sharp young man, inheriting some of his father's traits. The concluding part of Shakuni's letter was as follows:

> *'Putra, I hereby entrust you with a very important and secret task, hoping you have, in the meantime, become qualified enough to be equal to it. Though I have irreconcilable differences with your mother, I have full confidence in her that she must have brought you up the right way.*
>
> *Anyway, you may not be aware that one Brahmin scholar, named Shri Arstisena, used to visit our place often to meet your late grandfather. Not many people in Gandhara now are aware of him. I need to know his antecedents, present whereabouts and all other relevant details about him. You have to be very discreet and must never consult with any of your uncles or ministers on this matter.*
>
> *I shall wait for your feedback with all eagerness as it is much more important than you can ever imagine.'*

Shakuni handed over the letter to a messenger and ordered him to ride towards Gandhara that night itself.

Once Shakuni became sceptical about their prospect in the war, he started getting into a muddle. His own objective was now becoming hazy to himself. One evening, he felt the need to put his convoluted thoughts in order.

Should a war be fought, the Pandavas are more likely to defeat us as they have Krishna. So, where do I go now? Is my mission destined to fail? Shall we all be killed after thirteen years? Will Pritha have the last smile? Will her sons drag my mutilated corpse along the rugged ground to her feet? Is a terrible fate awaiting me to absolve me of my sins?

Shakuni felt cramps in his stomach. He was feeling utterly nervous. Was he supposed to accept such a dreadful possibility lying down, doing absolutely nothing to avert it?

No! My name is Shakuni. I can't surrender to my destiny so meekly. I am not scared of death at all. As such, life has long ceased to have any meaning for me. So what if Duryodhana loses the war? Am I doing all these for his sake? Let him be damned. And so what if I am killed in the war? Do I really need to live past the war? Why should I live that long if Pritha will never be mine? I must not be wary of the future. I have nothing to lose. But I must not float down the stream like a lifeless log either. I shall leave my mark even while accepting the inevitable. Even if I lose, I shall make my defeat as expensive as possible. I shall ensure that Pritha's victorious sons find no peace even in victory!

But how? Shakuni started walking around in circles inside the room. As always, the 'right' idea came to his mind at the right moment. He suddenly remembered the parting words of Ashwasen—'If you want to destroy an enemy completely, you must annihilate his descendants too….'

Shakuni had goosebumps.

Why am I targeting Pritha's sons only? Why not her grandsons, too? If I can destroy their next progeny right in front of their eyes, won't the Pandavas suffer like hell? It will be personally far more gratifying for me. What the hell will the Pandavas do with this bloody kingdom with their dear children going up in flames? Ashwasen was right. Regardless of the outcome of the war, the line of the Pandavas must not survive.

The idea lulled Shakuni into a sinister calmness. Even if he lost the battle, he would still manage to serve his enemies an unimaginable blow that they were never prepared for. But he needed someone to do this for him.

Shakuni knew that only one man on their side could do this. That person was apparently demure, low profile but was immensely capable. What he needed was a spark that could make him explode. But Shakuni also knew that it was not the right time to tell him about this. That man would not agree to do it unless the situation became that much provocative.

It would be Shakuni's last strike, anyway. It would inflict on his enemies a wound much more grievous than what his notorious dice had done. Shakuni had no dearth of patience to keep waiting for the right moment to deal his final and most brutal blow to Pritha and her sons.

11

Time was flying fast. In fact, that was what Duryodhana, his brothers, Karna and Dhritarashtra were feeling. For the Pandavas, the days seemed to be crawling ahead at a snail's pace. They had been exposed to the extreme harsh face of the reality. Each day was posing before them stiff challenges. They had to survive fending off wild beasts, brigands, natural calamities, diseases, hunger and frustration. They never knew that living, by itself, could be such a daunting task. The gruelling experience was actually doing them a great service. It was binding them to each other more inseparably and was making their resolve stronger. Each of them was growing wiser by leaps and bounds to develop into better human beings while Dhritarashtra's sons were spoiling themselves away in their opulent lives.

The Pandavas were roaming from jungle to jungle. Their survival in the wilderness became possible solely due to their exceptional fighting skills. They encountered *Rakshasas* almost regularly. Bheem used to treat them as good wrestling partners and enjoyed fighting them. He became a notorious *Rakshasa*-hunter. They started to stay away from him. Wild beasts and bandits were never a match for the Pandavas. However, they always had to remain alert. Arjuna paid a brief visit to Lord Indra who was said to have a special affection for the former. Indra gave him a wide repertoire of celestial weapons. Arjuna returned much more equipped and stronger.

Duryodhana, in the meantime, invited an utterly embarrassing and humiliating situation for himself ignoring Shakuni's forbidding. He planned a pleasure trip to the jungle where the Pandavas were living at that time. Duryodhana actually wanted to witness their suffering. For obvious reasons, Shakuni did not approve of such an immature and useless adventure. He feared that the Pandavas might try to assault Duryodhana and his men. However, Duryodhana paid no heed to him to his own peril. On the way to the jungle, their clamouring convoy disturbed some Gandharvas who were camping in the vicinity. They got into a heated altercation with the armed retinue from Hastinapur. The arrogance of Duryodhana's men irritated them and a fight ensued. The mighty Gandharvas thrashed them severely and captured Duryodhana, while his other brothers and Karna managed to run away. The Gandharvas would have killed him had the Pandavas not reached the place in the nick of time. They defeated the Gandharvas to free Duryodhana. He returned home unharmed but utterly humiliated. He was mortally upset—so much so that he even contemplated suicide. It took a prolonged counselling session from Shakuni to bring him back on track.

To allay Duryodhana's fear, Shakuni first made up a fake story that the Gandharvas actually had attacked the convoy on the request of the Pandavas and after capturing Duryodhana, deliberately lost to them in the battle before setting him free. Shakuni presented the incident as a clever Pandava ploy to humiliate Duryodhana. The subsequent friendship between Arjuna and the Gandharva king Chitrarath helped Shakuni cook up the story more convincingly.

Shakuni initiated an extensive recruitment drive for the army and announced many lucrative perks for the soldiers. On his advice, Duryodhana started sending delegations under Kanik's leadership to powerful states with the intention to forge fast alliances. At least politically they were in a good position. The Pandavas, in spite of their individual brilliance, were not in a very comfortable position in the matter of a full-scale war. Shakuni explained this to Duryodhana in detail in order to bail him out of the depression. Duryodhana was returning to his swaggering self, much to Shakuni's relief.

Another very important event was gradually unfurling in the mean time. Duryodhana's only daughter, Lakshmana, fell for Krishna's handsome son Shambo. The feeling was mutual. Duryodhana was against the alliance. But Shakuni saw a golden opportunity to bring Krishna to their side and convinced Duryodhana to approve the match. Grudgingly, Duryodhana accepted it as he understood the importance of securing Krishna's support. Shakuni's only fear was that Krishna might oppose the alliance. Surprisingly, Krishna did not meddle and stayed out of it.

Although relieved, Shakuni could not understand this detached Krishna. Why did he not try to dissuade his son from this marriage? Perhaps he wanted to respect his son's choice without foisting himself on his son. It was another telling evidence of Krishna's extraordinariness. Shakuni admitted to himself that if Devavrata was difficult for him to understand, Krishna was impossible.

On the completion of the twelfth year of exile, the Pandavas went into the year-long '*Agyatvaas*' and started living incognito. Duryodhana unleashed spies all over Bharatavarsha but the Pandavas were nowhere to be found. As their capture entailed another twelve years of exile over them, Duryodhana became increasingly restless and impatient as the year was breezing past. His spies were leaving no stones unturned to find the five brothers and Draupadi. The spies were even trying to find out their remains, in case they had died.

Only a few days short of the year's completion, news came from the west that Keechak—the mighty military commander of the Matsya kingdom had been brutally killed. His dead body was so unrecognisably mangled that it seemed to be the handiwork of some incredibly powerful creature. Shakuni and Duryodhana had a suspicion that it might be an act of Bheem. Otherwise also, Keechak's death interested Duryodhana as Matsya had long hostilities with the Trigartas, who were Duryodhana's closest ally. The Matsya army regularly defeated the Trigartas thanks to Keechak's able military leadership. Now, the Trigarta king Susharma requested Duryodhana to attack Matsya immediately to avenge his earlier losses. Duryodhana placed the issue for a discussion in his cabinet and it was unanimously decided that Matsya be put under seige. Even Devavrata showed interest and agreed to lead the Kaurava army. On Devavrata's advice, the Trigartas were asked to attack the southern frontier of Matsya and engage them in a fight while the mighty Kaurava army would strike from the unguarded northern side.

But they could never imagine in their wildest dreams what awaited them at Matsya.

The Trigartas were routed by four mysterious warriors who led the Keechak-less Matsya army to yet another thumping victory over their arch rivals. And on the other side, the famous Kauravas were thwarted single-handedly by a curious-looking person—apparently a eunuch whose chariot was being driven by the Matsya king Virat's youngest son, Uttar.

Shakuni had no doubt that the eunuch was none other than Arjuna in disguise and those four men the other Pandavas. But the revelation was just one day too late. Devavrata calculated that the *Agyatvaas* period had been duly over only the previous day implying that the

Pandavas had successfully complied with the terms of the *pasha* game.

'They must get back their legitimate property now. There should be no more disputes; we have had enough of it already. Period,' Devavrata announced in a firm, authoritative voice.

Returning from a disastrous Matsya campaign, an emergency meeting had been called at Dhritarashtra's assembly hall. Devavrata said the above to conclude the discussion that had been going nowhere. He turned around to leave the assembly room. But he could not.

'Which legitimate property did they ever have, *Pitamaha*? What they had was a gift that my father mercifully bestowed on them. Now, I am in charge of everything and I now decide that the meaningless charity be rescinded. So, they are not getting anything on their return—not even a needlepoint of earth unless I have any change of heart which seems highly unlikely at this moment.'

Everybody sat on their seat's edge expecting an explosion. Duryodhana's vicious words seemed to have stabbed Devavrata in the back. He turned back very slowly to face Duryodhana who was sitting on his throne with one leg cheekily placed over another, in a deliberately provocative pose to make his disregard for seniors evident.

Shakuni had been strumming his fingers over the hand rest of his seat, watching and enjoying the show this far. Now he became taut and watched Devavrata's reactions with rapt attention. *Was there a momentary upward bend at the corner of Devavrata's lips that had some semblance to a sly smile?* Shakuni could not believe his eyes. He looked closely again at his face but now there was no trace of that mysterious curl any more. Instead, Devavrata's face looked frighteningly grim now. His eyes were bulging and lips trembling. He glowered at Duryodhana and pointed his index finger at him. But what he said was addressed to Dhritarashtra, not Duryodhana.

'Dhritarashtra, I know it is already too late for you to clip this boy's wings but still I caution you that this evil son of yours will spell disaster for this house if he is allowed to continue like this!' Devavrata's voice was trembling in anger.

Dhritarashtra rushed towards Devavrata unsteadily and stammered with folded hands, 'I-I shall take him to task, *Tatshri*. Please, calm down.'

Devavrata stormed out of the hall. His bold footsteps were being heard from afar. Dhritarashtra and Duryodhana got engaged in a heated exchange of words. Bahlik, Drona, Kripacharya, and even Kanik were criticising Duryodhana's atrocious attitude. Quite expectedly, Duryodhana's own coterie came in his support now. Duhshasana, Karna and Dushpradharsha[1] angrily accused the seniors for conspiring against Duryodhana and Dhritarashtra.

Shakuni was sitting aloof, for he had no need to participate in it. He was thinking instead whether Devavrata's anger was genuine or feigned. *How many masks does this man wear? Is his real face itself a mask too?*

Suddenly, Shakuni realised that Vidur was surprisingly silent. Shakuni turned his attention towards him now. What he noticed was yet another surprise.

Vidur was staring unblinkingly at Bahlik. He was looking at the old man in such a way as if he was seeing

---

1 Another son of Dhritarashtra and Gandhari.

him for the first time. Vidur's eyes were shining. What novelty did he see in Bahlik today?

Shakuni looked at Bahlik to find if anything was amiss. There was nothing unusual in him today, except for the fact that he was speaking a little too much. In fact, he was Duryodhana's most vocal detractor today. This seemed slightly curious because Bahlik, usually a reticent man, never talked much in public and was rather fond of Duryodhana. But that did not mean that he could not open up if necessary. Shakuni found nothing irregular in him now. Then what had struck Vidur?

Vidur was now looking at the floor, completely unmindful about the excited altercation going on inside the room. Deep worry lines appeared on his forehead.

What was he thinking about?

Shakuni found this pensive mood of Vidur no less intriguing than Devavrata's enigmatic half-smile.

12

'Come *Putra*, come. I was thinking whether you have completely forgotten the way to my humble hut. It seems nowadays you don't have much time to waste with this senile old man,' said Vyasadeva in a slothful voice with his back to the door. He was busy lighting a lamp in his hovel.

Vidur bit his lips. He was standing at the threshold of the flimsy door. Vidur knew he deserved this. These days he had been too pre-occupied to visit his mentor. It was a fact that Vidur had made himself indispensable for Duryodhana, notwithstanding their mutual dislike.

Vidur, instead of apologising straightaway, responded with a naughty compliment in an attempt to please the great sage. 'I didn't make any sound, not even did I breathe near the door. Still you could understand I have come, that too without turning back. That is amazing, *Maharshi!*'

Vyasa understood Vidur's funny intention and smiled. This was the only place where Vyasa always struggled to remain ascetic. The very sight of Vidur filled him with affection. He said, 'I don't need to see you, Vidur. I can smell you from several *yojanas* away. I can hear your heartbeat from a distance, *Putra*. You are my seed...you are my...leave it,' Vyasa controlled the uncharacteristic burst of emotion that he felt quite unbecoming of him.

Vidur's vision became hazy too.

'So, the war is on?' Vyasa asked dourly, raising his bushy eyebrows.

'You know everything,' Vidur said.

'I'm afraid I do. That's my problem. Everything becomes my business at the end of the day, even if I want to remain aloof.'

Silence fell in the dimly lit hut. Father and son sat quietly facing each other.

Vidur broke the uncomfortable silence, 'How do you analyse the situation in Hastinapur, *Maharshi*?'

'What's left to analyse? It is simple. The Pandavas are coming back with fire in their heart. Duryodhana is sufficiently ill-advised by Shakuni to deny them their rights. The only solution is a war.'

'But the Pandavas have no army. How can they....'

'Who said they don't have an army? The Panchalas and the Matsya army will fight for them. All allies of the Panchalas and the Srinjayas will be theirs. Satyaki and his Vrishni army will be supporting them. And they have Krishna, above all. What more does one need to win a war?'

'You mean to say the Pandavas can win this war, *Maharshi*?' Vidur asked with bulging eyes.

'Not "can". They "will". They will win, most certainly. With Krishna's support, they simply cannot lose.'

Vidur was surprised by the confidence of the old man. Though he knew what Vyasa had just said was but true, something was hurting him. He badly wanted the Pandavas to win but it was very difficult for him to witness a bloodfest in the house he so passionately loved. His face was overcast with sadness.

Vyasa was observing his reaction. 'What makes you so tense, *Putra*? Don't you want a Pandava victory?'

Vidura replied hesitantly, 'You know that I do. But a battle will destroy the family for sure, *Maharshi*. That makes me very worried.'

'What has this family ever given to you, Vidur? What have you got from here? You were much more talented than Dhritarashtra and Pandu, yet you are nowhere near the throne. And never will be. Today that imbecile Duryodhana dares insult you at every opportunity. That foreigner, Shakuni, is wielding all the power under your nose. Your astute advices fall on deaf ears. Why are you still so loyal to Hastinapur? Is there anyone more devoted to this bloody kingdom than you? You should not have been this good. You shall get grievously hurt one day, I tell you.'

Vidur was too astonished to react. *Maharshi* had never talked like this before. Vyasa suddenly appeared very unfamiliar to him now. Why was he saying so? Was he upset? Vidur realised that he had just been exposed to a dark labyrinth of Vyasa's personality. Probably, Vyasa's private frustration coloured his words that were apparently meant for Vidur. 'Is there any one more devoted...than you?'—Vidur found this remark especially curious.

Does he mean to say even Tatshri Devavrata is not as devoted to Hastinapur as I have been? Does he have any reason to doubt Tatshri Devavrata's loyalty?

'Now tell me why you have come to me today. I know you haven't come to enquire about my health or well-being. Talk business now,' Vyasa said brusquely.

Vidur himself was in some hurry to do so. He asked, '*Maharshi,* what's your opinion about King Bahlik? Does he bear any grudge against Hastinapur? Was he content with his Vahik kingdom while his younger brother Shantanu got the more prosperous Hastinapur?'

The question surprised Vyasa. He said, 'As far as I know, Bahlik himself refused to take Hastinapur. He preferred to rule Vahik *Desh* as he was raised in the north-western regions. I think he was quite happy with whatever he got. But why do you ask?'

'The other day, I noticed something that I should have much earlier. Do you remember many years ago I once told you that Shakuni and I met a peculiar old man outside the city? He was reciting some odd lines. It seemed to me then that I had seen a similar face somewhere before. Just the day before yesterday I noticed a strange thing while Bahlik*ji* was speaking in our assembly. Suddenly it appeared that he has an uncanny resemblance with that mysterious old man. I had met Bahlik*ji* many times before but never had such a feeling. But that day, he looked exactly identical to that old man from a particular angle. My head reeled but I simply can't make anything out of it. Please help me, *Maharshi*.'

With a grave expression on his face, Vyasa mumbled in a gravelly voice, 'Exactly what I doubted.'

Vidur looked on blankly, unable to betray any reaction.

Vyasa asked him, 'What do you feel?'

'I suspect now that Bahlik disguised himself as that old man. But why would he do so?' said Vidur.

'He was not Bahlik. He was someone whose face resembled Bahlik's.'

'Who?' Vidur asked the question almost in whispers.

'I think he was Devapi himself, Bahlik's elder brother.'

Vidur took some time to recover from the shock. It was too much for him. He took some more time to arrange his thoughts. 'Okay. Even if I assume that he was Devapi, or the fact that he is still roaming like a vagabond around the city, why should it cause us any serious concern? After all, he is now a decrepit, disabled man not capable of harming even a fly.'

'There is nothing to fear if you see him as a person. But if you see him as a curse looming over Hastinapur, you shall lose your sleep,' Vyasa said.

'A curse?' Vidur's lips parted in astonishment.

'Remember I had told you that Devapi predicted about an intra-family war in our house? His prophecy influenced a section of people, including your grand-uncle Bahlik, so seriously that they even started preparations for the speculated war completely neglecting the present. And in effect, their crooked machinations have really brought the Kuru dynasty on the brink of a war today. They took the prophecy for granted and made it become a reality, dancing to Devapi's tunes like puppets. Another thing, was it really a prediction? Intra-family disputes are the most common thing in any royal house. Just look around at your neighbouring kingdoms and you shall understand. Everywhere there is open or discreet tension inside the house. And the Vrishnis are historically close to the Kauravas. I think Ugrasen (the then Vrishni king of Mathura) and Shantanu (the then Kaurava king of Hastinapur) even had a pact between them. So, it is quite expected that in case of any feud, the Vrishnis are likely to get involved and take a side. It does not take a seer to foretell such things. You understand what I am saying?'

Vidur had been listening breathlessly. He asked, 'Do you want to say that it was actually not a prediction, but a clever ploy to pollute the minds of the future progeny?'

'The very meaningful lines of that old man point towards that. He cryptically reminded all of you that the future will recall the past events. Devapi possibly nursed a malice in his mind for being thrown out of the Kuru family and tried to take his revenge. And, as you can see, he has been spectacularly successful.'

'I can't understand one thing, *Maharshi*. How could Devapi correctly predict about a great Kuru scion's sacrifice? Wasn't it about *Tatshri* Devavrata's noble act? He was absolutely correct about Krishna's birth and time too! And the "foreign agent"? It is clearly Shakuni!'

'Ha ha ha ha…,' Vyasa burst into a peal of laughter. 'Apply your mind, *Putra*. All these are post-dictions, not predictions! Did he specifically name that Kuru scion or mention the nature of sacrifice? In all great dynasties, you shall find at least one magnanimous character who acts unselfishly in the interest of the family or the kingdom. The house prospers around such personalities. And you talk about Krishna? Did Devapi specifically name him? No. He mentioned "eight years" based on a loose calculation about the advent of the next generation. And Krishna was born after nine years, not eight—to be precise. Go check your calculations. And mind you, the word "foreign" can be defined in many ways. Even the women married into a family are foreigners as they hail from other kingdoms. For that matter, the children born through *Niyoga* may also be foreigners, just like the Pandavas are—having no Kaurava blood in their veins. So, the expression "foreign agent" is not very specific although it appears so. People are actually trying to prove the predictions accurate by supporting them with suitable future events. This is nothing but hindsight explanation. Frauds cheat gullible people by such ambiguous yet almost obvious statements that they claim as predictions.'

Vidur did not know why he could not fully agree with Vyasa. He asked in a hoarse voice, 'You mean Devapi was a fraud? That he didn't really have any mystical powers. So, did he wilfully misguide several generations just to settle a score with the great Kuru house?'

'Wait, my boy. Wait!' Vyasa raised his voice quite abruptly surprising Vidur. 'Devapi was never any ordinary guy.

He really had mystical powers. He mastered the black arts, I know. That's why, he was taken so seriously. But I still suspect that his so-called prophecy was contrived—at least partially. It was due to his stature and fame, that he could manage to plant the ill will so deeply into the psyche of his next generations. No ordinary man could have done that.'

'But...,' Vidur was cut short.

'I have long doubted this. Today, it has been confirmed as you told me about Bahlik's similarity with that man. The Kauravas have so far been dancing to his tunes and ruining themselves—completely unwittingly. It is not a prophecy, Vidur; it is actually a terrible conspiracy of Devapi. Or you can say it is a curse. I was afraid of this. But now I somehow feel sympathy for him.' Vyasa said grimly.

'Sympathy for Devapi? Why?' Vidur sounded confused.

'I too was severely let down by these Kauravas, you know. This family used me, humiliated me and forgot me. My own mother reduced me to something like a male prostitute! I still can't forget how those two proud women—Ambika and Ambalika—reacted on seeing me in their beds. There was so much hatred. Only *your* mother gave me my due but she didn't belong to the family. I never deserved this insult, Vidur. I secretly admire Devapi because he has done what I myself could not. He has hit back; he has brought the Kauravas down to their knees.'

Vyasa lay down on the ground. He was of late not used to talking so much at a stretch.

Vidur asked softly, 'Isn't there anything we can still do to save the situation, *Maharshi*?'

Vyasa ignored the question. There was now a funny smile on his face. He muttered in a low voice as if talking to himself, 'It will be interesting to see what Devavrata does now. His life is even more pathetic than mine. I feel he will assume the command of the Kaurava army and occupy the battleground for some days, pretending to fight. He will keep the battle in a stalemate allowing neither side to win or lose. Then one day, he will commit suicide or let himself be killed when his lust for life will completely drain out.'

Vyasa's smile was fading through his speech and by the time he stopped, despair was writ large all over his face. He slightly raised his body from the lying position and made a craven request to Vidur, '*Putra*, please do stay away from this battle. It is a father's last request to his dearest son. It will be a great, unforgettable war. The Kauravas are unstoppably running into it. Let them. They deserve it. This war may avenge me, Devavrata and Devapi. But you are honest and innocent. This war is not worth your blood, *Putra*.'

'Then what do you want me to do, *Pitashri*?' Vidur deliberately addressed Vyasa as father now. He knew Vyasa would not forbid him anymore. The dispassionate sage had already been consumed by earthly emotions.

After a little pause, Vyasa replied unmindfully, 'Give your wisdom and knowledge to Yudhisthira after the war is over. He is a good boy. Your counsel will be useful to him. But don't live in this kingdom anymore. Renounce this material world and pursue *moksha* in obscurity, far away from civilisation. You shall become a much revered icon in your own rights.'

Vidur remained quiet for some time with his head lowered. Then, he raised his head slowly and said, 'As you wish, *Pitashri*. I shall do what you ask me to. But what will *you* do now?'

Vyasa smiled.

This is his best expression today, Vidur thought.

Vyasa said with misty eyes, 'Me? I shall embark on an extremely ambitious project now. I shall author a chronicle of the troubled history of this Kuru family. I shall write about how the men and women of our time lived, loved, thought, felt and fought. I shall write how blissfully we found our gods, how miserably we lost them. I shall leave records of everything. And if I can by any chance get Lord Ganesha to scribe my story, I swear I shall make all of you immortal. All of you shall live long beyond your deaths. It will be my tribute to the great Kuru family.'

Vidur fell at Vyasa's feet. Vyasa enfolded Vidur in his arms. The two outstanding men, both teary eyed, clasped each other with great passion.

13

It was noon. Shakuni was resting in his bed. He was not sleeping, though. Sleep had been a rare visitor to him these days. He was not keeping well too. He had had a bad sprain some time ago while dismounting from a steed. The pain relapsed with greater intensity in the past few days. He had lately developed some breathing trouble as well.

Bad health was a new thing for him. Born and brought up in a mountainous region, he had always been physically fit, although not particularly imposing. In his youth, however, he had been temperamentally volatile. But with conscious efforts, he was able to dominate his mind to a great extent. That dark motive remained the only extant truth in his life that kept him going. Nothing else mattered to him anymore. But time was taking an inevitable toll on his body. And that was something even he could not do anything about.

Shakuni got up from his bed and stood in front of a mirror, examining his own reflection. What he saw cast a shadow on his face. His lean, straight body was now noticeably bent with the awkward sag of his shoulders. The greenish eyes were set deep into the sockets. There were dark circles under his eyes and fine wrinkles crisscrossed his face. The aquiline nose loomed over thin lips like the hooked beak of a tired vulture. It had now become the most prominent feature of his emaciated face. White streaks were dominating his flowing beard and long tresses. Shakuni was ageing. And withering.

A wry smile twisted his lips. Shakuni said to himself, *time is running away fast, Saubala. Now, it is a race to the finish!*

'*Prabhu*, a messenger from Gandhara awaits you outside. Should I let him in?' The guard's query entered Shakuni's ears and jerked him out of his thoughts.

'A messenger from Gandhara? And you have kept him waiting? Bring him in, immediately,' snarled Shakuni.

Uluk must have sent in his response. Has he been able to collect the information I need so badly?

A portly man with a scroll in his hand was ushered in. Shakuni almost snatched it away from his hand and issued an instruction to the sentry, 'See this man off with a good meal and five gold coins.'

Shakuni unrolled the scroll hurriedly. It was indeed a letter from Uluk. He glossed over the mandatory pleasantries and family talks and fiercely read up the portion of his interest in a single breath.

As you wished, I have managed to learn some interesting facts about Shriman Arstisena through secret enquiries from various sources. I came to know that Arstisena was not originally a Brahmin; rather a Kshatriya. He was a Brahmin convert who was originally a descendant of the great king Kuru. He was the eldest son of King Pratip and his wife Sunanda. He was disowned by the Kuru family due to his deviant beliefs. He was also suspected to have contracted leprosy. He later assumed the Brahminical way of life. He mastered the occult also. His birth name was Devapi Pratipeya.'

Shakuni sat dumbfounded. So, Arstisena and Devapi were the same person! But how could Devapi live this long? Shakuni thought, *if Devapi's younger brother Bahlik can still live and remain fighting fit even today, why couldn't Devapi?*

Shakuni was sure now that Arstisena (or Devapi) had deliberately appeared before Vidur and him that day.

He thought, *why did Devavrata turn so pale when I informed him about Devapi immediately after meeting him that day? What was Devavrata's fear? Does he see Devapi as a threat? Possibly, Devapi bears a grudge against this family for being disowned and Devavrata is aware of it....*

Another strange thought was disturbing Shakuni. The particular event that made the present dispute absolutely irreconcilable—the fateful *pasha* game—had been played with the *pasha* set that Devapi himself had given to Shakuni. And it was the same *pasha* set Shakuni had tried to gift Pritha at Mathura many moons ago earning the life-changing humiliation.

Shakuni bit into his lip and wondered, *how astonishing it is that this particular pasha set repeatedly gets involved into contentious incidents at different points of time. Is this merely a co-incidence? Isn't it strange that I never lost any game played with that pasha set? Did Devapi actually pack any occult power into that particular set to use it as a totem weapon? But why did he give it to me? Did he believe only I could be able to use it most effectively? But how did he guess that I would be entangled in the affairs of a faraway Hastinapur some day? Was it sheer clairvoyance, or a far-sighted political calculation that Gandhara and Hastinapur would have to come close to each other in their best interests? Does it mean that Devapi actually stitched a colossal conspiracy, thread by thread over the years, looking so far into the future?*

Shakuni was sweating. He became thirsty. He picked up a jar full of water and guzzled it. While gulping the water, his eyes fell on the *pasha* set that was kept with great care on a marble rostrum at one side of the room.

Shakuni got up and walked towards the rostrum in an unsure gait. He was slightly limping as that pain in his leg seemed to have come back. He looked at the ivory dice with a very different eye today. He had always treated them as if they were living beings—much like his loyal slaves who obeyed him unfailingly. Today, he felt that their loyalty had actually remained with someone else and they followed Shakuni's orders only at that person's behest.

The thought hurt Shakuni's ego. He was very much aware of his notoriety as an unbeatable *pasha* player and took great pride in it. It was difficult for him to believe that his dice were controlled less by his nimble fingers and more by Devapi's spell.

Shakuni took the dice in his right palm. Their touch felt very unfamiliar now. Shakuni brought his palm near his eyes to take a closer look at them. They looked the same as before. But Shakuni was not at all confident today. The mysterious Devapi had cast a long shadow over Shakuni's personality.

Shakuni rolled the dice over the board with his typical finger movement. Quite unexpectedly, one die slipped out of his fingers and fell down straight on the floor. It was immediately shattered to smithereens. The other rolled over the board. But it too fell down on the floor after bouncing off the rostrum and broke into two halves.

Shakuni could not believe his eyes. These dice had been like his weapons. And now, he could not even keep them on the board. He was looking wide-eyed at the broken fragments strewn on the floor as if he was watching a mutiny of his soldiers.

It was evening already. The broken ivory shards were glittering in the moonlight that sneaked into the room through the blinds. Shakuni felt as if the broken dice were mocking him.

He started breathing heavily. Open mouthed, he was gasping for air. He was badly in need for a support right now. With much difficulty, he called the guard, 'Chitrarath…Chitrarath…help me…help…please….'

A distraught Chitrarath rushed in. Shakuni fell on his chest in a faint.

Shakuni had been bed-ridden for over a week, following his collapse that day. It was not at all to his liking but the *vaid* was very strict and meant business. He was sharp enough to understand that Shakuni was suffering from a deep complex that created a monstrous mental pressure. Shakuni had consciously killed many of his finer sensibilities, but never cared to dispose of their rotten corpses from his mind. As a result, his mental hygiene was slowly becoming poor.

The bed rest was doing him good though. He himself understood that he was in dire need of this. For years, he had been hyperactive. People said Shakuni remained awake even in his sleep! A brief sabbatical was very much overdue.

Duryodhana was taking very good care of him. He would visit his *Mamashri* umpteen times a day and enquire about every minute detail of his health and medication. Shakuni found Duryodhana's concern very endearing and was enjoying it.

Another strange thing was happening to Shakuni. Lately, Arshi was coming to his mind quite often. And even more strangely, Pritha never did. *How is Arshi doing now? How does she look now? I haven't seen her for years! Is she feeling lonely there? Or, is she enjoying her freedom from me? Does she still maintain her relationship with Arjak? Does she remember me sometimes? Does she feel guilty? Should I write to her one last time before the war? But what should I write? We have long buried all words between us, haven't we?*

Shakuni felt this brief ailment had made him more humane in more ways than one.

In Hastinapur, things were unfolding exactly the way *Maharshi* Vyasa had anticipated. On the completion of their exile, the Pandavas demanded their kingdom back which Duryodhana summarily refused. Seeing Duryodhana hopelessly adamant, Yudhisthira even asked for just one village for each of the brothers instead of the city of Indraprastha but Duryodhana rejected that too. Even Krishna's peace mission failed to break Duryodhana's resolve. The two sides were left with no other options than to fight it out.

By the time Shakuni was completely fit, the war was settled. Although Shakuni was sure that Krishna would never waver in his support for the Pandavas, he felt the need to formally approach Krishna for his support as Krishna's son Shambo was married to Duryodhana's daughter. At his persistent bidding, Duryodhana, somewhat reluctantly, went to Dwarka to request Krishna to take his side.

Shakuni had a faint hope that Krishna might stay neutral in the battle, his sympathy for the Pandavas notwithstanding. Should that happen, the Kauravas then would go to war with a huge advantage.

Returning from Dwarka, a visibly excited Duryodhana stormed into Shakuni's room.

'*Mamashri,* I think my visit to Dwarka has been greatly successful. Krishna won't fight—neither for me nor for Yudhisthira!'

'What?' Shakuni sprang up from his bed. He could not believe his ears. *Krishna won't fight for the Pandavas. Really!*

'What is more, he has given me a mighty contingent of the *Narayani sena*. This massive, powerful unit of soldiers will fight for me!' Duryodhana cried out like a delighted child.

It took some time to sink in. Shakuni could not understand why Krishna was so kind to Duryodhana.

'Why has he given you his army? He was never very pleased with you. Do you know whether he has given anything to the Pandavas as well?'

'Well, he actually gave me and Arjuna an option to choose between the *Narayani sena* and himself. He said he will only be present on the battleground unarmed and will not fight. I never knew Arjuna was such a fool. He chose the unarmed Krishna over that fearsome army and requested him to drive his chariot. Your Krishna will be Arjuna's charioteer...ha ha ha...and I was surprised to see that Krishna agreed, with a happy smile at that! I hid my happiness and accepted his army with a glum face...ha ha ha... But I tell you *Mamashri,* it was very difficult for me to pull a face at that time, ha ha ha....'

Shakuni sat on the bed with a thud. His mouth was wide open as if a yawn had frozen midway. He felt like tearing his hair. *What a moron this Duryodhana is! Who can make Duryodhana understand how he just squandered away a golden opportunity to win this war?*

'What bothers you now, *Mamashri*? Aren't you happy? We got a strong army contingent, they a good charioteer. We shall destroy them in a few days, just you see.' Duryodhana brandished his sword taking it from its sheath and swung it in the air.

Shakuni felt too tired to laugh at such tomfoolery. It was both useless and too late to argue with Duryodhana over the matter. He only said in a low, timid voice, 'Your army was already larger than that of the Pandavas. I think you should have chosen Krishna instead.'

'Why? Are we short of good charioteers? What can Krishna do on a battleground empty-handed?' Duryodhana asked angrily.

Shakuni's eyes flashed. He said, grating his teeth, 'My dear Suyodhan, you shall never understand that one unarmed Krishna is mightier than an entire army. You may remember his remarkable exploits right from his childhood. Anyway, let's hope for the best and pray that your decision proves right.'

'Don't worry, *Mamashri*. Have dinner and take rest. From tomorrow onwards, I want to see you fighting fit. We are going to fight the biggest war the world has ever witnessed,' saying this, Duryodhana stood up and walked towards the door. He was beaming with enthusiasm and happiness.

'Thank you, *Putra,*' said Shakuni in a feeble voice and added, 'Please ask Ashwatthama to meet me now.'

Duryodhana turned around, surprised. Ashwatthama was never quite close to Shakuni. Their relationship never extended beyond formal talks and pleasantries. They did not even appear to be much fond of each other.

'Ashwatthama? Now? Why?' Duryodhana asked, raising his eyebrows.

'He is the one I have had least interactions with so far. I want to gauge him a bit.'

'As you wish, *Mamashri*,' Duryodhana left with a shrug.

Shakuni knew Krishna would make all the differences. He was sure that the war was lost. He was now just trying to make the victory as costly for the Pandavas as possible.

'May I come in, *Mama* Shakuni?'

'Come, *Kumar* Ashwatthama. I was waiting for you. Come,' Shakuni welcomed Ashwatthama cordially and asked him to sit on a chair while he seated himself on a settee near him.

Ashwatthama took his seat and looked at Shakuni. Shakuni examined Ashwatthama's facial expressions. His comely demeanour hardly betrayed his curiosity. Shakuni liked it. Ashwatthama's eyes were interesting. They were big, deep, intense yet calm. They looked like a placid sea revealing much less than what they hid. Shakuni thought, *my choice seems to be right.*

Shakuni cleared his throat and said in a low voice, 'Drouni[1], you must be aware that we have a great battle in our hands now. Right?'

'Yes, it seems so,' Ashwatthama's reply was dry and emotionless.

'How do you assess the strength of the two sides?'

'Ours is obviously much stronger. They have only Arjuna, Bheem and to some extent Dhrishtadyumna and Satyaki as top-rank fighters whilst we have *Pitamaha* Bheeshma, *Pitashri*, Karna, Shalya[2], Somdatta, Bhurishrava, Bhagadatta, Brihadbal....'

'And you.'

'Yes, obviously.' Ashwatthama smiled a little, for the first time since he came to this room.

'So, we should win, right?'

'We should, but...,' Ashwatthama appeared pensive.

'But?'

'I am wary of Krishna, frankly speaking. In fact, he is the only person on their side I am wary of. Although he

---

[1] Son of Drona.

[2] Although maternal uncle of Nakula-Sahadeva, Shalya was tricked into the Kaurava side by Duryodhana and Shakuni.

won't take up weapons, his very presence can make the difference. What do you think, *Mamashri*?'

Shakuni thought, *this man is at least more intelligent than my Duryodhana.*

With a smile, he said, 'Much the same as you think, Drouni. Only difference is, I am pretty *sure* that Krishna will not let us win. We are actually going to fight a lost war. And that's the unsavoury truth your friends can't understand.'

'Oh!' Ashwatthama was visibly perturbed. Shakuni's plain speaking disturbed his composure.

'That's why I sent for you. First tell me, why will you fight in this war? You have no enmity against the Pandavas. On the contrary, they admire you, I know. Then why?'

'I am indebted to Duryodhana and his family. He has given us shelter, respect and amenities. In my childhood, even a glass of milk was a luxury for me. And look at me today! It is all because of Duryodhana. I have pledged my life to him,' Ashwatthama suddenly became little emotional.

'Good. That's what I wanted to hear. Now tell me, what can we still achieve from this war?'

'Except victory what else is there to achieve from a war? I can't understand, *Mamashri*,' Ashwatthama said.

'I want to make a secret agreement with you. This is strictly between you and me.' Shakuni was feeling a strange excitement. *My last strike!*

'Agreement?' Ashwatthama parted his lips in astonishment.

'Yes. Listen carefully. If the battle turns against us—which I am sure will—I shall ask you to do a certain thing. Only you can do that. You shall not refuse me even if it sounds bizarre. Promise me,' Shakuni's green eyes were shining too much for Ashwatthama's comfort.

'But what shall you ask me to do?' Ashwatthama was at his wit's end.

'Sorry, I cannot tell you that now. This is not the right time. You're not yet prepared for this. But when I do tell you that, you may be in the perfect shape to carry it out. And it will make your Duryodhana proud, I can assure you. Now, please ask no more questions and give me your word.'

'Okay,' said Ashwatthama hesitantly. 'If it serves Duryodhana's interest, I shall do it, whatever be it. I promise you.'

'Sure?' Shakuni's eyes were shining like pearls.

'I am a Brahmin, *Mamashri*. I am the only son of *Acharya* Drona. I value my words above any other thing in the world.'

'Perfect. You may go now. And please remember this. Good night.'

'Good night.'

14

The Last Day of the War

It was dawn. The eastern horizon had just become pink. Birds had started chirping. A gentle breeze was blowing from the north.

Shakuni put an *uttariya* around his upper body and came out of his tent. He had not been able to put his eyelids together even for a moment last night.

The vast expanse of Kurukshetra greeted him outside. The battleground where the Kaurava and the Pandava armies were engaged in a fierce battle was littered with countless dead bodies and animal carcasses. Seventeen days had already been spent fighting. The ground had turned brownish red. The air was filled with the stench given off by rotten corpses.

Shakuni stood alone on the edge of the ground. Today's fight would commence shortly. Shakuni knew this eighteenth day would be the last day of the war. The Kaurava army was hopelessly staring at a devastating defeat. The Pandavas were all set to clinch the matter today itself. Not even a miracle now could protect the ramshackle Kaurava army from the marauding Pandava troops. Just yesterday, Karna had fallen after putting up a glorious fight with Arjuna. Arjuna had struck him ungraciously while Karna's chariot was stuck in a cranny. And with Karna's death, the Kaurava defeat was just a matter of time now.

But at the beginning of the war, the Kauravas had been much better placed. Duryodhana had amassed a monstrous army, obtaining support from almost all major powers in

Bharatavarsha except Panchala, Matsya, Magadh, Chedi, a few other eastern states and of course the Vrishnis. The Kaurava army was more than one and a half times the Pandava force.

Duryodhana had taken his victory for granted at the beginning. His confidence, however, would recede fast as the battle progressed. One by one, all formidable Kaurava warriors fell to Krishna's guiles—just as Shakuni had feared. Devavrata's fall triggered the irreversible downfall of the Kauravas. He was the first generalissimo of the Kauravas. Even after nine days of desperate efforts, the Pandavas failed to unsettle him. Then suddenly on the tenth day, the Pandavas pitted Shikhandi—the transgender son of King Drupad—against him. Devavrata refused to fight an opponent who was not a complete man. From behind the cover of Shikhandi, Arjuna assaulted him with numerous arrows. Struck all over the body, Devavrata fell down. Although he did not die, he lay incapacitated on a 'bed of arrows'. It was rumoured that Devavrata himself had given a clue to the Pandavas about his disdain to fight an unarmed or unmanly opponent.

After Devavrata Bheeshma's fall, Drona became the next general. He was cheated by the Pandavas with spurious information about his son Ashwatthama's death. As a griefstruck Drona dropped his arms, Dhrishtadyumna (Drupad's son) beheaded him. It was another machination of Krishna who convinced Yudhisthira to mislead Drona with the lie.

Then, it was Karna's turn. When Arjuna hesitated to strike an unprepared Karna, Krishna instigated him with an inflammatory speech that effectively changed Arjuna's mind. Ashwasen the *Naga* prince, as promised to Shakuni, tried to help Karna during the fight against Arjuna but was killed by the latter.

King Bhagadatta and King Jayadrath also died in Arjuna's hands with Krishna intervening on both the occasions. Shakuni, in his mind, could not help admiring Krishna. This one man won the Pandavas the war singlehandedly without even picking up any weapon. No wonder he was an *avatar* of Lord Vishnu! How correct Devapi had been in his prediction—*The war will be won by the side with the most intelligent man*.

The Vahik prince Somdatta's old scores with Shini could not be settled. Somdatta's son Bhurishrava was all set to avenge his humiliation by defeating Shini's grandson Satyaki, but Arjuna intervened to save Satyaki at Krishna's bidding. Thereafter, Bhurishrava too was unfairly killed by Arjuna and Satyaki. An enraged Somdatta attacked Satyaki later but was killed by him.

Bheem, on the other hand, killed King Bahlik. He also singlehandedly killed all the brothers of Duryodhana one by one. Remembering Draupadi's humiliation, he was particularly brutal with Duhshasana. He ripped open Duhshasana's chest with his bare hands and drank his blood. The macabre incident completely destroyed the morale of the floundering Kaurava army.

The Pandavas too lost some valiant warriors like Shveta, Abhimanyu, Ghatotkach, King Virat and King Drupad but their mainstay was intact.

Last night, when a completely routed Kaurava army was returning to the camp, Shakuni avoided looking at Duryodhana. He knew he would find the visage of a ghost in his nephew's face. Karna had been his greatest strength. Duhshasana had been his dearest brother. Losing both of them on the same day was too much for Duryodhana. Shakuni heard Ashwatthama tell Duryodhana, '*Raja,* now please be sensible. All of our best warriors are down. The Pandavas are far stronger than us now. Who shall lead our charge now? You should better surrender immediately. Yudhisthira is a kind man. He will still pardon you and may even give you back the half-empire. Don't be so stubborn.'

'He is right, Duryodhana. Do as he advises,' seconded Kripacharya.

Shakuni's heart shrunk. Ashwatthama's peacemongering did not go down well with him. He became very anxious.

Ashwatthama is my last bet. Will he prove unequal to the task? Will my last blow remain undelivered? Have I chosen the wrong man?

But Duryodhana's reply was courageous, 'You're possibly right, Drouni. We have lost to Krishna. But it's already too late to think of a truce. Tell me why should they forgive me? Their hearts are burning with rage. Draupadi will never let them forget the past. And why should I live anymore? All my dear relatives, brothers, friends are lying there lifeless. No, *Mitra*. I cannot beg for their mercy. Better, I shall die fighting. I shall die with pride. What do you think?'

Duryodhana's brave, spirited words were applauded by everybody. Ashwatthama hugged Duryodhana and said in a choked voice, 'Right you are, *Raja*. I am proud of you. Your Drouni shall fight for you until his last.'

Shakuni closed his eyes. *Fools!*

'*Pitashri*!'

Shakuni turned around. Uluk was standing behind him. He raised his eyebrows. Uluk had come all the way from Gandhara with a large contingent of the Gandhara army on his father's demand. He had fought hard all through, though his efforts had not been enough to make a mark.

'*Senapati* Shalya has requested you to prepare for today's fight quickly. We are getting late.'

'Oh yes. I'm coming,' said Shakuni with a smile and started walking towards his camp hurriedly. He had fallen in love with this last morning of his life. He was sure that he would not survive the day and therefore wanted this incredible morning to stretch as long as possible. He wanted to take a good look back at his life before parting with it. But alas, time was running fast.

Shalya—the king of Madra—blew his trumpet to commence the fight of the eighteenth day. He was appointed as the general succeeding Karna. Although his sister Madri had been married to Pandu, he fought for Duryodhana. Dhrishtadyumna, the Pandava general, responded with his conch. The two armies started marching towards each other.

The upbeat Pandava soldiers pounced on the dilapidated Kaurava army. A fierce battle ensued. Shalya, flanked by Ashwatthama and Kripacharya, was leading his side well. Duryodhana showed surprising valour on the day. Shakuni too desperately ran his chariot into the enemy formation. They knew they had nothing left to lose but still had glory to achieve. The Pandavas were surprised by the indomitable spirit of the Kaurava army even after suffering such heavy casualties

But soon the Pandava commanders took control of the situation. Yudhisthira confronted Shalya. However, the eldest Pandava was ably escorted and assisted by his brothers. Shalya was soon surrounded by the Pandava brothers. He was fighting bravely, though. Finally, he was fatally struck by a javelin thrown by Yudhisthira and fell dead.

More than half a day's fight was still left. Now, Duryodhana took charge and regrouped his completely disarrayed troops. Kripacharya and Ashwatthama were fighting hard at different sectors. But the fight was grossly unequal. The Kaurava soldiers were being slaughtered everywhere.

Shakuni sensed the urgency. He took his chariot towards Ashwatthama's and called him for a quick conference.

'Yes, *Mamashri*. Speak,' a panting Ashwatthama said busily.

'Do you remember we made a secret pact?'

'Yes, I do,' Ashwatthama suddenly became grim and composed, diverting his full attention to Shakuni now.

'It is time. Listen very carefully. This war will be finished by this afternoon, I am sure. Those wicked sons of Pandu will kill us. But, they will spare you. They have no enmity with you in particular. Moreover, you are their *Guru's* son....'

'How can you say so, *Mama* Shakuni? Did they even spare their *Guru*? Didn't those mindless brutes deceive my old father—their revered *Acharya*? When he had renounced his weapons, those cowards held him by his hair and cut off his head! Oh, if I ever get that misbegotten Dhrishtadyumna, I shall smother the bastard to death, I swear!' Ashwatthama exploded like a raging volcano.

Shakuni clapped and said, 'There you are! There you are, Drouni. Won't you avenge your father's death? Shame on you, if you don't!'

'Yes, but how? I can't do it now. They are numerically superior. I alone cannot....'

'Who asked you to do it now? Do it in the night when they will be fast asleep in their camps.'

Ashwatthama had never known how the hound of hell looked like. He now believed it should resemble the man standing in front of him. But thanks to the bitterness caused by the war, Shakuni's obnoxious plan touched the right chord in Ashwatthama's mind instead of causing repulsion. But he hesitated as the last vestiges of a fast disappearing conscience were still troubling him a bit, 'But...but....'

'No "buts"! The crooks must be dealt with in crooked manners. When the war will approach its final moments, you must leave the battlefield securing yourself. Wait at a safe distance. Let the night fall. Then in the midnight, enter their camps and butcher them as mercilessly as you can. Leave no one—I repeat, no one. But I have one doubt myself. The clever Pandava brothers and Krishna may sleep elsewhere. In that case, you must ensure that not a single member of their next generation survives. The line of Pritha's sons must be completely annihilated.'

'Line of who?'

'Leave it. That does not concern you. You concentrate only on your job. Don't let those bloody Pandavas have the last laugh. If you don't find them, kill their sons and relatives. Spare no one. That's all. Best of luck.' Shakuni asked his charioteer to rush towards the enemy line.

Ashwatthama stood dumbstruck. He had goosebumps all over his body. He had never lost his poise before even in the craziest moment of the war. But now he was losing it. He himself could feel that he was fast degenerating into a qualmless monster.

The mighty king of Shalwa *Desh* was trying to do something special. He was riding a gigantic elephant and wreaking havoc on the Pandava side. Dhrishtadyumna and Satyaki pursued him. Dhrishtadyumna hit the monstrous elephant on its head with his mace and killed it. Then, Satyaki cut off the Shalwa king's head with a short lance. His death effectively marked the end of all Kaurava resistance. The remaining soldiers were trying to run away but the Pandava horsemen were easily catching up and killing them.

Duryodhana, Shakuni, Uluk, Ashwatthama, Kripacharya and Kritavarma were still alive. With a nod, Shakuni signalled Ashwatthama to leave the battleground. Ashwatthama firmly held a limping Kripacharya's hand and they both scurried towards the faraway jungle. Kritavarma too went in the same direction.

Shakuni turned his face towards Duryodhana. A bloody-faced Duryodhana was standing beside his dead horse with a mace in hand. His eyes were overflowing with tears. Shakuni's heart melted.

'Run away, Su, run! For heaven's sake, run away. They are coming!'

'Where shall I go, *Mamashri*?' Poor Duryodhana was still in need of Shakuni's counsel.

Shakuni's tears gushed out now like a river on full spate. In a choked voice, Shakuni said, 'Go hide in that underground chamber beneath the Dwaipayana lake. You shall be safe there, my child. Wait there for a better tomorrow. Hurry up!'

'And you?' Asked Duryodhana, sniffling.

'Me?' Shakuni burst into a psychotic laughter. He hummed tunefully, 'I have no need to run, for my time has been done. . . .' It sounded like a cruel song that he was singing over his own imminent doom.

Then he composed himself a little and said in a measured, conversational tone, 'I can go nowhere now, Su. I can run away from them, but cannot run away from myself. Let me meet my destiny. Please, take my Uluk with you.'

Uluk hugged Shakuni tightly. 'I shall go nowhere leaving you, *Pitashri*!'

'Don't behave like a fool, *Putra*. You don't need to die. Go with Su. Go, I command you!'

Suddenly a hair-raising shout was heard from afar:

'THERE THEY ARE! CATCH THEM! DON'T LET THEM RUN AWAY!'

It was Bheem. He had just spotted them even from a great distance.

The five chariots of the five Pandava brothers, each followed by some divisions of their remaining army, started rushing in from three sides. Yudhisthira was coming from the north, Arjuna and Bheem from the east, and Nakula and Sahadeva from the west.

'RUN, SU! RUN!' Shakuni cried at the top of his voice. Duryodhana started running towards the south. Shakuni pushed Uluk but he would not leave his father behind.

Shakuni quickly decided what to do. *No! I shouldn't let myself be killed by Pritha's sons. I shall better be killed by Madri's sons.*

Shakuni selected his own assassin and spiritedly charged towards Nakula and Sahadeva. Of the two brothers, Sahadeva reached him first.

'YOU'RE LUCKY TO HAVE HIM, SAHADEVA! NOW DO IT,' thundered Bheem.

Both Shakuni and Sahadeva got down from their vehicles and started a fierce swordfight. Meanwhile, Nakula had also arrived. Uluk engaged Nakula in another duel. Nakula was fighting with a sword, Uluk with a spear.

Shakuni was panting. His chronic breathing problem aggravated due to the strain of the fight. A much younger and fitter Sahadeva clearly had an upper hand in the duel. He already had Shakuni on the ropes. Uluk noticed his father was in trouble. He made a heroic attempt to save Shakuni. He suddenly pushed Nakula aside taking him by surprise and pounced on Sahadeva with his spear in hand. Sahadeva was unprepared for this and both fell on the ground rolling over each other. But a smart Sahadeva managed to hold the spear and turn it towards Uluk although the latter was still holding it. The spear broke under Uluk's weight with a broken shaft piercing through his heart!

'ULUK!' An insane cry ripped through Shakuni's chest. 'ULUK! Uluk, my son!' Shakuni dived on Uluk's fallen body but could not reach it. Sahadeva held him by the scruff of his neck and made him stand straight. Shakuni was having a bout of coughing and was shivering out of exhaustion and grief. He saw his death in Sahadeva's livecoal eyes.

'Your game is over, scoundrel. You don't know, just this morning I promised your death to Kunti *Maa*! Let me keep my word—let me make her happy, for once.'

Kunti's name froze Shakuni. Sahadeva uprooted the piece of spear from Uluk's chest. It was dripping with the blood of Shakuni's son. In the wink of an eye, Sahadeva thrust the broken spear into Shakuni's neck as powerfully as he could.

Shakuni's eyes bulged and his tongue lolled out. A strange guttural sound was coming out from his throat. He fell down on the ground. Nakula and Sahadeva hugged each other jubilantly. They were so excited to deliver the good news to their brothers that they did not wait for the fallen Shakuni to breathe his last.

Fatally wounded, Shakuni was writhing in mortal pain. The excruciating dying moments caused him strange hallucinations. He saw Pritha appear in front of him out of nowhere. Standing over his fallen body, Pritha was beaming with manifest happiness. Her milky white *saari* and *angavastra* were fluttering in the reckless breeze like the audacious flag of a triumphant army. Her eyes seemed to be spewing fire. She was saying something wagging her index finger at him. But Shakuni could hear nothing. The flippant air of Kurukshetra seemed to be stealing her words away. Although he did not hear her, he knew very well what she was saying. She must be reminding him of his misdeeds. For the first time, Shakuni did not feel that irresistible craving for her. His earthly desires were also dying with him.

Pritha's image was melting down and slowly transforming into Arshi's. Arshi looked so different from the day Shakuni had left her. She was now almost unrecognisable with peppered hair, sagging skin and a devastated face. She had once been famously beautiful but today she looked so wretched. Shakuni desperately wanted to ask her how she was—although the question was utterly meaningless after so many years. She was only weeping. Shakuni tried to smile at her but tears filled his own eyes too instead, almost blinding him. Arshi too faded into thin air. Were they just images? Were they not for real?

Then he saw a very old man clad in white robes. Although the man seemed to have been quite robust once upon a time, he was now too old to stand straight. He rested his body weight on a thick stick which too had been bent like a bow. His face was covered with white beard and a wild mass of hair that had never been combed for years. Shakuni had never seen a man so old. Even Devavrata seemed much younger than him, evidently. His shadow fell over Shakuni's body.

The man was cat-eyed.

Shakuni recognised him.

He was Arstisena alias Devapi Pratipeya, the forgotten eldest brother of Devavrata's father Shantanu who never got to be the king!

He held Shakuni's trembling hand. Shakuni felt the touch of his coarse and feeble fingers. The man was not an image. He was real—unlike Pritha and Arshi.

Shakuni was not the least surprised to see him here and now. Perhaps he had no strength left to be surprised. Shakuni knew his time was fast racing towards the end. With much difficulty, he tried to raise his head a bit. An ominous darkness was slowly falling all around him. His field of vision was shrinking fast.

The man said in a gruff, almost mechanical tone, 'Thank you, Shakuni Saubala. I knew only you can do this. Well done, you really threw your dice well.'

Shakuni could smile this time and mustered all his remaining strength to respond in a heavily distorted voice, 'And you...yours!'

The man laughed out loud. It was quite surprising how this decrepit, ancient man could let out such a full-throated laugh.

That was all Shakuni could say. Whatever remaining strength Shakuni had was spent uttering those three words. His slightly raised body fell down on the ground and became still for good. His lifeless eyes were still wide open, though.

The old man put his fingers over the eyelids of the dead Shakuni and closed them. Then he removed the *uttariya* from his upper body and laid it over Shakuni's bloodstained body.

The man looked around. There were terrible scenes of devastation everywhere. The war had caused almost total destruction of the legendary Kuru dynasty.

His vengeance had reached its mark. He felt avenged. But strangely, he felt no happiness.

He still had one thing left to do. He wanted to meet his nephew—Devavrata 'Bheeshma'—one last time. Devavrata was still alive and was lying unattended on a bed of arrows at a far corner of the battleground.

15

Lying on a bed of arrows, Devavrata had now completely understood the meaning of that strange dream—the mysterious androgynous person, that piercing feeling, the subsequent calmness. It was clear to him now that it was his pre-ordained destiny that had been sending him messages through his sub-conscious. That strange being of his dream was none other than Shikhandi. Devavrata had been looking like a hedgehog when Arjuna pierced him with countless arrows using Shikhandi as a shield. The arrows were deeply embedded into his flesh causing excruciating pain and did not let his body touch the ground when he fell.

Devavrata shut his eyes. He knew this torturous phase was going to end soon. He would soon find the salvation. The dream had given him that hope. He was preparing to free himself from all the bitterness and the malice that had plagued him all his life, once and for all.

He heard footsteps.

He opened his eyes with some effort. His vision was not very much clear. Still he could make out that a very old, bare-bodied man, bent with the weight of his age and propped with a stick, was standing beside him. His face was not clearly visible against the west-bound sun. The man came closer and put his palm on Devavrata's sweating forehead.

Devavrata was curious. *Who can this man be?*

'Have you still some strength left to *forgive, Putra*?'

The gravelly voice and the strange words struck Devavrata like a thunderbolt. He became completely oblivious of his physical condition. He tried to bulge his eyes as much as he could. Fortunately, the pain had not yet affected his mind. He needed no introduction to recognise Devapi, the eldest brother of his father Shantanu, although they had last met each other in a past almost beyond the limits of memory.

'*Tatshri*, you? How...how come....'

Devapi raised his hand and said in a voice choked with pent-up emotions, 'I have come to ask for your forgiveness, Gangeya. You must know how this wretched uncle of yours plotted the ruin of this house. Pity, *you* have been the greatest casualty of my mission. That was the only thing I feel guilty about now.' The old man started coughing.

Devavrata looked on with sharp eyes. Many years ago, Shakuni's descriptions about a mysterious old man had affirmed his old suspicions about Devapi's malevolence. Devapi's words interested him. *Is he going to issue a confession?*

Devavrata closed his eyes. He felt a simmering excitement inside him. The extreme bodily discomfort was not troubling him anymore.

'I had long sensed your ill will. I can understand what caused this hatred. But tell me, exactly what did you do, *Tatshri?*'

Devapi smiled. The smile seemed to be laboured. In a very tired voice, he said, 'You know very well why my family and countrymen disowned me. But what you didn't know was that I never forgave them. My hatred fell on the throne of Hastinapur. My sole objective of life was to destroy the Kuru family that expelled me. You know I was a master of black arts and the occult. But I was not able to punish the Kauravas alone only with these special powers. I needed support. I already had a foresight about a devastating war involving the Kauravas and the Yadavas. I planted it on Bahlik's mind. He always valued my words.

I advised him to shift to Vahik *Desh* from Hastinapur because I loved him and didn't want to harm him. Then, I started making plans to create troubles in Hastinapur. I was determined to make sure that your father's natural heir did not get to succeed him either, just as I myself could not succeed my father. Poor you! When I met you, you were just a teenager. I understood immediately that you have all the qualities of making a great emperor. Trust me, Devavrata, I loved you. But I hated Hastinapur more, unfortunately.

One day, I was invited by a fisherman for a meal. Satyavati was serving food there. I was taken aback by her drop-dead looks. The fisherman informed me that she was his adopted daughter. You know what I did? I advised him to have his daughter seduce Shantanu. I knew your mother had long left him. I also knew that he had an eye for younger women. But as his health was failing, he was not getting a young bride of his choice. As he predictably fell for Satyavati, the fisherman came to me. I taught him how to negotiate with Shantanu. But as your father did not readily agree to it, our plans came to a roadblock. But you did the unthinkable and made my plan work. Thank you, Devavrata! Had you become the king, I am sure, the future of the Kauravas would have been secured and my mission would have failed. But still I was far from happy as you were still in command and managing things nicely,' Devapi paused a little to take a breath.

'Please continue. The story is fascinating,' Devavrata said sarcastically.

'Meanwhile, I had changed my identity to Arstisena and started posing as a Brahmin. I wanted to erase my name and my Kaurava identity from public memory forever. Then I wandered into Gandhara and the Gandhara king Subal took a strong liking for me. I kept visiting him almost regularly and met the young Shakuni there. The boy was outstandingly sharp and cunning. My hunch was that Shakuni would one day become very useful to me. And wasn't I right? I gifted him with a special *pasha* set. I put some special powers into that *pasha* set so that an expert player becomes unbeatable while playing with that set. When you started looking for a bride for Dhritarashtra, I suggested Gandhari's name to Bahlik with the sole intention to get Shakuni involved in the affairs of Hastinapur. Bahlik was initially reluctant but then accepted the idea when his son got thrashed by a Vrishni Yadava. Everything started falling in place. Quite funny, isn't it?'

Devavrata did not comment. Devapi continued, 'Bahlik was regularly in touch with me. He kept me posted all through. Meanwhile, through my supernatural powers I foresaw the advent of an epochal man and his involvement in Hastinapur politics. You all know now who he is. Krishna! One day, when I was camping near Hastinapur, I saw Shakuni and Vidur. I was aware of their intelligence and felt like playing with them a bit. I gave them the clue about Krishna. But they understood it too late.'

'I think you didn't have much left to do after that. Shakuni and others did it all on your behalf, right?'

'Wrong. My masterstroke was yet to be delivered. Kuntibhoja's guru was very close to me. Through him, I influenced Kuntibhoja to set up an alliance between Kunti and Pandu. I knew that it would make Shakuni even more vicious. I was aware of Shakuni's feelings for her. Kunti had confided this only in her sister Shrutakirti who would later tell her husband Damghosh[1]—the Chedi king about this. Damghosh was my disciple. He was kind of a

[1] Damghosh was Shishupal's father.

gossipmonger. I never liked him. However, he did me a great favour by sharing the information casually.'

'You had everything working for you, I see!'

'Do you know what went in my favour? It was the fact that you all found your own hate lines. You, Bahlik, Vyasa, Shakuni, Vidur, Dhritarashtra, Gandhari, Kunti, Duryodhana and his brothers, the Pandavas, Draupadi... all. My poison was already coursing through all of your minds. Oh, the poison reminds me of another thing....'

'What is it?'

'I sent Ashwasen—the *Naga* prince who was scurrying for revenge against the Pandavas—to Shakuni with the Karkotaka poison. I knew that only Shakuni's skill or my *pasha* set's special powers were not enough to create sufficiently serious troubles within the house. It was very necessary for Shakuni to wield total control over his opponent's thoughts. That poison was ideal for this. Shakuni cleverly had the unsuspecting Yudhisthira drugged before that *pasha* game. Everybody knows what happened thereafter. My choice of Shakuni as my agent proved to be a masterstroke, don't you agree?' Devapi stopped, looking exhausted after talking so long. Today, he had completely unburdened himself to the person he wronged most. He sat on his haunches holding the stick that had gone some length into the ground wet with the Kaurava blood.

Devavrata turned his face away from his uncle. Strangely, Devapi's confession did not evoke any bitterness in his mind. He had already arrived in a kingdom between life and death, beyond the reach of mortal emotions.

'Shall you forgive me, *Putra*?' A sobbing Devapi slurred on his words.

'I have already done so, *Tatshri*. Nobody else will ever get to know of this meeting. Does Vyasadev know anything about all this?'

'His mother Satyavati must have told him. He met me once many years ago.'

'Anyway, *Tatshri,* I have one request to you.'

'What is it, *Putra*?' Devapi had meanwhile stood up with great difficulty.

'Please don't live anymore. Our time is done. It is better for us to occupy places in the memory of this generation than share their places on this earth.'

'Right you are. I needed to live just for this moment that came far too late. Goodbye, Gangeya.'

'Goodbye, *Tatshri*.'

With a sad smile on his lips and tears in his eyes, Devapi Pratipeya—the oldest living Kaurava who outlived as many as four generations—slowly tottered across the gory battlefield of Kurukshetra towards Samanta Panchak. At that holy place, he would renounce his inordinately long life in search of another world to learn better things than what this bewildering planet had taught him.

◈◈◈

Epilogue

Duryodhana would soon be captured by the Pandavas. They were gracious enough to give him a chance to fight back. Duryodhana and Bheem were engaged in a violent mace fight. A desperate Duryodhana was giving a spirited fight to a much stronger Bheem. To save Bheem from a certain defeat, Krishna instigated him to resort to unfair means. Bheem hit Duryodhana below the waistline violating the rules of the engagement. Duryodhana fell down with crushed thighs. After spending an excruciating night, he died in the morning.

Ashwatthama kept his promise to perfection. He sneaked into the Pandava camp at midnight and butchered each and every one sleeping inside. The five Pandava brothers, Krishna and Satyaki survived the carnage as they had spent the night away. But they lost their sons, Dhrishtadyumna and Shikhandi in the massacre. Krishna would later curse Ashwatthama with a pathetic life spanning three thousand years to be spent in total isolation and suffering from repulsive diseases. Completely shunned by the society, Ashwatthama was never heard of again.

Yudhisthira became the king and an icon of righteousness in his own right. With the help of his brothers and Lord Krishna, he ruled the combined empire of Hastinapur and Indraprastha for thirty-six years with exemplary justness.

Devavrata 'Bheeshma' would live past the war for about two more months that he spent lying on the bed of arrows in Kurukshetra. Even in that condition, he gave priceless counsel to Yudhisthira. He kept his last meeting with Devapi a secret.

Vidur, as advised by Vyasa, took up the life of an ascetic and did hard penance. Before voluntarily leaving his mortal frame, Vidur imparted all his knowledge, experience and wisdom to his protégé Yudhisthira. A dead Vidur continued to live on in Yudhisthira in the form of an ideology and inspiration.

Dhritarashtra and Gandhari lived with the Pandavas for fifteen years before choosing to live like hermits in jungles. In a noble gesture, Kunti too accompanied them without savouring the victory of her sons. The three old people died when a fire broke out in the jungle.

Thirty-six years after the war, Lord Krishna died in a freak accident when he was inadvertently struck by a hunter's arrow. The entire Yadava race perished in a violent infighting. Balaram voluntarily relinquished his life. After the deaths of Krishna and Balaram, the entire city of Dwarka was gobbled up by the sea.

Yudhisthira rehabilitated the displaced Yadavas at Indraprastha. He then anointed Arjuna's grandson Parikshit as Hastinapur's king and Krishna's great-grandson Vajra as Indraprastha's. Then the five brothers and Draupadi renounced the material world and embarked on *Mahaprasthan* in search of salvation.

Parikshit ruled for many years before being killed by Takshaka—Ashwasen's father who could finally take a long-overdue revenge.

Maharshi Vyasadev completed his magnum opus with Lord Ganesha's help and named it '*Jaya*'. He gave his own narrative of the troubled history of the great Kuru house ensuring that the grand story would never be erased from human memory. Although Shakuni was portrayed as the chief antagonist in the story, Vyasa almost remained silent about Devapi for reasons best known to himself.

About the Author

Born at Naihati (a suburban town in North 24 Parganas in West Bengal) in a family of academicians, Mallar Chatterjee remains a quintessential small-town person despite staying in Delhi and Kolkata for a long time. Mallar had special interest in mythology right from his childhood. He did his schooling from Bhatpara Amarkrishna Pathshala and Naihati Narendra Vidyaniketan. He did his undergraduation and post-graduation (in Economics) from the University of Kalyani.

Shakuni and The Dice of Doom is his second book of the *Mahabharata* series published by Readomania. His debut novel is *Yudhisthira—The Unfallen Pandava* (Book 1 of the *Mahabharata* series). This is an imaginary autobiography of Yudhishthira who, like an ordinary man, retells the events of the *Mahabharata* in first person giving a first-hand account, as if he witnessed the incidents himself.

Mallar is a Central Government employee. He is based in Kolkata.

Mallar can be contacted at: mallar.chatterjee1@gmail.com.